Praise for Matt D

'Fast-paced, insightful and very, very funny' *Heat*

'Funny and witty, a great read that gives us a look into the workings of the male mind' *Sun*

'A well-crafted tale of when love goes wrong and loves goes right – witty, astute but tender too' Freya North

'Frighteningly funny and sometimes just plain frightening . . . the most realistic perspective on the average man's world view most women will get without hanging around in a locker room' Chris Manby

'Delightfully shallow and self-obsessed – that's the male psyche for you' *Elle*

'An amusing insight into the minds of men' *Daily Express*

'A warm, open and damn funny book' *Lads Mag*

'Both hilarious and touching' *Best*

'Hilarious' *Cosmopolitan*

By the same author

Best Man
The Ex-Boyfriend's Handbook
From Here to Paternity
Ex-Girlfriends United

About the author

Matt Dunn is the author of four previous bestselling novels, including *The Ex-Boyfriend's Handbook*, which was shortlisted for both the Romantic Novel of the Year Award and the Melissa Nathan Award for Comedy Romance. He has also written about life, love and relationships for various publications including *The Times*, *Guardian*, *Cosmopolitan*, *Company*, *Glamour*, *Elle* and the *Sun*.

Matt was born in Margate, but eventually escaped to Spain to write his first novel in between working as a newspaper columnist and playing a lot of tennis. Previously he has been a professional lifeguard, fitness-equipment salesman and an IT headhunter, but he prefers writing for a living, so please keep buying his books.

Visit the author at www.mattdunn.co.uk

the Good Bride Guide

Matt Dunn

POCKET
BOOKS

LONDON · NEW YORK · TORONTO · SYDNEY

First published in Great Britain by Pocket Books, 2009
An imprint of Simon & Schuster UK, Ltd
A CBS COMPANY

1 3 5 7 9 10 8 6 4 2

Simon & Schuster UK Ltd
1st Floor
222 Gray's Inn Road
London WC1X 8HB

www.simonandschuster.co.uk

Simon & Schuster Australia
Sydney

A CIP catalogue record for this book is available from the British Library

ISBN 978-1-84739-523-8

Typeset by Rowland Phototypesetting Ltd, Bury St Edmunds, Suffolk
Printed and bound in Great Britain by CPI Cox & Wyman,
Reading, Berkshire RG1 8EX

For Loz

Chapter 1

I'm in my studio when my mobile rings, and while the sound of heavy breathing is initially exciting, it doesn't take me long to realize that it's just Ashif.

'How'd you get on with her?' he asks, evidently panting from the effort of walking along the pavement, given the heavy footsteps I can hear in the background.

'Who, Ash?'

'You know – that woman who wanted you to paint that portrait of her.' I can almost hear him grinning down the phone line. 'Nude.'

Ash is my art dealer, although when I say dealer, in truth his family own the Indian restaurant on the seafront where I display my work in return for a ten per cent cut on any that get sold.

'Ash, she was about seventy.'

'So?'

'And more importantly, she wanted *me* to be nude, as it turned out.'

'Ah.' There's a pause, and then Ash clears his throat. 'But you're still doing it, right?'

'What do you think?' I say, realizing I probably already know the answer to that question. 'Of course not.'

'That, Ben, is the reason you're still what's known in the trade as a "struggling artist",' sighs Ash, no doubt picturing his commission disappearing down the drain. What else he does for money, I'm not exactly sure, but there must be something, as given the number of pictures I actually sell, or how few commissions that come my way as a result of his dealings, I can hardly live on the ninety per cent I get.

'Yes, well, as I've told you a hundred times, I'm not prepared to compromise my principles.'

Ash snorts loudly into the receiver. 'And as I've told you a thousand times, principles are for people who can afford them. And right now, that's not you.'

'Well, if you wouldn't mind perhaps qualifying some of these dodgy enquiries that you keep sending my way a little better, then maybe one day it will be.'

'So what if you have to kiss the occasional frog? It's a numbers game.'

'No, that's accountancy, and if you remember, I've given that up. This is *art*,' I say, conscious that it sounds more than a little pretentious.

'So, where does the term "painting by numbers" come from, then?' says Ash, feebly.

'Ash, that's …' I stop talking, and wonder again at the wisdom of letting someone who knows absolutely nothing about the art world represent me. 'Never mind. What did you want?'

'What did I want?' repeats Ash, as if he's forgotten the reason for his call. 'Oh. Right. I was wondering what you were up to.'

I stare at the painting on the easel in front of me, which I've spent most of the day tweaking, but just can't seem to get right. '*Working*, Ash. That's what I do when I'm here in my studio.'

'Ah,' says Ash. 'I did wonder. Anyway, let me in, will you? I need to talk to you, and it's freezing out here.'

'You're outside? What the hell are you doing calling me on the phone, then?'

'Well, I thought you might be doing her. Painting, her, I mean. That woman. And I didn't want to interrupt you.'

'Well don't, then.'

'Wait! I've got something important to tell . . .'

I click the phone off and slip it back into my pocket, then try to ignore the sound of banging from the front door, until it's clear it's not going to stop, before making my way along the hallway and down the stairs. My studio's in the upstairs part of an old shop, one of a few in this part of Margate's old town that the council is renting out for next to nothing to local craftspeople or artists like me in an attempt to regenerate the area, and, as I reach the ground floor, I can see Ash's face peering in anxiously through a gap in the whitewashed glass.

'Where's the fire?' I say as I let him in.

'Well, it's not in here, more's the pity,' he says, exhaling exaggeratedly, then nodding towards the fog breath he has produced. 'Why on earth do you work in these conditions?'

'Because they're cheap, Ash. And Turner lived just around the corner, you know?'

Ash frowns. 'Tina Turner?'

'No, Ash. Turner. The *painter*?' I shake my head slowly at Ash's blank expression. 'Besides, with you as my dealer, it's all I can afford.'

'Agent, please,' he says, still a little out of breath from his walk. Ash is a little on the large side, but then so would I be if I lived above the Indian Queen. 'Dealer sounds a little, well, druggy.'

'Sorry, Ashif.' I give him a mock salute. 'Agent. And what's with the suit?'

'Why? What's wrong with it?' says Ash, picking an imaginary bit of fluff from his jacket.

'Nothing. I just hope the judge was impressed.' Ash got a new BMW a few months ago – a thirtieth birthday present from his parents – and already has nine points for speeding on his licence.

He opens his mouth as if to respond, then evidently thinks better of it. 'Where have you been?' he says, as I lock the door carefully behind him. Not that there's much in here to steal, but last time I left it open, someone actually put a bin-liner full of old clothes inside, obviously harking back to the charity shop it once was. 'I've been phoning you all afternoon.'

I follow him upstairs, retrieving my mobile from my pocket and looking at the screen, where Ash's two missed calls are clearly visible. 'All afternoon? I hardly think a couple of calls five minutes apart qualify as "all afternoon".'

'Yeah, but you never, er, don't answer your phone,' says Ash, frowning at his own bad English. 'If you know what I mean?'

'I'm sorry,' I lie, having ignored his earlier calls on purpose, then point towards my painting. 'I was just a little preoccupied with this. Plus I must have left my phone on "vibrate".'

Ash raises one eyebrow. 'Kinky.'

I can't help but make a face back at him. 'It's about the only pleasure I get nowadays.'

'Well, if you'd have taken up that old woman on her offer . . .'

'As if.'

'For the millionth time, it's pronounced "Ash-eef".'

'Very funny, Ash.'

'So have you never, you know, *done it* with someone you've painted?' he asks, walking over towards the window and wiping the condensation off one of the panes.

'Of course.'

Ash looks round in surprise. 'You have?'

'Oh yes.' I nod. 'Because that's what always happens. In porn movies.'

Ash looks a little disappointed. 'So, no one new on the horizon?'

'Nope. The women I meet nowadays don't seem to think that "Ben Grant – struggling artist" is much of a catch. And to be honest, it's getting to the stage that whenever I do meet someone, even if I can be bothered to ask them out on a date, there's a part of me that's hoping they won't turn up.'

'Why ever not?'

I sigh. 'Because it'll just be the same again. We'll have a bit of fun, and then it'll start to go bad, and it's back to square one. And I'm getting a little tired of it all.'

'Yes, well, perhaps you shouldn't have made Amy dump you, then, should you?'

'Let's not go down that particular conversational road again, please.' Amy and I split up about a month ago, and there's hardly been a day since then that Ash hasn't reminded me of the fact. 'And, anyway, I didn't *make* her dump me. The decision was mutual.'

'Mutual?' Ash laughs. 'As in she decided to split up with you, and you had no choice but to agree.'

'No, because it was the right thing to do. For both of us. She wanted a commitment out of me. And I wasn't prepared to give her one.'

Ash nods slowly. 'I can see why she dumped you, then.'

'Get your mind out of the gutter, please. A *commitment*.'

'Why not?'

I shrug. 'She just wasn't *the one*. There was no spark. No thunderbolt.'

'No? So why can't you stop thinking about her, then?'

'I don't think about her, really. Just . . . well, about *us*.'

Ash raises both eyebrows, and takes a step backwards. 'Us?'

'No. Our relationship, I mean. Amy and me. And why it went the way of all the others.'

Ash gives me a weary look. 'Because you weren't prepared to marry her?'

'Yes, but why? She was my twenty-ninth girlfriend, you know. That's one for every year of my life. You'd have thought I'd have learned something about relationships by now. At least enough to keep one going.'

'But you can always go back to her, right? I mean, you said she was keeping that particular door open for you?'

I make a face. 'Yes, but it wouldn't simply be going back to her, would it? It'd mean giving all this up.' I gesture around my sparsely furnished studio, trying to ignore the cracked panes of glass in the window. While I've always loved art, in actual fact, I trained as an accountant, and worked as one up until last year, at a medium-sized firm here in Margate, which was where I met Amy. But, recently, I'd begun to feel more than a little restless – in both my job and personal life – so six months ago I decided to leave, to try to make a go of it as a painter. Leaving Amy came a little bit later, but I can't pretend the two were unrelated.

'Amy said that, did she?'

'Not in so many words. But I think she always assumed that my painting was just something I needed a little time off for. You know, to get it out of my system.'

'Get it out of your system?' Ash laughs. 'What, like glandular fever?'

'I'm serious, Ash. Accountancy wasn't for me. And if Amy couldn't see that ... Well, that just proves that she wasn't either.'

'But she wanted to marry you, Ben.'

'No, Ash. She wanted to marry the me I wasn't happy being. There's an important difference. And this ... It's always been my dream. And you've got to go for your dreams, haven't you?'

He walks over to the painting I've been working on for most of the day and studies it for a moment or two. 'Ben, your trouble is that you're a perfectionist, who expects everything to meet your exacting standards,' he says, picking it up and turning it through a hundred and eighty degrees, before placing it back on the easel. It's an abstract, with one large blue rectangle next to a smaller, darker one, and I'm a little annoyed that it actually looks better that way up. 'And if it doesn't ...'

'You're talking about my work, right?'

'If you like.' Ash grins at me, then picks the painting up again. 'What's it supposed to be, anyway?'

'It's a self-portrait.'

Ash squints at it. 'Really?'

'Of course not, Ash. It's not *supposed* to be anything. It's *abstract*.'

'You're telling me,' he says, grimacing at the canvas.

I snatch it from him exasperatedly and place it against the wall, face-inwards. To be honest, I don't sell many of these. It's mainly the portrait work that Ash gets me that pays the bills – when it's genuine portrait work, that is, rather than pervy old ladies who want to sit *on* me, rather than for me. And when the bills aren't very big. 'Anyway, as pleasant as this little artistic debate is, what was it you wanted to tell me?'

Ash thinks for a moment. 'Come on. I'll buy you a drink.'

I glance at my watch. It's five-thirty, and although I'm due to be teaching my art class in an hour, the offer of a beer – and one I don't have to pay for – is too good to turn down. 'You're on.'

'Excellent,' says Ash, as I follow him back down the stairs. 'There's someone I want you to meet. And we've just got time for a swift one before they arrive.'

I get a sudden feeling of *déjà vu*. 'Don't tell me – another potential "client" who wants me to show her more than my etchings?'

Ash smiles. 'Well, you're right about the "female" part.'

I stop on the bottom step, and lean heavily against the bannister. Ash has tried to set me up on a number of occasions, none of which have worked out. Our tastes in women, like our tastes in art, are a little different. 'This better not be another prospective ex.'

'No,' says Ash, pursing his lips enigmatically. 'At least, I hope not.'

'So why do I need a drink before I meet her?'

'You don't.' Ash looks up at me nervously, before making for the front door. 'But I do.'

Chapter 2

Five minutes later, I'm sitting at a table in The Cottage, the pub just around the corner from my studio. On the wall next to the bar, a large hand-written poster is appealing for people to sign up for the pub's five-a-side football team, but seeing as they've decided to call themselves 'The Cottagers', not surprisingly, there's not many takers.

'Here you go.' Ash puts a pint down on the table in front of me, then – and not for the first time – glances anxiously at the door. Given how nervous he's looking, I'm starting to get a little worried about what he might be up to.

'Checking your escape route?'

'What? No.' He looks at his watch, then gulps down a large mouthful of lager. 'Listen, Ben, I've got something to tell you. Well, it's more of an announcement, really.'

When Ash doesn't continue, I put my beer down and study his face, wondering what it is he's having so much trouble saying. He's perspiring slightly, and it's hardly hot in the pub, so either the brisk walk here took more out of him than normal, or he's really worried about something. For a moment, I wonder whether the 'woman' thing was just a ruse to get me here, and he feels he needs to be in a public place – with witnesses – before he can say what he's got to say. But what? I know he's not gay, and from what I can tell, he's not been having girlfriend problems – particularly since as far as I'm aware he hasn't had a girl- friend for the best part of a year – which just leaves one thing. And it's the thing closest to Ash's heart. Money.

'Hold on, Ash. I can guess what this is.'

He looks a little surprised. 'You can?'

'Your cut.'

Ash reaches a hand up to his face anxiously. 'Where?'

'Your percentage, I mean. Of my sales. You want to negotiate.'

'I do?'

'I mean, I really appreciate you letting me show my work in the restaurant, and all that, but it works both ways, doesn't it? Otherwise, you'd have to go out and get some other paintings to cover the walls, which you'd have to pay for, and . . .' I stop talking, because Ash still hasn't said anything, and then start to feel a little sick. Maybe that's what's happening. Perhaps his mum and dad have decided they don't like my stuff any more, and want to replace it with something a bit more, well, Indian. 'That's it, isn't it? You want to replace my work with some rubbish prints from IKEA, don't you? Well, what's it going to take? Fifteen per cent? Twenty? My firstborn child? Because . . .'

Ash suddenly holds both hands up, as if he's trying to fend off a beach-ball. 'Your firstborn child? I can't wait that long. And, anyway, it's nothing like that. I'm getting married.'

'What?'

Ash nods. 'Yes. Can you believe it?' he says, evidently not quite believing it himself.

For a moment, I can't think what the appropriate response should be, my relief at not losing my only exhibition space overshadowed by my complete and utter astonishment. 'When? Why?' I start to say, then fortunately manage to turn them into a hurried 'Who to?', before draining most of my beer in one gulp. 'I mean, I didn't even know you had a girlfriend.' I shake my head, and then realize that as surprised as I am at his news, Ash is even more stunned at my reaction. 'I'm sorry, Ash. What I mean to say is "Congratulations", of course.'

He breaks into a relieved grin. 'Thanks.'

We clink our beer glasses together, then regard each other across the table, grinning like idiots, until I actually have to ask. 'But seriously, who is this woman? And what's she like?'

'Priti,' he says, glancing at his watch again, and then at the door.

'Is she?'

Ash frowns. 'Is she what?'

'Pretty.'

'No, that's her name. It's spelt P-R-I-T-I.' Ash reaches into his wallet, then hands me a photograph of an extremely attractive girl dressed in a sari. 'Although as a matter of fact, she is.'

I whistle appreciatively. 'You're telling me. She's Indian, right?' I say, studying the photo closely.

'No, Ben. That's her at a fancy dress party. Of course she's Indian.'

I shake my head incredulously. 'Well, you certainly managed to keep that quiet. And why haven't I met her?'

Ash shrugs, then adjusts his tie. 'I've only met her a couple of times myself, to be honest.'

I nearly drop the photo into my beer glass. 'What? And you're getting *married*?'

Ash snatches Priti's picture from me and carefully slides it back into his wallet. 'Well, okay, maybe more than a couple.'

'How many more than a couple, exactly?'

'Including today?'

'Yes, Ash,' I say, finally understanding who today's mystery guest is going to be, and why Ash is so nervous. 'Including today.'

'Well . . . Three.'

'Three? And when was the last time you saw her?'

Ash frowns into his glass, as if the answer's in there. 'I dunno. Must have been five or six . . .'

'What? Days ago? Weeks?'

'No. *I* must have been five. Or six. I can't remember. But that's not so surprising, seeing as we don't live in the same country.' He takes another sip of his beer. 'But my mum and dad have been planning this for ages – they were friends with her parents before we moved here – and we've been emailing and speaking on the phone for the last few months, so it's not as if we're complete strangers.'

As Ash's voice tails off, I stare across the table at him, still trying to get my head around the whole concept of what I assume is his mum and dad shipping a girl in from India for him to marry. 'So your parents have . . . *arranged* the whole thing?'

Ash nods. 'Well, yes. That's why it's called an arranged marriage. She's arriving today for a visit – to see where I live, and everything. And assuming we get on face-to-face, then we probably will. Get married, I mean,' he says, matter-of-factly.

'And you don't think it's a bit . . . Weird?'

'Nah. My lot do it all the time.'

It's my turn to glance nervously at the door. 'And she's on her way here? Now?'

Ash unbuttons his jacket, then does it up again, obviously preferring to keep his stomach covered. 'Yup. My folks picked her up from the airport this afternoon. We've got a big family meal planned this evening, then she gets to meet the cousins tomorrow.'

'But you haven't seen her yourself yet?'

'Nope. But she'll be along any minute.'

'Hang on. So you haven't seen her for the best part of, what, twenty-five years?'

'That's right.'

'And you've arranged to meet her here? This evening?'

'Yup.'

'With me?'

'Well, I wanted to make a good impression.'

'Don't you think you'd have made a better one by picking her up from the airport yourself?'

'Nah. She thinks I'm a businessman. So I said I had a client meeting.'

'With your only client.'

Ash grins. 'I may have neglected to mention that particular fact. But you're a famous artist around these parts.'

'Well, that's very nice of you to say so,' I say, swelling a little with pride, 'but I hardly think that's true.'

'Maybe not,' says Ash, immediately bursting my bubble. 'But she doesn't know that, does she?'

'And what does she know about you? That you're . . .'

'Like I said, a businessman,' repeats Ash. 'And a successful one.'

'I was going to say "fat",' I counter.

Ash pats his stomach self-consciously. 'Yes, well, I've been trying those diet milkshake things, and they don't work.'

'That's because you're supposed to have them *instead* of meals. Not as well as.'

'I was hungry.' Ash sighs. 'Besides, I'm not fat. I'm big-boned.'

'I hope you haven't told Priti that.'

'Why not?'

'You don't want her to be disappointed on her wedding night.'

'Very funny.'

As Ash fixes his gaze on the pub door, I don't quite know what to say. For all his outward anxiety, Ash seems to be treating this as a pretty normal sequence of events. 'Listen. Are you sure you wouldn't prefer to be meeting her on your own?'

'You're joking. I'd be a nervous wreck.'

'As opposed to the cool, calm, collected person sitting in front of me?'

Ash grabs a serviette from the dispenser on the table and dabs at the sweat on his upper lip. 'Is it that obvious?'

'No, Ash. You look fine.'

'Great, because this is important, you know? And I'd hate to mess it . . .' He suddenly stops talking and breaks into a huge smile, and when I look over my shoulder, I can see the reason why. Priti looks just like her photo – although she's not dressed in a sari this time, but a pair of jeans and a duffel coat – and to Ash's obvious delight, she certainly lives up to her name.

Ash waves at her – a pretty unnecessary gesture, seeing as he's the only other Indian in the pub, and in fact, apart from me and the barman, the only other person in the pub – and as she walks over to our table, he leaps out of his chair with an unusual athleticism.

'Hi,' he says.

'Hi, Ashif,' replies Priti, smiling shyly up at him. Her

accent's quite strong, and a little hard to place, although of course, having never been to India, it wouldn't make any difference to me even if I could place it.

Ash half holds a hand out, not sure what the correct greeting is – although I have to say I'd be just as clueless given the circumstances – and they do an awkward little dance, before Priti grabs his arm and kisses him lightly on the cheek. I can't help feeling like I'm intruding, and wonder whether I should just sneak away, but don't think I'd be able to get past Ash, so instead, after I've left a suitable pause, just clear my throat awkwardly.

'Oh yes. Sorry,' says Ash, looking round suddenly, as if he's just remembered that I'm here, 'Ben, this is Priti. Priti, this is Ben.'

'Nice to meet you.' I shake her outstretched hand, and concentrate on speaking very slowly, in the hope she'll understand me. I know that they're bilingual in a lot of India, but Ash doesn't always speak to his parents in English, so I can't just assume that Priti's going to be fluent.

'Hello,' says Priti, breaking into a broad smile, and almost immediately I can see why Ash is so smitten. 'Nice to meet you too.'

'Let me get you a drink,' says Ash, looking like he's in need of another one himself.

'Thanks. A half of lager, please.'

'Lager?' says Ash in an impressed tone, as if Priti's just admitted to being a fan of the same football team as him. 'Right,' he adds, winking at me, before scampering off to the bar like an excited puppy, albeit a rather well-fed one.

As Priti watches him go, I find myself staring at her, wondering what kind of woman would up sticks and move halfway round the world to marry someone she's only met a couple of times. But Priti doesn't look desperate – far from it, in fact. As she sits down in the seat opposite, I'm conscious that I'm still staring, so I quickly sit back down myself.

'Not too chilly for you, is it?' I ask, noticing she hasn't taken her coat off. 'Here in England, I mean, rather than this particular pub.' Great. Thirty seconds after meeting her, and I'm already talking about the weather. And I wonder why I'm single.

'Oh no,' says Priti, sitting down at the table. 'I'm used to it being colder, actually. Plus, it's nice to get away from all that rain.'

'Ah yes,' I say, assuming she must mean the monsoons. 'So are you finding it weird? Being in England, I mean? And in *Margate*.' For some reason, I adopt a funny voice when I pronounce the town's name, maybe to make it sound exotic.

Priti shrugs. 'No. Although is it always this quiet here?'

I peer around the pub's gloomy interior. Even though there's just the four of us in the place, Ash still seems be having trouble attracting the barman's attention away from whatever minority sport he's watching on the big-screen TV in the corner.

'This is actually quite busy for a Friday night,' I say, realizing it must contrast somewhat with the billion or so in Priti's homeland.

Priti laughs. 'You're kidding?'

I suddenly realize that I shouldn't be saying anything that might put Priti off – after all, it's not just Ash she's come here to check out – so decide to change the subject. 'That's a lovely accent, by the way,' I say. 'Where exactly are you from?' But when she replies, her answer is somewhere I've never heard of.

'Dhundhi?' I try to pronounce it in the same way she just has. 'Whereabouts is that?'

'On the east coast.'

'Ah,' I say. 'I've never been to India.'

'Oh?' Priti looks a little surprised. 'Well, Ash and I might visit for our honeymoon. Assuming he'll have me, of course,' she adds, more for the returning Ash's benefit than mine.

'What are you two talking about?' he says, carefully placing a half of lager down on the table in front of her.

'I was telling Ben we might go to India. On honeymoon. After we're, you know, *married*,' she says, as if testing out the last word to see how it feels.

Ash picks his pint up, and regards her over the top of it. 'So, the wedding's still on, is it?'

'For now,' says Priti, nervously holding her glass out for him to clink his against. 'Although you've still got to get through the rest of the weekend.'

As the two of them gaze shyly at each other over the

tops of their respective drinks, and although surely it should be Priti who's jet-lagged, it's me who's more than a little confused. And I must be looking like I'm feeling, because Ash puts his beer down and frowns across the table at me. 'Something the matter, Ben?'

'No, I'm sorry. It's just . . .' I'm wondering where to start, when Priti interrupts me.

'Ben was just asking me about home. And how it compared to Margate,' says Priti, giving the word the same emphasis that I did.

Ash shrugs. 'Well, that's one of the reasons you're here this weekend. To see if you like it.'

'We could always live there,' suggests Priti. 'Move in with my parents.'

'And leave my favourite client, just when he's on the verge of the big time?' Ash digs me in the ribs. 'Besides, I wouldn't understand a word anyone said.'

I'm even more confused now – although admittedly, that's partly because I didn't know I was on the verge of the big time. 'But I thought you spoke . . .' I stop talking again. What's the language called? 'Indian?'

Ash smiles. 'Ben, for the millionth time, there's no such thing as "Indian". It could be Gujarati, or Urdu, or Hindi, but technically . . .'

'Okay, okay. Sorry.'

Ash turns back to Priti. 'And it's not as if your parents live a million miles away, is it? I mean, they're even planning to drive here next month for the party.'

I look at the two of them in turn. 'Party?'

'Oh yes,' says Ash. 'We're planning a big engagement party next month. At the restaurant. Which you'll be coming to, of course.'

'And your parents are going to drive?' I ask, ignoring Ash's kind invitation. 'All the way?'

'Oh yes,' says Priti. 'You can do it in a day.'

Ash swallows a mouthful of beer. 'As long as you don't take the scenic route, and use the bridge. Which your parents are happy to do, now that it's free.'

Priti pokes him playfully on the arm. 'They're not that tight. After all, they'll be paying for the wedding.'

'Which is going to be here too, right?' I say, still wondering what I'm more astonished about – the fact that anyone would consider driving here from India, and that they could do it in a day – or that someone's gone and built a *bridge*.

'Oh yes,' says Ash. 'Who wants to get married in Scotland? It rains all the time, for one thing.'

'Like I was telling Ben,' says Priti.

'In . . . Scotland?'

Ash shakes his head. 'Keep up, Ben. Where Priti's from?'

'But . . . Dhundhi?'

'Dundee,' says Ash. 'That's right.'

'Of course,' I say, finally recognizing her accent as from north of the border. 'And the bridge would be . . .'

'The Forth Road Bridge,' says Priti.

'Right. That's, er, what I thought. Obviously.'

Priti looks at me for a second, then starts to laugh.

'You didn't . . . India?' she says, in between gasps. 'A *bridge*?'

I feel myself start to redden. 'No. I mean, yes. But Ash hadn't mentioned, well, *anything* about you until about five minutes ago. And I thought these arranged marriages were all about . . . Well, I don't know what I thought, to be honest,' I say, to no one in particular, before picking my beer up and pretending to be interested in something floating in the glass.

Ash smiles. 'Think of it like an introduction service,' he says. 'Like I said, we knew each other as kids, and our families have kept in touch over the years, and they get on well . . .'

Priti nods. 'And so it's natural to see whether we might hit it off as adults.'

'Exactly,' says Ash, smiling across the table at her.

'Plus, Ash's parents made it worth my while,' adds Priti. 'Financially. Which is really where the *arrangement* part comes from.'

'What?' I stare at the two of them in disbelief. 'So Ash's mum and dad *paid* you to . . .'

'Of course they didn't,' says Ash quickly, as Priti starts sniggering.

'You should have seen your face,' she says, although I'm not sure whether she's referring to me or Ash.

'I'm sorry about Ben,' he says. 'He's an artist. He doesn't know much about the real world.'

'Of course. You're the painter,' says Priti, struggling to regain her composure. 'Perhaps you could paint me?'

'In the nude, maybe?' says Ash. 'Sorry. Bad taste joke,' he adds quickly, when he sees Priti's expression.

I excuse myself and head off to the toilet, leaving an embarrassed Ash to explain what he meant, hoping for his sake that he hasn't fallen at the first hurdle. But my fears are unfounded, as by the time I come back, they're gazing into each other's eyes like lovestruck teenagers.

I finish the rest of my beer quickly, then clear my throat. 'Well, as much as I'd like to stay here and play gooseberry, my art class beckons. Priti, it was lovely to meet you. Ash, thanks for the beer. And congratulations. Both of you.'

'Thanks, Ben,' says Priti, standing up, and giving me a peck on the cheek. 'Great to meet you too. And I'd love to see your work sometime. Maybe you could do a picture of the two of us?' She smiles down at Ash.

'Sure,' I say. 'A wedding portrait, maybe?'

'Thanks, Ben,' says Ash, as I make my way towards the door. 'But I was kind of assuming we'd get a photographer.'

Chapter 3

Still a little stunned at Ash's news, I pull the pub door shut behind me, then make my way up the High Street, and I'm taking a short cut through Boots – not because I want to take advantage of the fact that it's late-night shopping, but because I could do with a blast from their heating – when I spot an attractive girl about to walk in through the opposite door. And when I say attractive, I don't mean in a pretty, er, Priti kind of way – even though she's Asian too – but rather jaw-droppingly stop-me-in-my-tracks attractive; long dark hair that offsets her coffee-coloured skin, a cute nose, and full, kissable lips. For a moment, I don't know what to do. I could hold the door open for her, of course, but she might turn out to be one of those raging feminists who then decides to punch me in the face for being sexist enough to imagine she couldn't possibly manage this big heavy door without male assistance. Alternatively, I could just walk on through, thus making her wait, which would give me longer to stare at her. But by the looks of her, she's in a bit of a hurry, and whilst I quite enjoy bumping into attractive women on the street – especially since it's the only physical contact I get with the opposite sex at the moment – given the speed she's going, I might come off worse.

I make an executive decision to hold the door open, and stand to one side, bracing myself for a verbal onslaught, or a physical one, or even worse, a complete lack of acknowledgement, but instead, the girl smiles at me, and actually says *thanks*. And her smile is so warm, so genuine, so *intoxicating*, that perhaps foolishly I mistake it for more than just politeness, and so after I've waited for a couple of seconds, I turn round and follow her back into the shop. I'm single, after all, as Ash's recent announcement has reminded me, and besides, I owe it to myself to check her out.

As the security guard gives me a funny look, I quickly make the 'I've-forgotten-to-buy-something' face, and head off in the direction the girl's gone, although when this turns out to be along the 'feminine hygiene' aisle, I have to make a quick detour. But when I emerge from the 'skincare' section, she's nowhere to be seen. Hurriedly, I peer around the store, but there's no sign of her, and I'm just thinking about giving up and heading outside when I spot her, now dressed in a long white coat, emerging from a door behind the pharmacy counter and taking over behind one of the tills.

There's a queue of customers, which I instinctively join the end of, while wondering what my approach should be. Only problem is, I don't have a prescription like the rest of them seem to be clutching, so I quickly step back out of the line and stand there, looking at the cold remedies, while trying to work out what to do. I've got to see whether that initial smile was anything more than that, which means going over and talking to her, but about what? I've never been good at this chat-up lark, and especially under pressure. And I know why: it's the fear of rejection – the worry that the moment I lay myself bare, she'll send me scampering shame-faced from the shop, my ego crushed by a simple 'no'. Because by suggesting something like a coffee, or a drink, or even dinner, what I'm really saying is 'I want to get to know you better, then have sex with you, with a view to maybe us spending the rest of our lives together.' And that's a scary thing for anyone to propose – even when it's disguised as a latte at Starbucks – and especially when you're making that proposal after something as simple as a smile.

Mindful of my earlier conversation with Ash, I realize that I have a decision to make, and it's one that every single *single* man makes at least once a day – do I risk the humiliation of crashing and burning in an attempt to rid myself of my unattached status, and what's worse, risk it when I'm pretty sure any new relationship's going to go the same way as all the others? Well, given how attractive she is, and the alternative, there's really just one answer to that.

I pick up a bottle of Night Nurse and pretend to study the label, while actually studying the queue. Amid the coughing, spluttering, and limping line – and God knows what medicine they think they're going to get to help them – there do seem to be a few people who are just buying deodorant, maybe because the queue here is shorter than the one at the tills at the front of the shop. But that raises another issue – do I risk my own well-being by queuing up with this unhealthy lot? Given that I need an excuse to talk to her, I don't seem to have any choice, so I grab the nearest toiletry and rejoin the end of the queue. But then it occurs to me that simply walking up and paying for a tube of Lynx shower gel isn't going to do the trick, so I put it back, then pick it up again hurriedly as I edge closer and closer to the till.

I'm desperately starting to wonder how much conversation I can eke out of the purchase of a packet of Nurofen as well when I have an idea. There's a sign above the counter that says 'Ask Your Pharmacist', and while I know they don't mean 'for a date', this at least gives me a chance to have an actual conversation with her. So, in theory, all I have to do is invent an ailment. But what? Because thinking about it, there's a very short list of ailments that will show you in a positive light. A simple cold or flu, maybe – but trouble is, I don't sound like I've got any symptoms. What about something not wrong with me, but with my dad. Or my mum? No – I can't use her, and risk coming across as a mummy's boy. And if I pretend I'm here for either of them, will she think that I'm a caring son, or more likely, that I still live at home? Best not to risk it. In that case, I need to come up with something that's amusing. The bad curry I had last night? No. Insulting her national cuisine might not be the best idea.

There's only one person in between me and the till now, and I'm starting to panic. Excessive sweating? No – not good, especially since the combination of the store's heating system and my heavy coat means that I actually am, and the last thing I want to do is draw attention to that. My mind is playing tricks on me, suggesting the most embarrassing ailments. Athlete's foot? No – she might think I need the cream for another itchy area. Piles? Best not. The runs? The runs! That's it. Or at least, a sports injury. Women like sporty guys, right? And although apart from the odd game of tennis, the most sporty I get is when I watch the football with Ash, it might just work.

Happy with my plan, I slip the shower gel back onto the nearest shelf, and when I eventually get to the till, surreptitiously check the name badge pinned to the lapel of her white coat – Seema Mistry – and prepare to launch into my story. But as she looks up at me, my mind goes blank.

'Can I help you?'

'Er, yes,' I say, followed by 'yes', but an octave or two lower than my first, nervously squeaked reply. Trouble is, I can't think of how, and the only thought that leaps to mind is why didn't I hold on to the shower gel? I look around, but it's too far away to reach without me losing my place in the line. What if I buy something else – something that at least doesn't have aloe vera in it – that suggests I'm a real man? But what? 'I'd like to buy some, I mean, I need ...' I stop talking, because she really is very pretty. And, more importantly, I can't think of anything.

Seema smiles at me sympathetically, then taps the glass counter in front of her. Where the condoms are.

'What size?' she whispers.

'Pardon?'

'Condoms,' says Seema, slightly louder this time. 'What size do you need?'

This takes me by surprise, not only because I'm pretty sure I hadn't said anything out loud about actually needing some, but also because I've been buying condoms for fifteen years, and never knew that they came in different sizes. But all of a sudden, it strikes me that buying a packet of condoms is an excellent idea. Two, maybe, to suggest that not only am I getting a lot of sex, but I'm responsible as well, and what's more, if I go for 'ribbed', it'll make me out to be a considerate lover too. But then again, it's embarrassing buying condoms at the best of times. And especially from a girl you fancy.

'Er ...'

'Yes?' says Seema.

There's a murmuring from the queue behind me, and I realize that I don't have long. Maybe I should just go with the condoms after all. But the *Who-Wants-to-Be-a-*

Millionaire? million-pound question still remains, and it's a lot harder to answer than anything I've ever seen on the programme.

'I'm not sure. I mean, I'd like to say "large", obviously. But being honest, I'm probably more of a medium. Not that I've ever had any complaints.'

Seema looks at me levelly. 'What size *packet*?'

I'm a little stunned at her directness. I mean, I know she's a medical person, but surely this is a bit, well, forward. 'That's what I've been trying to explain.'

'Well?' says Seema, patiently. 'Three? Six? Twelve?'

I want to say that I've never actually measured it, but I'm sure most women would know that to be a lie. 'Er . . . Do you mean in "inches"?'

'No,' says Seema, producing a selection of different-sized packets of Durex from beneath the counter. 'How *many*.'

'Ah,' I say, although *aargh* might be more appropriate. 'Well I, er, don't actually need any. Condoms.'

'You don't?' says Seema.

'No. I wanted some advice.'

'Advice? Are you sick?'

'Not exactly,' I say, although I'm beginning to worry that yes, I am. 'I've got a, um, sports injury.'

Seema looks at me suspiciously. 'Really? What have you done?'

Don't say groin strain. *Don't say groin strain.* 'It's a, er, groin strain.'

Seema raises one eyebrow. 'How on earth did you get that?' she says, tapping the top of the largest condom box with her index finger. 'Or daren't I ask?'

As I try and come up with a valid scenario, one of Seema's colleagues opens up the next-door till, and the people in the queue behind me move across to that one. Which of course means I've got no reason to hurry up. Even though now, I actually want to.

'No, it was from playing . . .' Playing what – the piano? 'I mean, I was in the gym. And I, er . . .' I stop talking, as I'm in danger of getting myself into more trouble. What's more, it's clear that Seema's not buying any of this. 'So, what would you, you know, advise?' I say, pointing at the 'Ask Your Pharmacist' sign above her head, just in case she thinks I'm acting inappropriately.

Seema thinks for a second or two. 'Well, generally, with any kind of strain, we advise something called RICE.'

I'm a little confused. 'What – like *Basmati*?'

'No,' she laughs. 'It's an acronym. R-I-C-E stands for rest, ice, compression, elevation. Though given that it's your groin, I think we'd better forget the ice, compression, and, you know . . .'

'Elevation?'

Seema nods. 'Exactly. So just make sure you rest the affected area.'

'Oh. Right,' I say, trying to ignore the fact that the way she's looking at me suggests she doesn't think that'll be a problem. 'Thanks.'

'So you won't be wanting these, then?' she says, nodding towards the bumper pack of Durex.

I give the box a cursory glance, then suddenly feel guilty that I haven't bought anything, though why, I don't know. It's not as if Seema owns the shop, or is on commission, or anything. 'No, I'll take them anyway. For when I'm, you know . . .'

Seema picks up the box and scans it through the till. 'Better?'

'Yes. Better. And thanks.'

'For the condoms?'

'No. The advice.'

'It's what I'm here for,' says Seema, although perhaps a touch ironically, before extending a hand towards me.

I take it, and give it a shake. 'I'm Ben. Nice to meet you,' I say, realizing that now's my chance, and if I am going to ask her out, then I won't get a better opportunity. But whether it's from a lack of confidence from all the failed relationships in my life, or the knowledge that I'll have to buy my toiletries from Superdrug from now on if she turns me down, or simply that I'm overwhelmed by how attractive she is, I just can't get the words out.

Reluctantly, I let go of Seema's hand, but she keeps it extended. 'It's nice to meet you too, Ben, but I was actually after your nine pounds ninety-eight.'

'Oh. Right. Sorry. Of course.' I feel myself blushing, and hurriedly fish around in my pocket for a ten pound note. 'Here.'

'Thanks,' she says, handing me my change, along with the condoms, which she's mercifully put in a plastic bag. 'And in the meantime, take care of that groin.'

'Sure. Will do. Bye.'

She smiles. 'Bye, Ben.'

Reluctantly, I turn and start to walk away from the counter, only remembering that I should perhaps be limping when I'm halfway out of the store, and when I look back over my shoulder to see whether I've been sussed, I guess the answer must be 'yes', because Seema's smiling to herself, while shaking her head.

When I get outside, I peer into the bag to see exactly what it is I've ended up spending nearly ten pounds on, but the first thing I notice is the use-by date on the box. Even though it's a good two years away, given the way things have been going, my first thought is that I might end up having to throw most of them away.

Chapter 4

Cursing myself at my pathetic chatting-up skills, I make my way towards the library, and head upstairs to the Adult Education floor. To be honest, I couldn't live off my painting alone, and so I'm grateful for the two hours a week at thirty-six pounds an hour that the council pays me for the class. But they're a fun – if mixed – bunch, even though their general skill level is somewhere below what you'd see displayed on the average family refrigerator door, and given that I spend the majority of my week with just my paintbrush for company, I actually quite look forward to these sessions. As usual, when I get to my classroom, Taxi Terry is already there.

'Cheer up.' Terry grins at me. 'It might never happen.'

I catch sight of my expression in the large mirror along the back wall of the room, and see what he means. 'Evening, Ta . . . er, Terry,' I say, stopping myself just in time. I give all my students a tag, as I'm terrible with names, and I read somewhere that if you associate their name with what it is they do or something about them, and even give it the same first letter, then it helps you to remember it. Unfortunately, I usually just end up calling them that instead, which is okay when it's something like 'taxi', because Terry's actually quite proud of what he does for a living, but I have to be careful that I don't make the same mistake with Hoodie Harry. And especially Lesbian Lizzie.

'What's up with you?' asks Terry, getting a box of pencils out of his bag.

'Sorry, Terry.' I try to force a smile, wondering whether I should tell him what's just happened in Boots, but I've had enough embarrassment for one night. 'I've just found out a friend of mine is getting married,' I say, trying to sound upbeat.

'Ah.' Terry's face darkens a little. 'I thought you might have heard some bad news. Can't you talk him out of it?' Terry's in his mid-forties, and, having been divorced last year for the second time, seems to have lost his faith in the institution of marriage. I suspect he signed up for this class to meet women, but seeing as the only women here are either old enough to be his mother, or would prefer to go out with his mother, I'm always a little surprised he keeps turning up. And early, too – unlike on the odd occasion I've used his cab company.

'I don't want to talk him out of it,' I say, walking across and switching on the electric heater in the corner. 'He seems very happy.'

Terry makes a face. 'Won't last,' he says, sitting down behind his easel.

I'm just about to take issue with him as Sad Sarah, Mad Mavis, and, er, Lizzie walk into the room. They always arrive together, and at exactly the same time each week, though God knows how or why. One night, Terry and I watched at the window to see whether they all came in the same car, or had some unwritten agreement to wait for each other outside until they were all there, but even the fact that they arrived from different directions didn't seem to make any difference. *Maybe it's like when women live together and their periods start to coincide*, Terry had suggested, although I hadn't wanted to know how he knew that particular fact.

'Evening, Ben, Terry,' they chorus, taking their places behind their respective easels.

'Evening, guys,' says Terry, although he's already been told off several times by Lizzie for saying that.

'Ladies,' I say quickly, wanting to head off any potential disagreements. 'Shall we get going?' I look at my watch, wondering whether we should wait for Harry, the other member of our little group. He's only here because he has to be – part of his community service order, apparently – although I wouldn't have known that if he hadn't turned up one summer evening wearing a pair of shorts that clearly displayed the electronic tagging device on his left ankle. He seems like a nice lad, though, if prone to the occasional flash of anger, especially where Terry is concerned – although that's possibly as much Terry's fault as his. Once Harry's finished the course, he wants to go on and design cars, apparently. Although it was having designs on other people's cars that got him the ASBO in the first place.

As if on cue, Harry rushes in. 'Sorry I'm late,' he says, a little breathlessly.

Terry peers at the still-swinging door behind him. 'Someone after you?'

'Nah.' Harry sits down behind his easel. 'Car broke down.'

Terry raises one eyebrow. 'Yours? Or someone else's?'

Harry grins at him. 'Brakes went. Crashed into some old cab out front.'

Terry's jaw nearly hits the floor. 'What?' As he leaps up and runs to the window to check on his taxi, which he always parks right outside so he can keep an eye on it, Harry winks at the rest of us.

'Not really. My girlfriend's. Piece of trash.'

Mavis shakes her head. 'Harry! That's no way to talk about a woman,' she says, then emits her trademark laugh – the high-pitched braying noise that she makes after everything she says, as if she's just heard what she's said for the first time, and it's the funniest joke in the world. In fact, it was when she made the same sound after simply introducing herself to the group at the first session that she earned her rather un-PC nickname.

'Depends on the woman,' says Terry, still scowling at Harry from across the room.

Harry looks at the two of them, a confused expression on his face. 'Nah. My girlfriend's car, I mean. A crappy old Fiesta. She's selling it to pay for the wedding.'

'I didn't know you were engaged,' I say, wondering whether everyone is getting married except me. 'Congratulations, Harry.'

Harry frowns. 'I'm not.'

'Ah.' I decide not to ask further – the only thing Harry is interested in more than other people's cars is other people's wives or girlfriends, and I've long since given up trying to keep track of the various girls I see him with around town. Instead, I point up at the clock on the wall. 'Let's get started, shall we?' I was going to start them on sculpture today – in fact, I've been thinking about moving on to it for a couple of weeks, but I don't particularly want to give Harry any sharp implements – so I just nod towards their easels. 'Continue with your portraits. And remember, you're trying to capture the essence of the person. Not just how they look on the outside.'

As they get down to work, I wonder what the real story is with them all, and why – apart from Harry – they've chosen to be here on a Friday night. While I'm not sure what Harry's love life is about, apart from what seems to be a quantity rather than quality approach, Terry, on the other hand, couldn't be more cynical. And whether that's because he's tried and failed – twice – who knows? As far as I'm aware there's a Mister Mavis at home, but given that I know she does this class on a Friday, pottery on a Thursday, creative writing on a Tuesday, and computer studies on a Monday, I can't imagine they have much of a home life. As for Lizzie,

I've seen her out a couple of times with another woman, but she never introduces her as 'my partner', or whatever is politically correct nowadays, and in fact doesn't introduce her at all, so I don't feel I can ask.

But of them all, Sarah is the one I feel the most sorry for. Her husband of fifty years died last year, and she's given up all hope of meeting someone else, even though she's a well-preserved seventy-one. I'd asked her why at our Christmas drinks bash, when Harry had brought in half a dozen bottles of Moët which had 'fallen off the back of a lorry' — evidently without getting smashed, unlike we did that evening — but Sarah had just shrugged. *Because I'll never meet anyone like him again*, she'd said, matter-of-factly, and I'd felt instantly guilty for boring her with my and Amy's 'problems' beforehand. And the way she obviously believed that fact so strongly, and what that said about how great their marriage had been, had put a lump in my throat so large that I couldn't force another drop of champagne past it.

I walk slowly around the room as they paint, offering advice here, or a comment there, though fortunately I manage to stop myself from asking Terry whether his portrait is something from the *Alien* films, as he tells me later it's one of his ex-wives. But as I watch them work, I can't seem to concentrate, given this afternoon's developments.

Because while I'm happy for Ash, there's another emotion nagging away at me, and when I finally work out what it is, I'm a little surprised to realize that it's jealousy. I mean, I know he's had a bit of help, but given our respective relationship histories, I really, genuinely thought that I'd be the one who'd get married first. After all, compared with him, I've been out with loads of women – well, not loads, exactly, but probably at least the national average, and yet, out of them all, there wasn't one – Amy included – I wanted to make an 'honest woman' of.

While I realize that it's pretty selfish of me to be thinking about my shortcomings rather than Ash's good news, I'm also slightly worried that he's happy to leap into something so serious with someone who, let's face it, he doesn't really know that well. But then again, given *my* relationship history, maybe that makes sense? After all – and ironically – with most of my girlfriends, the longer our relationship lasted, the more we got on each other's nerves, meaning that the prospect of marriage got less and less likely as time went on – something Amy obviously recognized too. Which is possibly why she tried to force my hand.

Yet here Ash is and – judging by the look on his face earlier – after little more than five minutes, he's sure he wants to make the kind of commitment that I've not even come close to for most of my life. Although the fact that he's so excited by the prospect, and I wasn't, makes me realise that Amy and I splitting up was the right thing to do.

And while Ash has always been the leap-before-you-look type, what I can't understand is why Priti is so keen on the idea too. She certainly doesn't seem desperate, and by the look of her, she could have her pick of men. Is there something Ash has got that I haven't – apart from a mysteriously unlimited cash supply, a flash car, and parents who own the best Indian restaurant in town, of course? But then again, Priti doesn't seem the gold-digger type. And even from the brief conversation I've had with her, I can tell that she seems level-headed enough to know that a marriage needs more than material things to work.

Maybe it's a timing issue? Perhaps she's simply ready to get married, and Ash, as usual, is the lucky one, and just happens to be in the frame at the right time. He's always been an opportunist, and maybe *given* his relationship history – or lack of it – he's realized he'll never get a better opportunity.

And yet, at the same time as I'm congratulating myself on such a clever analysis, I start to feel more than a little depressed. Because it's not as if I haven't had an opportunity either. To be honest, I've been keen to settle down and get married for a good few years now, and I know that a couple of ex-girlfriends of mine – Amy included, of course – have felt the same. And they've been nice girls: good-looking, fun, sexy – everything that Priti seems to be, but for some reason they just haven't been right.

For the rest of the class, I can't seem to get a handle on *why*. Have I been picking the wrong kind of girls to go out with in the first place, hoping that the thunderbolt will strike as the relationship progresses, then losing interest when it – not surprisingly – doesn't? Or am I being stupid in wanting to be knocked off my feet by someone, and not being prepared to make a commitment, particularly now that, given my recent change of career, and therefore financial status, I might not get as many opportunities any more? And if that's the case, have I been foolish in letting other – perfectly satisfactory – relationships pass me by?

But it's not until I'm walking back home that I realize that whichever of those questions is right, there is one common factor in all of my failed relationships. One thing that's stopped me from getting down on one knee. And the probable reason for my current single status:

It's me.

Chapter 5

When I wake up the next day, the first thing I do – and I know it's stupid, but I do it most mornings – is turn to my right, then slowly open my eyes, just to see whether I'm on my own or not. And as I blink in the morning sunlight, I realize that of course I am; as Ash reminded me yesterday, Amy and I split up. Just like I split with the rest of them, so why I'm still surprised to wake up alone more often than not, I just don't know. I also realize that the simplest way to avoid this feeling is, of course, to sleep in the middle of the bed – that way, the first thing I'd see every morning wouldn't be this huge great space next to me. But that's not really what double beds are for, is it? Besides, it'd feel a little too weird, as if I was admitting that the vacancy next to me was never going to be filled. Either way, and irrespective of how I try to deal with it, the problem with waking up alone is that it puts you in a bad mood for the rest of the day. Because even though you can get out of any side of the bed you like, you always seem to end up getting out of the wrong one.

This morning, however, feels even more depressing, as for the first time I feel that if my relationships keep going the way that mine and Amy's did, then this is how it might be every single day of my life – with the emphasis on the word 'single'. For a moment, I contemplate not getting up at all, but then suddenly change my mind. Today, I tell myself, I'm going to play things differently. Instead of moaning to myself about the fact that I'm alone again, I'm going to enjoy it. Celebrate it, even. Please myself. After all, I can do what I want with my day. And while my initial thought is that I want to spend it with someone else, someone *special*, I decide that, actually, I'm going to do exactly that. It's just that the special person is going to be, well, *me*.

For a start, I decide not to get dressed, and so, after a quick visit to the bathroom where I leave the toilet seat up on purpose, amble into the kitchen wearing just my boxer shorts, before flicking the kettle on and wondering what to have for breakfast. However, this feeling of elated semi-nakedness lasts only as long as it takes me to open the fridge door and discover that I'm out of milk. And seeing as I can't stand black coffee, and the staff in the corner shop might frown on my turning up there dressed as I am, I reluctantly head back into the bedroom and throw on yesterday's jeans and a sweatshirt.

But this is still great, I think, as I stuff a handful of small change into my pocket and walk out through the front door. I live right in the centre of town, on a street called, ironically, Love Lane, and while my flat's not that big – which is one of the reasons I need to rent a studio to work in – it's handy for the shops and the sea. Mind you, given the size of Margate, and the fact that we're on the coast, so are most places, I suppose.

I haven't shaved, or even showered – which would explain the slight odour I detect as I walk along the road, surreptitiously sniffing my left armpit – and I'm just about to sniff the right one, then stop myself, realizing that if one's bad, the other one being not-so-bad is hardly going to make up for it. I've also got no socks on, which is perhaps not such a good idea given that it's chilly, and when I catch sight of my reflection in a shop window, my look is a little more 'homeless' than 'hasn't been home', which wasn't really my intention. But then again, I'm not trying to look like anything for anyone.

There are no other customers in the corner shop, which is probably fortunate, considering my level of hygiene, and as I take my purchases to the counter, the girl behind the till looks me up and down a little strangely – although that could also be something to do with the fact that I'm buying a pint of skimmed milk, some HobNobs, and a packet of hot cross buns, thus maybe sending out mixed messages as to my healthy eating plans. But I don't care, I remind myself, as I start to count my change out on the counter in front of her. I'm not dressing up for her – or any woman. Because I am single, and proud of the fact. So what if I don't meet my ideal woman today – or any day, come to think of it? Besides, what is it they say – whoever 'they' are? When you're not looking for it, that's when it comes along? Well, I'm definitely not looking – either for it, or like it – so today could just be my lucky day.

'Hello, Ben.'

Or perhaps not.

'Amy. Hi.' She's dressed in her gym gear, although whether she's pre- or post-workout, it's difficult to tell, because Amy always looks immaculate. I haven't seen her since we split up, and while I'm pretty sure she's not checking up on me, this particular shop is a little out of her way. 'What are you doing here?'

'Same as you,' she says, holding up a carton of milk and a packet of sugar-free muesli, as I try and hide my shopping behind my back. 'In principle, at least. Another healthy breakfast?'

Amy always despaired of my eating habits. In fact, when we broke up, she told me that she was looking forward to going out with someone whose idea of a starter wasn't to pop open a packet of Pringles. 'Well, you know. My body is a temple, and all that.'

She gives me a look as if to say that if it is a temple, then no one would want to worship there this morning. 'Same old Ben. How have you been?'

'Oh, fine. Busy. Working.'

'Working?' Amy raises one eyebrow. 'Oh, you mean your *painting*. How's that going?'

I bristle slightly at her dismissive tone, but then again, I suppose she's got a right to be resentful of my change of career. After all, in her eyes, I chose it over her.

Possibly because that's what I told her in an attempt to
spare her feelings when we broke up. 'Good. Great, in
fact. How's *your* work?' I say, keen to emphasize that it's
not mine any more.

'Oh, you know. At least it pays the bills, I suppose.'

Normally, I'd laugh at this. Amy's so focused on
climbing up the corporate ladder that to pay the bills is
probably the last reason she goes to the office each day.
But the insinuation that what I do doesn't cuts right to
the bone.

'Yes, well, everyone's got to start somewhere,' I say,
counting the exact money out of the rest of my coppers,
and sliding them across to the shop assistant.

'Well, it's good to see that there's *something* you're
prepared to stick at. When the going gets tough.'

For a moment, I don't know how to respond to that.
Amy's obviously referring to our relationship. But before
I can answer, she glances down at my pile of change and,
added to my unkempt appearance, obviously puts two
and two together, but unusually for someone who's as
good an accountant as she is, makes five.

'You know you can always come back,' she says,
resting a hand on my arm. 'If things are *that* bad.'

'You mean to work, right?'

Amy removes her hand and smiles sympathetically at
me. 'You know what I mean, Ben.'

'Well, they're not *that* bad, actually,' I say, before
realizing that sounds a little nasty, as if I'm implying that
things would have to be really desperate for me to

consider going back out with her. 'Work-wise, I mean. In fact, hang the expense ...' I glance around the shop, then as nonchalantly as I can, pick up the nearest newspaper, which happens to be a copy of the *Sun*, before flinging another thirty pence recklessly down on the counter.

'Well, that's good to hear,' says Amy, pulling a cashpoint-crisp twenty-pound note out of her purse to pay for her purchases. 'Really it is.'

We stand there awkwardly for a moment, until I break the uneasy silence. 'Anyway,' I say, tapping the top of my left wrist, before realizing I've forgotten to put my watch on this morning. 'Must run.'

Amy looks a little put out. 'Hot date?'

I could say yes, of course, but that would be a lie. And cruel. And being cruel, or lying to women – particularly a woman I once cared about – isn't really my style.

'Nope.' I smile back at her, and gather up my shopping. 'Hot cross bun.'

As Amy rolls her eyes at me, I head out of the shop, then make my way back down the street and into my flat, taking a swig out of the milk carton as I shut the door behind me, then – after checking no one's looking, for some reason – wipe my mouth on my sleeve. I'm a little bit shaken after our chance encounter, but pleased that she seems to be okay. And while I can't quite work out how that makes me feel, one feeling I am sure of is hunger, so I slice a couple of the buns in half and stick them under the grill, scanning the front page of the paper while I wait for them to toast. I don't normally buy a newspaper, and I soon realize why, as it appears to be full of stories about the latest celebrity divorce, and an 'exclusive' about how someone I've never heard of has been caught cheating on someone else I don't recognize, while the first bit of proper news seems to be relegated to page two. And what's the common factor in all these misery stories? Women. Yup, I tell myself, I'm better off without them. Until I turn to page three, that is.

I make myself a coffee, then rush to the grill, where I've forgotten about the hot cross buns, which are now a little hotter than I'd have liked. And as I eat them, I start to wonder whether in fact Terry's viewpoint on women is the right one. After all, why on earth do I feel the need to spend my whole life, all day every day, with someone else anyway? It can't be sensible. And the more I think about it, the more I try and rationalize it. And fail.

I find a piece of paper and a pen and sit down at the table, then write the words 'single' and 'married' at the top, and draw a line down the middle so I've got two columns. In the 'single' column, I start listing all the things that are great about being, well, not married, using this morning as a prime example. You can eat what you want, I think, finishing off the last of the charred buns, before moving on to the HobNobs. And wear what you want. Go to bed whenever you like, and get up whenever too. Oh, and you don't have to shower, I add, remembering my armpits, then hurriedly cross the last three things out when I realize that they look more like the kind of thing a five-year-old would highlight for their ideal weekend. There's the extra money, of course, having not wasted it in over-priced restaurants on a series of dates that'll never go anywhere, or expensive presents to compensate for a lack of 'emotional giving' – Amy's words, not mine.

I add a couple more, and although they're mainly observations about particular women I've been out with, like not having to sit through *EastEnders*, or being able to watch a DVD without pausing it every five minutes to explain the plot of any film that isn't a 'chick flick', I suspect they're probably generally applicable, then refill my coffee mug and turn my attention to the right-hand column. Given the amount of things listed on the left, surely this can't be difficult?

I start with the obvious one: regular sex. Then cross it out again, because from what I've heard from Terry over the past few months, the reason it's called 'tying the knot' is because you might as well tie a knot in a certain part of your anatomy, given the amount of sex you have once you've slipped a ring on her finger.

Okay ... Someone to share my life with. Good one. Assuming I want to share it, of course. I mean, I quite like being alone in my studio. Although someone to share the bills with would be good, I think, listening to the clunk of a number of brown envelopes coming through the letterbox.

Er ... Someone who loves me? Well, I've got my mum and dad, although they're not going to be around for ever. But then again, I could always get a pet, I suppose, crossing it out.

Kids. *Of course*. I love kids. Except for those two little buggers who visit Mr Williams, the divorced dad in the flat upstairs, every other weekend, and seem to spend most of their time jumping around on the wood laminate floor that according to the lease he's not supposed to have. Oh, and the unruly lot that my dad teaches, who he often mentions in the same breath as when he's talking about bringing back capital punishment. But your own are different, aren't they? Or at least, that's what my dad always says, admittedly through gritted teeth.

I stare at my piece of paper for a while, wondering why the 'married' column is so much harder to fill up than the 'single' one, and I'm on my fifth HobNob when it hits me – someone to love. The one item on the list that makes everything else irrelevant because it's so important, and at the same time, means I was wrong last night, and that it *isn't* me. Because the thing about being married is that you've got someone to love.

And the more I think about it, the more I realize that that's all I want. Because up till now, that's been the problem – what's missing from every relationship I've had. And while that realization is a relief, because it explains why I didn't want to move things on to the next level, I also find it quite shocking that in thirty years, I've never actually said those three little words to anyone – apart from a member of my immediate family, that is – and meant them.

I have said them, you understand. To Amy, for instance. And it's not that I was lying at the time. For example, I love HobNobs, but I can certainly live without them – especially when I've got a packet of those Fox's super-chocolatey biscuits in the cupboard. So in actual fact, when I told Amy I loved her, I wasn't lying, because I did – even though there weren't any Fox's in reserve, so to speak. But I realize now that I loved her in the HobNob sense, rather than being *in* actual, literal, romantic love, whatever that is. And that's fundamentally why, when she gave me her ultimatum, we split up. Because loving someone like you love a biscuit is really not the soundest basis for a marriage.

Desperately, I do a mental run-through of my previous girlfriends, trying to think of someone, but the sad fact is that there's no one I've ever dated who's made me feel how I imagine love should feel. Sure, I've missed a few of them when we've been apart, or been eager to see them at times, although that's usually been for other things, like sex, or because I've been looking forward to seeing a particular film we'd planned to go to together, and, well, just sex, really. But even though I search as far back as I can remember, there's no one who's really made my heart go, well, whatever hearts go like when you're in love. And all of a sudden, that strikes me as the most depressing thing in the world. With a shake of my head, I crumple my sheet of paper into a ball and throw it towards the bin in the corner. And miss.

Oh well. There's nothing for it but to get on with my

day, I decide, but to be honest, by the time I've finished the paper, a couple more HobNobs, had a shower, then checked through the Saturday TV listings, it's still only lunchtime, and this 'celebrate your single status' lark has started to get pretty boring. In fact, the more I think about it, the more I'm craving *any* company, let alone female.

I can hardly phone Ash – he and Priti are probably busy working out what the names of their kids are going to be – and by one o'clock I'm starting to run out of options. Seeing as there's no food in the fridge, and I can't be bothered to trudge round Tesco, there's only one thing for it. One place where I'm guaranteed a warm welcome. And where there's a good possibility that I'll get fed too.

Chapter 6

As I walk in through the kitchen door, my mum looks round from where she's unloading the dishwasher. 'Don't tell me it's lunchtime already?'

I look at my watch as innocently as I can, relieved that I remembered to put it on after my shower. 'Is it?'

As I shut the door behind me, she peers over my shoulder. 'On your own today?'

There are a hundred answers to that question, but I settle for a simple 'Yes, Mum.' I love my mother to death, but the disappointment in her voice whenever I admit that I'm not getting married, and therefore not presenting her with grandchildren yet, is getting a little hard to bear. Which is probably why I haven't told her that Amy and I have split up yet. 'Where's Dad?' I say, deciding that there's no time like the present. Plus, I might get some sympathy food too.

My mum shrugs. 'Probably outside in his shed. Though God knows what it is he does in there.'

She always says this, and I know the answer. He doesn't actually 'do' anything in there, apart from tidy it up, or sort out his toolbox. But the real reason he goes out there is to get away from her. Not that my mother needs to be got away from – in fact, both of them would be lost if they had to spend more than a day apart. It's just that my dad, like most people, occasionally needs his own space. And it's ironic that in this rather large four-bedroom house that he's worked all his life to pay for, the space he's chosen is a draughty eight-by-six wooden construction at the bottom of the garden.

'It's just, well, I wanted to tell you something. Both of you.'

My mother freezes, then drops the pan she's been wiping into the sink with a loud clang and rushes out into the garden. I walk over to the kitchen window just in time to see her hurry down the path and almost drag my dad bodily out of the shed, silencing his protests with a kiss, before escorting him smartly into the kitchen a few moments later. They've been married for almost thirty years, and yet sometimes their relationship seems so fresh, so much fun, that you'd be forgiven for thinking that it had only been thirty minutes.

As she closes the door behind him, he gives me a long-suffering smile. 'How's my favourite offspring?'

'Dad, I'm your only offspring. So that's not much of a compliment, is it?'

'Sorry, son,' he says, ruffling the hair on the top of my head as if I'm about five years old. For some reason, my dad never calls me by my name, as if perhaps 'Ben' wasn't his first choice all those years ago, and therefore he refuses to acknowledge it. But then again, he usually refers to my mother as 'your mum', so I suppose I shouldn't take it personally. 'Your mum says you've got some sort of announcement to make?'

I take a deep breath. 'Well, it's to do with Amy. We've, well . . .' I glance at my mother's face, trying to ignore the look of expectation, as if she's hoping I'm going to say that we're engaged. 'We've decided to go our separate ways.'

'Oh, Ben, how could you?' My mum pulls out a chair and slumps down at the kitchen table, and I immediately feel guilty.

'Who's decided?' asks my dad, sitting down next to her, and beckoning for me to follow suit. 'You? Amy? Or was it one of those "mutual" decisions you keep having forced upon you?'

'Well, to be honest, she decided,' I say, wondering whether to try explaining the circumstances of our parting. 'She wanted us to think about getting married.'

'Think about?' asks my dad. 'Or actually get married.'

'Well, both, I suppose.'

'But I thought you *wanted* to get married?' says my mum accusingly.

'I did. I mean, I do. Desperately. I just wasn't sure whether I did to Amy.'

'So this parting of the ways was your fault again?' says my mum crossly. She's always really liked Amy, so it comes out as more of an accusation than a question. 'You'll be the death of me, you know?'

'It's no one's fault,' says my dad, leaping to my defence. 'Sometimes these things just happen.'

My mum doesn't look entirely convinced. 'Well, why do they always happen to *Ben*?'

My dad and I stare at each other, unsure who that question is actually directed to. 'I don't know, Mum. And thanks for your support, Dad, but maybe Mum's right.'

She looks surprised. 'I am?'

'Well, maybe. I mean, not necessarily about me and Amy, but generally. I'm starting to think it's *all* my fault.'

She frowns. 'What is?'

'The reason I'm not married yet,' I say, feeling suddenly embarrassed.

'How do you mean?' asks my dad.

I take a deep breath, and try to explain. 'Well, you know how I've had rather a lot of girlfriends? And none of them have really, er, done it for me.'

Out of the corner of my eye, I can see my dad smirk. 'That must have been frustrating.'

'Not like that,' I say, as my mum tuts at him. 'You know what I mean. So I'm just starting to worry that I might be . . .' My mouth goes a little bit dry, and the two of them exchange worried glances.

'Go on, son,' says my dad.

'Well, I think that possibly I'm . . .'

'What?' says my mum, desperately.

'I don't know. G . . .' My voice cracks a little after the

first letter, but before I can clear my throat and finish the sentence, my mother leaps out of her chair and rushes round to my side of the table.

'Oh, *Ben*,' she says, enveloping me in a huge hug.

'Get off him, woman,' says my dad. 'What were you going to say, son?'

'Going about this relationship lark the wrong way,' I say, attempting to prise my mum's arms from around my neck, but she refuses to let go, and in fact, squeezes me even harder.

'Oh, thank goodness,' she sniffs, finally letting go of me. 'I thought you were going to tell us that you were, you know, *gay*. Which would have been fine, of course.' Although they're distinctly middle-aged, my mum and dad are not at all stuck in the Middle Ages when it comes to, well, modern life, and thinking about it, my mum's only objection to me being gay would be the grandchildren issue.

My dad smiles. 'In what way, son?'

I shrug again. 'I dunno, really. I just kind of thought that I might have been, you know, doing it all wrong.'

My mum frowns at my dad. 'Alan, I told you we should have had that birds and bees conversation with him, and not just left him to his own devices. I mean, I know we let you keep that stack of magazines under your bed when you were a teenager, Ben, but those weren't *real* women.'

'More's the pity,' jokes my dad, as I try to stop myself from blushing furiously. 'But if you wanted some tips in the bedroom department, then of course. Happy to offer my fatherly advice.' My dad always refers to sex as 'in the bedroom department', and I wish he wouldn't. In fact, I'd actually rather he didn't refer to it at all. He nods towards the tray of sausage rolls that are visible through the glass oven door. 'Although perhaps best wait until after we've eaten, though.'

I stare at the two of them for a couple of seconds before what they've said actually sinks in. 'No. Not *that*. God no. Eurgh. I know what I'm doing in, er, *that* department, rest assured.'

My mum smiles sympathetically, and sits down next to me. 'Are you sure, Ben? Because it's very important. I mean, one of the things that first attracted me to your father was his ability to . . .'

'Mum, please!' I shudder. 'It's not that at all. I just mean, well . . .' This is harder to explain than I first thought. 'You know how I changed my position recently?'

She folds her arms. 'If it's positions you're worried about, Ben, then your dad's got this book that . . .'

'Mum, for the last time, I'm not talking about sex. I'm talking about relationships.'

'Oh,' she says, standing up abruptly. 'I'll put the kettle on, then.' We're not one of those families who talk about this kind of stuff very often, but whenever we do, my mum always likes us to be drinking tea.

'I mean, I've probably gone out with most of the eligible women my age in Margate . . .'

'That's my boy,' interrupts my dad, proudly.

'. . . and not found one who I've wanted to settle down with. Or who's wanted to settle down with me.'

'Ah,' says my dad, a little less proudly.

'Except for Amy,' says my mum, removing three mugs from the mug tree and banging them down noisily on the granite work surface.

'But that's the real irony. The one who did want to marry me also wanted me to go back to being something that I'm not. And I wasn't prepared to compromise.' I shake my head slowly. 'Which is why I'm starting to think my whole approach is wrong.'

'Rubbish.' My dad laughs. 'You just need to show them who's boss,' he says, slapping my mum on the backside as she walks past him.

'Dad, I worked with Amy for over a year. She's pretty . . . Formidable. Even her actual boss can't show her who's boss.'

He smiles. 'Son, you just have to be a man about it. Leave them in no doubt as to who wears the trousers. Isn't that right, Sue?'

My mum and I exchange glances. We both know who actually runs their relationship, and it's certainly not my dad, even though she lets him think he does – which I suspect is a rather clever ruse.

I sigh. 'But that's the problem.'

My dad frowns. 'How is it a problem?'

'Quiet, Alan,' says my mum. 'Let Ben explain.'

As my dad shuts up obediently, I try to put it into

words. 'What you just said. "Be a man about it". I'm not sure I know what that means any more.'

My dad opens his mouth to answer, but my mum shushes him again. 'Go on, Ben.'

'Well, back when you and Dad got married, the roles were pretty clearly defined, weren't they? The man went out to work, while the woman looked after the house and the children. And sure, women could maybe do a bit of part-time work, but fundamentally, they knew what their real "job" was, and that arrangement worked.'

My dad shrugs. 'So, what's your point?'

'My point, Dad, is that nowadays, that's all changed. Women have careers. Ambitions. Higher aspirations than maybe just being "her indoors". And that's great. But the trouble is, it also means their expectations for us are different too.'

As I say this, I wonder if I'm talking about men and women in general, or just me and Amy. Because that was always one of the issues I had with her, or rather, she had with me. She loved her job, and could never quite understand why I'd given mine up to follow this 'pipe dream' – her words – of mine to become an artist.

'It's not so different,' argues my dad. 'I mean, your mum's got a career, and we're from a different generation.' As well as my dad teaching, my mum works part-time in You've Been Framed, the picture framing shop on the High Street. Which is handy for me, of course.

'Mum's got a *job*, Dad, which she's only been doing

since I left home. And no offence, Mum, but it's not the same thing.'

'None taken, Ben,' she says, fetching a packet of PG Tips from the cupboard and dropping three teabags into the teapot.

'But I'd have been happy if she'd wanted one,' says my dad defensively. 'After all, men are perfectly capable of raising children.'

'Oh, are they?' interrupts my mum. 'Not in your case, they're not.'

My dad looks like he's about to answer her, then evidently thinks better of it, as he knows he doesn't have a leg to stand on. On the odd occasion growing up, when Mum was ill, or away visiting sick relatives or something, I'd come home from school, and Dad would be standing cluelessly in the kitchen, wondering exactly which pan to use to make the only thing he knew how to make for dinner. And while his omelettes always tasted good, that was because *he'd* made them, not because they were particularly light, or fluffy, or even eggy, come to think of it. But that was just the way it was back then. Because men knew their place. And people made allowances because of that. So while I'm pretty sure that if you asked my dad whether he'd be happy that a wife of his had a career, and of course he'd say yes, he'd still have expected his dinner to be on the table when he got home from his.

'So why does that make a difference, son?' asks my dad.

'Because the problem is, women aren't quite sure exactly how to behave with this new-found liberty themselves, and because – if we know what's good for us – we follow their lead, then we sure as hell aren't. And that's what makes relationships so difficult.'

My mum stands up and shakes her head. 'But surely all a woman can ask for in a man is someone who'll be a good husband and a father?' she says, resting a hand on my dad's shoulder.

'You'd think so, wouldn't you? But nowadays, tell a woman that that's your biggest ambition and she won't look twice at you, or even worse, she'll probably castigate you for not wanting to be some captain of industry, even though underneath it all, that's what she wants for you too. Would you have wanted Dad to be some high-powered businessman instead of a teacher, if it had meant he'd miss out on seeing his child grow up, and didn't see much of you either?'

'Of course not,' admits my mum, walking over to the oven and removing the tray of sausage rolls. 'Although the money would have been nice.'

'But that's because the relationship's what it's all about,' says my dad, smarting a little at the 'money' comment. 'The family. And out of that comes everything else.'

'But that's what I've been trying to tell you. It doesn't work like that any more. Try and chat up a woman nowadays, and if you're not a "new man", who's just as happy running a multinational company as he is wearing a sarong, they don't want to know. Or even worse, if they do agree to go out with you, they spend the whole relationship trying to turn you into that. So the fact that I don't have a high-paying job any more, or a flash car ...' I stop talking and look at them both helplessly. 'Maybe it's me. Maybe I have just been going out with the wrong kind of women. Or maybe, by giving "it" all up to become an artist, I've actually gone and painted myself into a corner.'

'Never mind, Ben,' says my mum, pouring some hot water into the teapot. 'You'll soon meet someone else.'

'Haven't you been listening to anything that I've said? It's tough out there. Particularly for someone like me. Someone who's a little ... Unconventional. I used to be sure there'd be someone out there who'd let me be me, but now I'm not so sure. And to be honest, I'm starting to feel too tired to keep on looking.'

My dad puts a consoling hand on my shoulder. 'There's no rush, son.'

'Yes, there is,' I say, a little too loudly. 'I mean, I'll be thirty this year. And you were already married to Mum, *and* had me, when you were my age.'

My mum glances across to where my dad's sitting. 'Ben, we—'

'Feel for you, son,' interrupts my dad. 'What can we do to help?'

'Nothing, Dad,' I sigh. 'It's just what with Ash getting married, I ...'

My mum stops what she's doing. 'Ash is getting married?'

'Yup,' I say, miserably, realizing I've accidentally opened another can of worms.

'Oh,' she says. 'And have they set a date yet?'

I shrug. 'I don't know. I only found out they were engaged yesterday.'

'But it'll be before you?' asks my mum, getting some plates out of the cupboard.

I try to ignore the disappointment in her voice. 'Obviously, Mum. Unless some miracle happens.'

My dad walks over to the fridge, and removes a carton of milk. 'Look on the bright side,' he says, pouring some into each of the mugs. 'If Ash can find a girl who'll marry him, then there's hope for you yet.'

'Well, that's reassuring,' I say sarcastically, while trying to work out whether my dad's observation is more insulting to me or Ash. 'But then again, he had a little help.'

'Help?' My mum sits down next to me. 'What sort of help?'

'It's an arranged marriage, Mum. His parents sorted out the whole thing for him.'

My dad frowns. 'How do you mean?'

I shrug. 'They found a suitable girl, sounded out her parents, introduced the two of them, and now they're getting married.'

'Well, that sounds like a wonderful idea,' says my dad.

I pick up a sausage roll from the tray my mum's just

put on the table, then drop it again, blowing on my fingers at the unexpected heat. 'It's very common in the Indian community, apparently.'

'No,' continues my dad. 'A wonderful idea for you.'

I let out a short laugh. 'I hardly think that Ash's parents would be interested in finding me someone to marry.'

'Ben,' says my mum. 'Your dad means that *we'll* do the same thing. For you.'

'What?'

'Why not? It's the Easter holidays. I don't have anything else planned,' says my dad, warming to the idea. 'So just say the word, son, and your mum and I will find you a bride.'

Just say the word? Plenty of words leap to mind, but not one that I can say in front of the two of them. 'But . . .'

'No buts, son.' My dad smiles reassuringly at me. 'In fact, no time like the present.'

I frown up at him. 'What do you mean?'

'This evening. Let's go out on the town. Just you and me.'

'What? On the pull?' I say half-jokingly.

'Exactly. I'll show you how it's done. See if we can't find you the future Mrs Grant.'

I know he probably feels he's doing me a favour, but I can't think of anything worse. 'Dad, with all due respect . . .'

'What?' He looks suddenly affronted. 'I managed to pull your mother, didn't I?'

For some reason, I can't come up with a single suitable response to that statement. I look desperately across at my mum for help, but she seems to be nodding in agreement. 'Well, I . . .'

'You've got nothing else planned, have you?'

I think for a moment or two. 'Well, I was going to watch *Match of the Day* . . .'

'So, tape it.'

'But . . . Tomorrow's Sunday.'

'And you've got to get up early to go to church?'

'Well, no, but . . .'

'Great,' he says, grabbing himself a sausage roll. 'It's a date, then.'

And as I stare into the steaming mug of tea my mum's just placed in front of me, I realize something about being in Boots yesterday, when I thought my life couldn't get any more embarrassing.

I was wrong.

Chapter 7

It's nearly nine o'clock when my dad finally appears downstairs. He's looking a little uncomfortable, although whether that's down to him having second thoughts about this evening, or the fact that he's wearing a pair of trousers that appear to be at least two sizes too small, it's hard to say.

As my mum and I try hard not to laugh, he looks at each of us in turn. 'What?'

'Dad, it's ...' I don't quite know what to say. The wide-lapel pastel-blue suit he's wearing might have been the height of fashion thirty years ago, but nowadays, he's more likely to trip over his flares than cut a dash with them.

'Something wrong with my get-up?' says my dad, admiring his reflection in the hall mirror.

I walk over and stand next to him. 'Well, the fact that you refer to it as a "get up", for a start.'

He looks a little hurt. 'This is my best suit. The one I met your mother in, in fact.'

'And it would be fine if we were going to a seventies revival night, but we're not.'

'No,' says my dad. 'But we are going to a "Ben's Love Life" revival evening. So it doesn't really matter what I wear, does it?'

'The way those trousers are restricting your breathing, you'll be the one in need of revival before the end of the evening,' I say. 'Besides, it's the twenty-first century. And you have to dress a bit more, well, appropriately.'

My dad looks me up and down. 'What, like you?' he says, indicating my jeans. 'In my day, we dressed up to meet women. Not down. And we certainly didn't wear plimsolls. It's no wonder you're having women trouble.'

'Dad, they're called "trainers" now. And everyone wears them. All the time. They're quite "the thing", in fact,' I say, trying to talk in language he'll understand.

'For PE, maybe,' he says, folding his arms, which causes the stitching on the back of his jacket to rip slightly.

'PE? Plimsolls? Please don't talk like that. It's embarrassing enough that you look like my dad, without sounding like him as well. And what's that round your neck?'

'It's called a *tie*, son. Although your generation seems to have forgotten all about them.'

'With good reason. You look like you're going to a parents' evening, so please take it off. Don't you have any jeans?'

My dad thinks for a moment. 'Well, there's the ones

I use for gardening, but I don't think they're very clean. And, anyway, I thought you said we were going to a night club?'

'We are.'

'Because in my day, those kind of places were strictly no jeans allowed.'

'Well, as you'll find out later, it's not your day any more,' I say, although I'm beginning to wonder whether, actually, it's not mine either.

Much to my mum's amusement, I send him back upstairs, with strict instructions to change into his best shirt and newest pair of trousers. When eventually, he reappears, at least he's looking a bit more neutral, although I do have to untuck his shirt, but that's less because it's 'with-it' and more because it'll hide where he can't quite do up the top button on what he keeps referring to as his 'slacks'. And while he doesn't quite look trendy, he doesn't look embarrassing either. Which is something, I suppose, seeing as I've realized that I'm going to have to go through with this evening, as I haven't managed to come up with a better reason to reject their offer than either 'it's embarrassing', 'it's demeaning', or the more obvious 'it'll never work'. Besides, it'll be far more effective to let them have a stab at it, then realize that themselves. If I can only prevent him talking, or dancing, and as long as I don't see anyone I know, then I might just survive the night without having to move towns. Or countries, perhaps.

'This is fun, isn't it?' he says, after my mum has

insisted on taking a photo of the two of us by the door.

'What is?'

'Father and son,' he says, making for the front gate. 'Out together. On a Saturday night.'

I follow him down the garden path, trying to think of a suitable response, and I'm just about to answer, when I stop in my tracks. My dad is walking with what I suddenly realize is the same kind of swagger that John Travolta adopted in *Saturday Night Fever.*

'Are your trousers too tight?'

'What? Why?' My dad stops bouncing on his toes, and turns to face me. 'I haven't ripped them, have I?' he asks anxiously, wheeling round and sticking out his backside, trying to see it in the reflection of my car window.

'Dad, *please*. No, I was talking about the way you were walking.'

'Walking?'

'Yes. Is it your bad knee?' My dad's got a dodgy cartilage – an old football injury, according to his version of events, although my mum told me he did it leaping out of his chair in excitement while watching the cup final.

He looks down at his leg. 'My knee?'

I sigh, realizing that this is going to be one long evening. 'Never mind.'

We get into the car, and drive off down the street in silence, my dad checking his hair in the passenger mirror. As we reach the corner, he clears his throat. 'So. A night club, eh?'

'Well, no one calls them night clubs any more. We're

going to do what's known nowadays as "clubbing".'

'Ah,' says my dad. 'Clubbing. Right.'

As I pull out onto the main road, I can hear him whispering the word 'clubbing' to himself several times, as if he's practising a new language. 'And what's the name of this "club"?'

'It's called "Tramps".'

'Tramps?' My dad snorts. 'That's not a very auspicious name for somewhere to meet a young lady.'

'Yes, well, most of them aren't ladies. Or that young, come to think of it. As you'll find out.'

My dad doesn't say anything for the rest of the journey, obviously mulling over my last observation, and starts whistling to himself as I drive, so tunelessly that it's a relief when I find a parking space just across from our destination. We get out of the car and head over towards a large white building on the pavement opposite, my dad thankfully walking a little more normally now – although that could be because his knee is actually playing up due to his exaggerated striding earlier – and stop under a large neon sign that displays the word 'Tramps' in vivid blue letters. It's still early, so there's no real queue, but when we go to walk in past the bouncer, my dad is halted by a big meaty hand on his shoulder, and a loud 'Oy!'

Before I can react, my dad turns round. 'Yes?'

'It's Mister Grant, isn't it?'

'That's right,' he says politely. 'And who might you be?'

As the bouncer removes his hand, I swallow hard. He's twice my size, and by the looks of the tattoos on his neck, about a hundred times as hard.

'I'm Martin Walters. You used to teach me.'

'Martin. Yes. Of course. Nice to see you again,' says my dad, clearly not recognizing Martin at all. It's his standard response, as he must have taught thousands of kids over the years, and therefore finds it impossible to remember all of them. 'So,' he says, looking at Martin's tight-fitting sweatshirt, which has the word 'Security' printed across it in large yellow letters. 'You're working here now?'

Martin nods. 'Yeah. My parole officer reckoned it'd be a good outlet for my violent tendencies.'

'Well, good for you,' says my dad. 'Everyone should play to their strengths. What was yours again?'

'Fighting,' says Martin. 'You used to put me in detention for it. Every week. I've never forgotten that.'

'Come on, Dad,' I say, anxious to get him out of range of Martin's not inconsiderable reach. 'Let's go on in.'

'Oh yeah,' continues Martin. 'Every day I spent in prison, I thought to myself, this is just like being in Mister Grant's detention class.'

'Ah, yes, well. I'm sure you deserved it,' says my dad, blissfully unaware of either the potential violent revenge that Martin might be planning to take, or the murmuring queue that's starting to build up behind us. I grab his arm and try once more to lead him through the doorway, but Martin doesn't seem to be getting out of the way. 'Detention, I mean. Though thinking about it, probably the prison sentence, too.'

I cringe, and brace myself for fight or flight, and although flight seems the better option, given my dad's bad knee I might be in for a pasting. But instead, Martin breaks into a grin.

'I did. I was a right little bastard.'

'Martin. Language please,' scolds my dad.

'Sorry, Mister Grant.' Martin suddenly seems to have reverted ten years in less than a second. 'And I reckon it did me the power of good. If I hadn't had your detentions, I never would have got through prison. So thanks,' he says, holding out one enormous palm.

'Quite,' says my dad, briefly inspecting Martin's tattooed knuckles, before shaking his hand firmly. 'And you're welcome.'

Martin steps to one side, so I breathe a sigh of relief, and start to walk over to the front desk to pay, but before I can get my money out of my pocket, he puts his massive arms around our shoulders, and escorts us straight inside. 'Have a nice night,' he says. 'Oh, and Mister Grant?'

My dad looks up at him. 'Yes?'

Martin flashes him a gap-toothed grin. 'Don't start anything.'

As we walk in past the coat check booth, my dad turns to me. 'Did we just get in for free?'

'So it seems,' I say, a little stunned, and in need of a

drink. 'Let's hope you used to teach some of the bar staff too.'

We make our way down the dimly lit corridor, and into the main dance area. There's a poster on the door advertising tomorrow night's 'Eighties Evening', but by the looks of the women on the dance floor, that's a pretty good description of some of tonight's clientele.

My dad makes a face at the noise. 'How on earth do you chat someone up in here?' he shouts.

'You don't,' I yell back, while leading him towards the bar. 'It's all about body language. Imperceptible signs. Letting them know you're interested. And hoping that they're drunk enough to respond.'

He looks at me as if I'm mad, although his expression could also be because his ears are hurting. As I get us a couple of drinks, he peers anxiously around the gloomy interior, perhaps hoping to find a seat marked 'please give up for elderly people'.

'So come on, then, son,' he says, taking the pint I've bought him gratefully. 'Tell me exactly how this works. What should I do?'

'Well, you can start by calling me Ben.'

'Okay, son. I mean, Ben.'

'Well, what I'd do normally is look around and see if there's anyone I, you know, *fancied*,' I say, indicating the various groups of women on the dance floor, or in the booths around the outside of the room. 'And then try to make eye contact. And assuming they didn't look away in disgust, go over and offer to buy them a drink.'

'Just like that?'

I nod. 'Yup.'

'But ... That isn't the way to meet women. What about the art of conversation?'

I shrug. 'As you say, that's a little difficult in here. Besides, it's just how it is in these kind of places.'

He sighs. 'Well, it's no wonder that the divorce rate is so high nowadays, if this is how most relationships start. I mean, it's all based on looks, rather than personality.'

'Or, more importantly, level of alcohol consumption. On both sides, sometimes.'

My dad makes a face, and then, embarrassingly, takes his glasses out of his pocket, puts them on, and starts scanning the room. 'So,' he says. 'What about her?'

'Please don't point.' I knock his hand down, then pick up my pint and take a sip so I can peer over the top of the glass towards where he's just unsubtly indicated a group of girls. 'Which one?'

'That one,' he says, pointing again. 'In the boob tube.'

'Boob tube?' I follow the line of my dad's index finger to where a group of girls are standing next to the fire exit. I'm guessing he means the one nearest to us, because she's wearing a strapless dress – although that's quite possibly because the straps haven't been invented that are up to the job. 'What *about* her?'

'She looks like she's got a nice, er, personality,' says my dad. 'Why don't you go and talk to her? Tell her you're an artist. Girls like sensitive men.'

'Dad, the last time I told a girl I was an artist, she thought I meant "recording". Besides, like I said, that's not how it works.'

'Rubbish.'

'Dad, please.'

By now the girls have noticed my dad staring, and I'm wondering if it's too late for us to duck behind the nearby pillar, but instead, and to my horror, he puts his beer down on the table, slips his glasses back into his pocket, and starts to walk over to where they're standing.

'Come on,' he says, beckoning me to follow him. 'I'll show you how it's done.'

'What? No!' For a second, I'm frozen on the spot, horrified by the prospect of him demonstrating the chat-up techniques he used on my mum, and my first reaction is to grab him, but I'm too slow. After a quick gulp of beer, I hurry after him, catching him up just before he reaches the group.

'Ladies,' I say, while surreptitiously trying to usher my dad away from them.

'Go on then, Ben,' he says, ignoring my attempts to move him on. 'Make the introductions.'

As the girls look at us curiously, I realize that I've got no choice. 'Hi,' I say, suddenly feeling five years old. 'As you've heard, I'm Ben.'

My dad clears his throat, and I'm just about to introduce him when I realize I don't have a clue how to. I can't say that he's my father, of course, and I've never introduced him as 'Alan' in all my life — it just doesn't seem, well, right. But just as I'm wrestling with what to say, one of the girls beats me to it.

'And who's this, Ben?' says the one closest to us, looking him up and down. 'Your dad?'

It's an unkind remark, but it's also true, although my dad cheerfully admitting to it doesn't turn out to be the best plan, as while it might be loud in the club, I can hear the girls' laughter for most of the walk back to where we've left our drinks.

'Ouch,' says my dad, picking his beer up gratefully and taking a sip. 'They didn't give us much of a chance.'

'Which is what I've been trying to tell you. You have to lead with a drink. And by the way, if there is any talking to be done, then please let me do it.'

'But you weren't,' he protests.

'Because, for the millionth time, that's not how it works.'

He starts tapping his foot to the music. 'Well, why not just go up to them and ask them to dance instead?'

'Don't you dare,' I warn him.

'So, you don't talk to them, you don't dance with them, and in fact your whole approach seems to be based around plying them with alcohol. It's no wonder you're finding this so difficult.' He looks at me disbelievingly, then puts a reassuring hand on my shoulder. 'You've got to come up with a line. Something to get their interest. And above all, don't be put off. Faint heart never won fair lady, and all that.'

I look around the interior of the club again. There are

very few of what I'd even describe as 'fair' ladies, and even 'fair-to-middling' would be pushing it. 'I'm telling you, Dad, it's hopeless.'

'Rubbish.' He glances over towards a pretty girl leaning against the bar. 'Mind if I have another crack?'

'Be my guest. And remember, ask if you can buy her a drink.'

'A drink. Got it.'

I start to walk after him, but then stop myself. After all, I want him to find out just what it's like nowadays. Just how hard it is for us single men. So instead, I lean against the pillar and pull my mobile phone out of my pocket, pretending to study the screen as if I've just received a text. When I look up again, my dad's back in front of me, a dejected expression on his face.

'What's wrong?'

My dad shrugs. 'I did as you said. Offered to buy her a drink.'

'And?'

'She looked me up and down, then asked if she could just have the money instead.' He shakes his head. 'Unbelievable.'

I try hard not to laugh. 'Isn't it just?'

'Okay. Onwards and upwards. What about that one?' He points towards a pretty redhead standing on her own next to the dance floor.

By now, I'm almost past caring. 'Help yourself.'

Thirty seconds later, he's back. 'I don't think you'd have liked her.'

'Why not?'

'Well ...' He leans in close to me, and lowers his voice. 'I think she – what is it you say? – plays for the other team. And she's a sex maniac, to boot.'

'What do you mean?'

'She said she was waiting for her girlfriends.'

'Dad, that doesn't mean ... Never mind.' I look at my watch, and see with horror that it's not even ten o'clock yet. 'Come on. Shall we go?'

My dad doesn't answer me, but instead just heads off towards another group of women who are sitting in a booth by the dance floor. He introduces himself, rather formally shaking each one of them by the hand, before – to my astonishment – sitting down at their table, and then turning and pointing in my direction. I'm mortified, and pull my phone out of my pocket again, studying it as intently as if someone's just texted me next week's winning lottery numbers, and by the time I dare to look up again, my dad's standing next to me. This time, however, he's got a smile on his face.

'What are you looking so pleased about?'

'Oh, nothing,' he says.

'Got blown out again?'

For a moment, I think my dad assumes that's something rude. 'No, actually.'

'Well, what are you doing back here, then?'

He turns round and waves at the girls, who wave back at him. 'Mission accomplished.'

'What? How?'

'I told you,' he says. 'You've got to be creative. Come up with a line or two.'

Uh-oh. 'And what was yours, exactly?'

My dad grins. 'I told them I didn't have long to live . . .'

'What? You won't if you carry on like that.'

'. . . and my dying wish was to see my only son get married,' he continues, triumphantly handing over a piece of paper. 'Ta-daa!'

'What's this?'

'This would be . . .' He pulls his reading glasses out of his other pocket, slips them on, and studies the name on it. 'Kerry's phone number.'

'And which one is Kerry, exactly?'

He changes over his glasses, and peers back at the table. 'The one in the black dress.'

I look over at the table, where a pleasant-looking girl in a black dress is smiling at me, then stare at the scrap of paper in disbelief. 'Thanks for nothing.'

'What's wrong?' he says, trying to press it into my hand. 'I got you her number, didn't I?'

'Which I can't call, of course.'

'Why ever not?'

'Oh, just because of the simple fact that if we do go out, and get on, and get married, and then you miraculously survive the wedding, and long after that as well . . .'

'. . . then it'll be a miracle. And you'll have a funny story to tell your children, won't you?'

I shake my head slowly. 'Dad, you might have checked that I actually fancied her first. Besides, you can't start a relationship from a position of deception. It's all about honesty nowadays.'

My dad sighs. 'Son, from the first days that women started putting make-up on, or wearing these new wonderful bras, honesty went out of the window. We all exaggerate a little at the beginning. Dress ourselves up. It's part of what's known as courtship. Now, give me your phone.'

'You're not going to call her, are you? I mean, she's just sitting over there.'

'Don't be stupid.' My dad takes my phone, punches her name and number into it, then presses *Save*, then hands it back to me, along with his glass. 'Now, look after my drink, will you?'

I look at him warily. 'Why? Where are you going this time?'

'To the toilet. If that's okay?'

'As long as you don't try and chat anyone up in there. And then can we go?'

'No chance.' My dad eyes the dance floor, then does a strange movement that I assume is supposed to be one of his dance moves, but looks more like someone's just dropped an ice cube down the back of his shirt. 'I'm just starting to enjoy myself.'

As he heads off in search of the Gents, I slump down at the nearest table, sick with the realization that here I am, reduced to going clubbing on a Saturday night with my fifty-five-year-old dad, and what's more he's having more success on the pulling front than I normally do. But just when I think my evening couldn't get any worse, I hear a familiar voice behind me.

'That's the spirit,' says Ash, clapping me on the shoulder. 'Back in the saddle.'

Horrified, I turn round slowly to see a smiling Priti, and Ash, with his arm round her waist, looking like the proverbial cat who's got the cream. 'What are you doing here?'

'Nice to see you too, Ben,' says Priti, sitting down next to me.

'Sorry, I didn't mean it like that. I thought you'd be out having fun.'

'We are having fun,' says Ash. 'I'm showing Priti the local hot spots.'

I nod towards the dance floor, where a woman my mother's age wearing little more than most people wear on the beach is attempting to dance without spilling her Bacardi Breezer. 'And this was the best you could come up with?'

'Well, it was this, or a night in with my parents,' says Ash, squeezing into the corner seat. 'No contest, really.'

'They're not that bad,' says Priti, digging him in the ribs affectionately.

'I suppose not,' says Ash. 'But speaking of parents, Ben, that bloke over there doesn't half look like your old man.'

I look round to where my dad is making a beeline from the toilets to our table, stopping every two or three steps to do a little shimmy. 'Can I get you both a drink?' I say, in a vain attempt to change the subject, and despite the fact that they're both holding full glasses.

'Hang on,' continues Ash, putting a hand on my arm to stop my escape. 'It *is* your old man. But what . . .' Ash stops talking, probably because the expression on my face has already answered the question he was about to ask. 'Oh, *Ben*.'

I put my head in my hands. 'Could my life be any sadder?'

'Well, I think it's lovely,' says Priti. 'You taking him out on a Saturday night. Has he recently lost his wife, I mean, your mum, or something?'

'He might do later, when I tell her exactly what he's been up to,' I say. 'No, it's nothing like that. He, I mean, we . . .' I stop talking, at a loss to explain any of this. But fortunately – or unfortunately, depending on your point of view – I don't get a chance to, as my dad swaggers over to join us.

'Aye aye,' he says, noticing Priti sat next to me. 'What's all this then? You pulled, son? I mean, *Ben*,' he adds, with a not-so-subtle wink.

I cringe inwardly. 'No, Dad. You know Ash, of course. And this is . . .' I'm wondering just how to introduce her, when Priti takes over.

'Hello, Mr Grant. I'm Priti.'

My dad fixes her with what he obviously thinks is his

most charming smile. 'You certainly are, young lady,' he says, shaking her hand somewhat enthusiastically.

'No, Dad, her name is Priti.'

'Oh. What is it?'

'What's what?'

'This pretty name of hers,' says my dad, still holding on to her hand, while looking at me like I'm one of his thicker pupils.

'It's Priti. Spelt P–R–I–T–I,' says Priti.

'Oh. Right.' He lets her hand go, and picks his beer up. 'Sorry.'

'Yes,' says Ash. 'My fiancée.'

'Fiancée, eh?' says my dad, looking at me accusingly. 'Well, congratulations, both of you.'

'Thanks, Mister Grant,' says Ash, proudly.

'Please,' says my dad, although he addresses it more to Priti. 'Call me Alan.'

'So what are *you* doing here?' asks Ash, no longer able to contain his curiosity.

'Well, Ben's been having some trouble on the girl-friend front,' says my dad, before I can stop him. 'And so I've been showing him how it's done.'

Ash chokes off a laugh. 'Really? And are you having much luck?'

'Luck, my boy, has nothing to do with it. It's all about technique. As I've been trying to tell him. Although it's easier for you lot nowadays.' My dad pulls the scrap of paper out of his shirt pocket, and shows it proudly to Ash. 'I mean, we didn't have mobiles in my day.'

'And in fact, the telephone hadn't even been invented,' I add.

'I'm not that old,' protests my dad. 'In fact, I'm sure I could still show you a thing or two out there as well,' he says, looking over towards the dance floor, where the same woman seems to be oblivious to the fact that her bottle is empty, and she's dancing in a puddle of Bacardi.

'Please, God. No,' I say, under my breath.

'How about it?' says my dad. 'Ben?'

'You must be joking,' I say. 'Besides, I promised Mum I'd get you home at a reasonable time.'

'Which is when?' he says dejectedly.

I stand up abruptly. 'Now,' I say, not even bothering to look at my watch.

'Ah,' says my dad, winking at Priti. 'She who must be obeyed, eh?'

'That's right,' says Priti, grabbing Ash's arm and smiling up at him. 'Which is a lesson you'll do well to learn.'

I escort my dad back outside, and set off on the short drive home, surprised to find that it's just gone ten, as even though we've only been out for an hour, it's felt like much longer. As we walk in through the front door, my mother meets us in the hallway.

'On your own?' she asks.

I assume that's directed at me. 'What did you expect, Mum? That I'd meet someone and bring them back here – with him in tow?' I jab a thumb in my dad's direction as he undoes another button on his trousers, then sighs with relief.

'You never know,' she says, walking into the kitchen and putting the kettle on. 'Your dad's quite a charmer.'

'I can think of other words for him.'

'So, no luck at all, then?'

I've told my dad not to tell her about the Kerry incident. 'Oh, yes. Thanks to him being there, I had to beat them off with a shi . . . I mean, a stick. In the end I just couldn't choose, there were so many.'

'Well, never mind. What is it your father always says when you get dumped? "Plenty more fish in the sea"?'

'But that's just it, Mum. I'm starting to worry that there aren't any more. Or that maybe I'm allergic to fish.'

She picks three mugs up off the draining board. 'It can't be that bad, surely?'

'I have to say, Ben was right,' says my dad, giving my mum an appreciative squeeze. 'It is tough out there.'

'Thank you.' I sit down heavily at the kitchen table. 'Finally.'

'Well, perhaps you shouldn't have left it so late. After all,' says my mum, sitting down opposite me. 'Like you said, you're nearly thirty. And most people are already married at your age.'

I stare at my mum for a moment or two, then lean over the table and give her a huge kiss on the forehead. 'Mum, you're a genius!'

My mum looks puzzled. 'For remembering how old you are?'

'Yes,' I say, fishing in my pocket for my car keys. 'Got to go.'

'Back to Amy?' says my dad, hopefully.

'A little bit further than that, actually,' I say, heading down the hallway, and out through the front door.

Chapter 8

The reason my mum's a genius? Because she's reminded me that I've got a back-up option. And it's not Amy, but a girl called Linda Martin.

Linda and I met at college – she was in the same year as me, and her parents lived about half an hour away from mine, meaning we'd often travel back with each other at the end of term. And even though I fancied the pants off her, and I think she felt the same about me, I never actually *got* the pants off her, mainly because whenever I was single, she was going out with someone, and vice versa. And because of this, the strangest thing happened. We became friends.

And I remember one drunken night, in the late stages of a party at someone's house. Linda was moaning about how her then-boyfriend thought she was too possessive, and we'd caught sight of my soon-to-be ex, whose name I'm slightly worried that I've forgotten, snogging Phil, a guy from the sports science course who Linda had gone out with the previous term, but who'd broken it off with her, telling her he thought she was a bunny-boiler – and we'd made a deal. And not just any old deal. Because Linda had turned to me – I remember it clearly – and said, 'Tell you what, Ben. If neither of us can find the right person to marry by the time we're thirty, let's marry each other.' And we'd shaken hands on it.

While back then I'd dismissed it as one of those drunken things you say from time to time, given my current situation – not to mention my impending birthday – it suddenly strikes me as something that deserves further investigation. I mean, I don't expect her to drop everything and marry me, but who knows? Linda and I were *good* friends. From what I can remember, she wasn't unattractive, even though the John Lennon glasses she used to wear back then made her look a bit like an owl. She was studying accountancy too, which means she's probably got a good job now. Plus, she was always very encouraging about my art, which means that right now, she's as good a bet as any. And even though I haven't seen her since then, thanks to the Christmas cards we exchange every year, I've got her mobile number.

I spend a restless night thinking about it, then after a couple of cups of strong coffee for breakfast, compose a text message, and press *Send*. I've decided not to remind her about our deal straight away – I don't want to scare her off, after all – so I just suggest a drink, then spend the rest of the day checking and re-checking my phone, on the odd occasion even calling it from my landline to make sure the ringer's still working. By late afternoon,

I've just about given up, when I realize with a start that I've missed a text message, and from an hour ago. I hurriedly scroll through the menu to find it, nearly deleting it by accident, then almost drop the phone in my excitement. It's from her.

Hi Ben it says. *Free tonite? Wd be gr8 2 c u.*

I gr8 my teeth a little as I compose a message back to her – I've never been keen on text-speak – saying tonight would be great, and suggesting a pub I know near where she lives. If she can meet me at such short notice, then that's got to be a sign that she's single – which is something I can take both ways, of course. But maybe, just maybe, she's been having the same trouble as I have. Perhaps she's even been holding out for me, in the hope that I'll get back in touch. But later, as I get ready, there's one thing I do know – whatever the reason she wants to see me, it's got to be better than being set up with a complete stranger by my mum and dad. We used to be friends – which is the best starting point, after all. She's sure to remember our discussion that evening, which is possibly why she's agreed to meet me. And if she's got a biological clock that's ticking, so much the better.

I'm a little nervous as I make the half-hour drive to meet her, and get to the pub a few minutes early, but Linda's already there, sitting in a corner, flicking through a magazine. I recognize her instantly, even though she's changed her old round glasses for some of those trendy, angular ones, and instead of the sweatshirt-and-combats combination she used to favour at college, is dressed immaculately in some sort of business suit. I immediately wish I'd worn something smarter than jeans – my dad's words coming back to haunt me – but then I remember that I don't actually have anything smarter than jeans, having symbolically taken all my suits to the charity shop the day I gave up my job. It's too late to go home and change anyway, so I just walk over and hover by her table.

'Ben?' She looks up from her copy of *Guns and Ammo*, which I'm hoping she's pulled out at random from the pub's magazine rack, rather than brought in specially.

I grin self-consciously down at her. 'Hello, stranger.'

She breaks into a smile, then gets up awkwardly to greet me, though her awkwardness is more to do with the fact that I'm standing a little too close to her, and she's got her drink in one hand and magazine in the other, so has to reach past me and put them down on the table before getting out of her seat, thus putting her face embarrassingly close to my groin.

It's clear we don't quite know what to do. A hand-shake's too formal, and while a hug might work if we had seen each other a bit more recently, an eight-year gap is a tricky one to judge. I settle for a kiss on the cheek, though have to embarrass both her and myself when she goes for the continental 'two-style' kiss while I'm already sitting down after the one.

'So, how have you been?'

'Good, thanks. You look . . .' I'm warming to my task now. 'G–R–8. I mean, great.'

'Thanks.' Linda blushes slightly. 'You've grown your hair.'

'That's not all. Not that I've grown anything else. I mean, I've made some other changes. In my life, that is . . .' I stop talking, wondering why I'm so bad at this. 'Can I get you a drink?'

'I'll get you one,' says Linda, reaching for her handbag and standing up. 'A lager?'

I shrug affably. 'Why not?'

I take a quick glance at her fingers as she walks past me. There doesn't seem to be any sign of a wedding or even engagement ring. This is looking better. And as the evening progresses, it gets better still, because as we swap details of who we still keep in touch with from college – which on my part seems to be no one, while Linda's a walking Friends Reunited, reeling off how so-and-so's just had a baby, or you-know-who's got married – not once does she mention a partner, or anyone who could be remotely perceived as a boyfriend. Once she's finished bringing me up to speed, I clear my throat.

'So, never married, eh?'

She laughs, then holds up her left hand and wiggles her ring-less fingers. 'Nope. I've been waiting for the right person. You?'

For a second, I wonder whether she's suggesting that *I* might be the right person, but then realize she's just asking me a question. 'No. Same here. Although, do you remember that one drunken night?' I say, deciding this is my opportunity to deal with the elephant in the room. 'At college. At that party?'

Linda smiles. 'There were a lot of parties, Ben. And a lot of drunken nights.'

'You know, at what's-his-name's house?'

'Well, that narrows it down.'

Ah. I can see that as far as Linda's concerned, the elephant's not actually in the room, and what's more, I'm going to have to drag it in, sit it down, and physically point it out to her. 'You know, the one when we promised to marry each other by the time we reached thirty? If neither of us had, you know, met someone else?'

I laugh, to try and make light of what, in the cold light of day, sounds like a ridiculous arrangement, and fully expect Linda to join in, but instead she looks at me a little strangely.

'No.'

Ah. This is a setback I hadn't counted on. 'Yes, you must remember. We were round at that party, where that bloke you used to go out with got off with . . .' Damn. What *was* her name? 'And so we decided that we'd get married. As a kind of fall-back plan. If we weren't married to anyone else. By, er, thirty.'

Linda starts to edge imperceptibly away. 'What are you talking about, Ben?'

'Our . . . agreement.' I'm getting insistent now, and it

seems to be scaring her off. 'We even shook hands on it,' I say, conscious that my hands are shaking now.

'You're joking, right?'

'Well . . .'

As Linda stares at me, I pick up my lager and take a sip, wondering whether I should just get up and leave, but then she suddenly lets out a short laugh. 'I do.'

I nearly spill my drink. 'Do what?'

'I was kidding you. Of course I remember.'

'You do?'

'I do,' repeats Linda, although the way she phrases those two little words makes them sound a little chilling. 'I just didn't realize it was legally binding.'

'Oh.' I put my beer down carefully, not quite know-ing what to say next. 'Right.'

'So, that was the reason for your text?'

'Well, not *just* that, obviously,' I say, trying des-perately to think of something else that might sound plausible. But before I get a chance, Linda laughs again.

'Yes it was. You thought that you could just get in touch out of the blue and make me honour some drunken "agreement"' – I can hear the speech marks around the word – 'that you and I made eight years ago?'

'Er, yes. Well, not *make* you, exactly. Just see if you, you know, remembered it,' I say, my plan to bring it up and, if she reacted strangely, just sweep it under the table suddenly seeming a little bit shaky too.

Linda fixes me with a disbelieving stare. 'How dare you think that I'd be so desperate that I'd drop everything to marry *you*. What if I was involved in a happy relationship?'

I'm a little insulted by her dismissive tone, and can't help defending myself. 'Well, you're not, are you?'

'Not what?'

'In a relationship. Happy or otherwise.'

'No,' says Linda. 'But that's beside the point.'

'It's exactly the point,' I say. 'And that's why it makes perfect sense to at least investigate the possibility. We were friends at college. Good friends.'

'So good that you didn't bother to keep in touch with me when we left.'

'Yes, well, ignoring that small point for a moment. We've both obviously gone through the ringer in terms of relationships since then, and still not managed to find someone.'

'No, but . . .'

'And let's face it, neither of us is getting any younger.'

'What do you mean by that?'

'Nothing,' I say, letting my eyes flick over to a woman with a baby in the corner. I do it in a subtle way, but Linda still follows my gaze.

'Oh, of course,' she says, widening her eyes. 'I'm a woman, I'm almost thirty years old, and therefore I must be desperate to have a baby. That's the best reason for marrying a virtual stranger I've ever heard. In fact, I've changed my mind. Quick – let's elope. Right now.'

'Elope?'

Linda shrugs. 'Why not? I mean, I've got a couple of

meetings scheduled for tomorrow, but I'm sure I can bump them back a day or two. Oh no, hang on, there's the honeymoon to think of. Where were we going to go?'

'Well, I hadn't really thought that far ahead, but—'

'Hawaii's nice. Or maybe the Maldives. One of those little huts on stilts. I've always wanted to stay in one of those.'

Ah. I hadn't really factored this in. And my credit card is nearly at its limit. 'Well, maybe we could forget the honeymoon,' I say, trying to lighten the mood a little. 'I mean, you just spend all of your time in bed, don't you? So it doesn't really matter where you go.'

'Of course, Ben. Silly of me. After all, like you so kindly pointed out, I'm just so keen to get on with making babies. Now how many shall we have? One? Two? What about four?'

'Well, I don't—'

Linda reaches across the table, and rests her hand on top of mine. 'Oh, Ben, I'm sorry. I'm getting ahead of myself, aren't I? I mean, we haven't even done it properly.'

'Done it?'

'No. And don't you think we ought to? Before we go any further.'

Surely she can't mean *sex*? Although that is pretty forward-thinking of her. I mean, what if we're not compatible in the, er, 'bedroom department'? 'Well, okay.'

'So, go on then.'

I frown at her for a moment. 'Go on then what?'

Linda glances down towards the carpet. 'You know. Down you get.'

I follow her gaze. To be honest, the carpet looks a little, well, mouldy. 'What, here?'

'Why not? I was drunk the last time you did it, and here's as good a place as any.'

'If by "it" you mean, er, sex,' I say, 'I'm not sure we ever actually did it.'

She smiles, then shakes her head. 'No, silly. I mean your proposal.'

'Oh.' I laugh, though it's more of a nervous laugh than an amused one. 'Right.'

Linda stares unblinkingly back at me. 'So go on then. Propose. And do it properly this time.'

'What – once more, with feeling?' I say, sure that she's joking now.

Linda laughs again. 'Of course. Now, get on with it,' she says, rather loudly.

'But—'

'Ask me again, Ben.'

'Linda, I—'

'Ask me again!'

As Linda starts to get a little hysterical, I begin to realize that perhaps I've made a mistake by coming here this evening, and what's more, I'm starting to worry myself whether our agreement *was* legally binding. 'Keep your voice down,' I say, aware that one or two of the other tables are looking round at us.

'Keep my voice down? But I want to share it with the world. After all, it's not every day you get engaged, is it?'

'Linda, we're not getting engaged today. I don't know what you—'

'You're right, Ben. I mean, technically we got engaged back at college, didn't we? It's just been a rather long engagement.'

I try to remove my hand from underneath hers, which takes a lot of effort. 'Listen, I didn't come here to ask you to marry me. I just wanted to see whether we had any basis to go forward. That sort of thing. But I can see that we haven't, and . . .'

Linda suddenly sits bolt upright. 'So, you're calling it off?' she says angrily.

I look at her across the table, wondering if she's actually a bit mad, rather than just mad at me. 'Well, er, no. I mean, there's nothing *to* call off.'

Linda stares back at me for a second or two, then bursts out crying. Very loudly. Huge, shoulder-heaving sobs, that have the effect of making everyone in the pub stop talking. I lean across and put a hand on her arm to try to calm her down, but she shrugs me off, and then next thing I know, the barman is towering over me.

'Everything all right, love?'

'Yes, thanks,' I say. 'She—'

'I wasn't talking to you,' he says, glaring down at me. 'Unless you're suggesting I'd be calling you "love"?'

'No. Sorry. Of course not.'

Linda sniffs a couple of times, and then blows her nose loudly on a serviette. 'He's just called off our engagement,' she says, practically to the whole pub.

'No, it's not like that,' I say, as an angry murmuring travels round the room. 'She . . .'

'How long have you been engaged?' asks a woman from the next table.

'Eight years,' sniffs Linda.

I start to protest, but the woman gives me a dirty look. 'Eight years?' she says, shaking her head. 'Well, if he hasn't made an honest woman of you by now, I'd say you're best out of there.'

'Quite right,' says an old man from the bar.

As Linda starts crying again, I'm wondering how on earth I'm going to get out of this, when fortunately the barman provides me with the perfect excuse. 'I think you'd better leave,' he says, folding his arms and nodding towards the door.

I glance anxiously around the pub, then look across the table at Linda, who's sobbing quietly into her wine glass. I'd like to think that she's putting on an act, but even if she isn't I'm still keen to make my escape as quickly as possible. 'Are you going to be okay?'

'Just go, will you?' she sniffs.

'Now,' adds the barman, helping me out of my chair.

And the truth is, unlike Linda, I don't need to be asked twice.

Chapter 9

It's Monday lunchtime, and I'm in my studio, having just come back from chasing up another of Ash's 'leads', when my mobile goes.

'How'd you get on with her?'

'Er ... Who?' I say nervously, although I'm pretty sure I didn't tell Ash I was going to see Linda last night. Not that I'm planning on telling anyone what happened. Ever.

'With that woman,' says Ash. 'This morning?'

'Oh. Right. Ash, for the millionth time, I don't do that kind of thing.'

'Why ever not?'

'It's demeaning.'

'So is having no money. Besides, painting pet portraits might not be high art, but loads of people ...'

'Ash, it wasn't her pet she wanted a portrait of. And in future, when a scary old lady asks you whether I'd be prepared to go round to her house and paint her pussy, please check that she actually owns a cat first.'

Ash laughs. 'Ah. Sorry,' he says, sounding anything but. 'Anyway, let us in, will you?'

I peer out of the window to see Ash and Priti standing outside, and I've half a mind to pretend I'm not here, but Ash is carrying three Styrofoam cups of coffee from Mr Bean, the cafe on the corner, and to be honest, given my current mood, I could do with a caffeine boost.

'Afternoon,' he says, handing over one of the steaming cardboard containers.

'Is it?' I look at my watch, before realizing I've forgotten to put it on again, then shut the door behind them. 'To what do I owe this pleasure?'

Ash makes a face. 'I'm just about to take Priti to the airport.'

Priti puts a hand on his arm, and smiles up at me. 'And I wanted to come and say goodbye.'

'Oh. Right. Well, goodbye, Priti.' As soon as I've said it, I realize how rude that sounds. 'Sorry. Just ignore me.'

Ash stares at me. 'What's wrong with you?'

'Nothing.' I take a sip of coffee. 'Everything. I only made the mistake of telling my mum and dad how the two of you met.'

'So what?' Ash shrugs. 'It's hardly a secret.'

'That's not what I meant, Ash. But now they've gone and offered to do the same for me.'

'Really?' Ash carefully hands his coffee to Priti for safekeeping, then starts to laugh, and before long he's fighting for breath.

'It's not funny, Ash,' I say, once he's finished, which only has the effect of starting him off again.

'No, Ash,' says Priti, shushing him. 'In fact I think it's rather sweet.'

'Sweet?' I roll my eyes. 'It's a disaster.'

'Why?'

'Because it's so embarrassing, that's why.'

Priti puts her coffee down on the windowsill. 'Well, we're not ashamed of it.'

'I don't mean it like that. And no offence, but your lot do it all the time, don't they? Mine don't. And the last thing I want is to be set up.'

'Why ever not?' asks Priti, a little naively, I feel.

'Well, for a start ...' I stop and think for a second. Why not, apart from the obvious taste issues? 'Well, because it's just not the way it works here, is it?'

Priti shrugs. 'Well, maybe it should be. I mean, it obviously does work, given that there's over a billion of us now. Plus I'll tell you something, for us women, it's a hell of a lot easier than going through the normal process. And incidentally, I don't see why it shouldn't be the same for you "lot",' she adds, borrowing my rather un-PC phrase, 'in fact, thinking about it, I've got lots of non-Indian mates who'd jump at the chance.'

'What — to go out with Ben?' says Ash. 'You don't have their names and addresses, do you?'

I ignore him. 'But isn't it a bit, well, false?'

Priti laughs. 'What, unlike logging on to some website and falling for a picture of some blonde babe, when in reality she's ready to collect her bus pass? I tell you, Ben, the world of dating is hard enough out there as it is. So any help you can get is a good thing, as far as I'm concerned. And most women would probably agree with me.'

'Really?'

She smiles. 'Really.'

I shake my head. 'Sorry, Priti. I'm just worried that any women I meet this way are going to find it a little, well, strange.'

'It's not strange at all.' Priti thinks for a moment. 'In fact, do you know the most refreshing thing about it?'

'What?'

'You don't have to go through all that disappointment. That long-term process where you meet someone, think they might have potential, and then end up losing them because they're unable to commit.'

'Sounds familiar,' says Ash.

'I'm serious. This way, you're being introduced to someone who you know is up for commitment from day one.' She grabs Ash's hand. 'And that makes the whole thing easier.'

'Easier?' I say.

Priti nods. 'Much. You should give it a go.'

Ash puts his arm round her shoulders. 'Ask my folks, if you like.'

'Ash, that's very nice of you to suggest it. And no offence to Priti, but I'm hardly going to want the rejects your mum and dad went through . . .'

'Not to set you up, Ben. I mean to tell yours how to go about it. Properly. Rather than coming out clubbing with you every Saturday.'

As Ash starts to snigger again, I shake my head. 'I'm not sure.'

Priti frowns at me. 'Why ever not?'

'You met my dad. I wouldn't trust him to pick out a shirt for me to wear, let alone a potential girlfriend.'

Priti sighs. 'It's not like they're picking out a shirt you don't like and then forcing you to wear it for the rest of your life. Like I said, it's more of an introduction service.'

'Exactly,' says Ash. 'I mean, think of the number of people your mum and dad know.'

Priti nods, encouragingly. 'They both work, don't they?'

'Well, yes.'

'Okay,' says Ash, taking a pen and pad out of his pocket and scribbling some numbers down. 'So, your dad's school has, what, fifty people working there?'

'Something like that.'

'All right. Well, say that two-thirds of them have kids. And two-point-four of them. That's maybe eighty offspring, of which half will be girls, right?'

'Of which some will be ugly.'

Priti digs me in the ribs. 'Don't be so sexist.'

'It's hardly sexist to state an aesthetic preference. I am an artist, after all.'

'Okay,' interrupts Ash. 'So say half of them are ug . . .'

I mean, you might not fancy them. And then, half of them are the right age band, and single. That still leaves ten unattached, attractive women that your dad can put you in touch with – just through his work. And that doesn't include his friends. Or the people your mum knows.'

'Well, when you put it like that . . .'

Ash finishes the rest of his coffee, and looks around for a bin, before throwing the empty cup into an old cardboard box in the corner. 'What have you got to lose?'

'Apart from my self-respect?'

Ash grins. 'But think of the plus side. You get to meet a bunch of women you wouldn't normally, and who knows – one of them may be Miss Right. Plus, you get to have sex with the others.'

Priti clears her throat. 'I'm still here, you know.'

'Sorry,' says Ash, blushing slightly, then winking at me so Priti can't see. 'But you see my point.'

'*Our* point,' says Priti, grabbing Ash by the hand.

And as I think about this after they've gone, I realize that perhaps they're right. Not about the sex part, although that is an obvious bonus, but in terms of what do I have to lose? Because let's face it, given what I was prepared to do with Linda last night, any self-respect I had has long since evaporated. So when five o'clock comes, instead of going home, I turn up at my parents' house instead.

My dad looks up from where he's doing something on

his laptop at the kitchen table. 'It's not dinner time already, is it?'

'Very funny. What are you up to?'

My dad swivels the laptop round so I can see the screen. 'I've just signed up for Facebook.'

I raise one eyebrow. 'Really? What for?'

My dad shrugs. 'We're setting up a page at school. You know, for ex-pupils, and so on. In fact, you should give it a go. Lots of single women on there. Apparently,' he adds, quickly, when he catches sight of my mum's expression.

'Listen,' I say, pulling out a chair and sitting down opposite him. 'I need to talk to you both about something.'

'Ben, you already told us about you and Amy, remember?' says my mum, putting down her copy of *Good Housekeeping*, and looking anxiously over towards the kettle.

'Not Amy, Mum. I mean the other night.'

My dad laughs. 'Don't tell me, you phoned that Kerry I chatted up, I mean, *spoke to* for you, went out with her last night, and she's dumped you already?'

'No. It's nothing like that. I wanted to talk to you about your . . . Offer.'

My dad shuts the laptop. 'Our offer?'

'Yes.' I look at the two of them, sitting there expectantly, and take a deep breath. 'I need your help. You know. Like Ash, remember?'

'You want us to set you up?' asks my mum.

'With a woman?' says my dad.

'Preferably,' I say, then realize that I'd better not joke around here. 'Of course with a woman. I mean, I just thought, who knows me better than my mum and dad? Plus, between you, you must know lots of eligible women. And you've not done badly yourselves, have you? Thirty years happily married, and all that. You must be doing something right.'

My mum and dad exchange glances, before my dad shrugs. 'I don't mind asking around at work. There's old Mike Richards. He's been trying to get his daughter married off and out of his house for ages. Apparently she just sits around all day, watching Jeremy Kyle and scoffing custard creams . . .'

'Or what about that girl who runs the café at the bowls club?' says my mum. 'The one with all the piercings. Though I must say, I don't know why she's got that one through her . . .'

I hold my hands up, wondering why what seemed such a good idea after I talked it through with Ash and Priti suddenly seems so ridiculous. 'Let me stop you there. I don't want your friends' reject or misfit daughters, or girls who have escaped from the circus. Let me explain how this works. It's a coming together of two families. One complimentary to the other. Each bringing something to the party.'

My dad smiles. 'I get it, son.'

'Get someone with a holiday home, Alan,' chimes in my mother, suddenly excited. 'I've always wanted a holiday home. In Spain. Majorca, maybe. Or a boat. See if there's anyone who's got a boat.'

'Mum, you're missing the point. This is someone for *me*. From maybe a family like ours. Not some rich lot who're going to let their new in-laws spend a couple of weeks on their floating gin palace in the Balearics every summer.'

'Oh.' My mum's face falls. 'But we could still ask. Or maybe put an ad in the paper.'

'No. No newspaper ads. In fact, there's one condition.'

'Which is?' asks my dad.

'You find out how to do this properly. So we'll get Ash and his parents over, and they can tell you exactly how to go about it.'

'Okay,' says my dad, getting up from the table and fetching a pencil and notepad from the sideboard. 'But in the meantime, what do we say about you.'

'Pardon?'

'If someone turns up before we get a chance to speak to Mr and Mrs Patel.' He licks the end of the pencil. 'You know. What's your ESP?'

'It's USP, dad. Unique Selling Points,' I say. 'If I had ESP I wouldn't be putting myself through this humiliation in the first place. And besides, I shouldn't have to tell you what they are.'

When my dad stares at his pad for a full minute but doesn't write anything down, it becomes clear that, actually, I do.

'Well, he's quite a catch,' suggests my mum.

'What, like measles,' says my dad, collapsing in a fit of giggles.

'Dad! Try and think practically.'

'And you're nice-looking,' says my mum, leaning over and pinching my cheek. 'And you dress very nicely. Although your iron seems to be broken.'

'Mum, for the millionth time, it's the look.'

'You've got your own teeth,' she says. 'And hair.'

'Although rather a lot of it,' adds my dad.

'And your own flat.'

I sit back in my chair. 'That's more like it.'

My dad raises both eyebrows. 'And a six-figure salary?'

'I wish.'

'Well, how much did you earn this year? From your painting?'

'Hang on.' I borrow his pad and pencil and make some hasty calculations, then slide them back across the table. 'Here.'

'There you go,' he says, turning it the right way up. 'Six figures.'

'Dad, you're not supposed to include the figures after the decimal point.'

He shrugs. 'Suit yourself. But at least that gives me something to work with. You leave it to us, son. We'll soon get you sorted.'

'Okay.' I stand up and make for the back door. 'But promise me you won't do anything until you've spoken to Ash's mum and dad.'

My dad reaches for his computer again and fires it up. 'I promise,' he says, although the glint in his eye suggests otherwise.

Chapter 10

At seven o'clock precisely, the doorbell goes, causing my mum to run around the kitchen in a panic. In truth, the meal's been cooked for hours, although it's been a big debate as to what she'd actually be cooking, of course, which had prompted several phone calls to Ash just to check that no, his mum and dad weren't vegetarians, and yes, they did drink alcohol. Which is a good thing, because I've got a feeling we'll be needing a lot of it. Or at least I will.

I open the front door and show Mr and Mrs Patel in, followed deferentially by Ash, who seems to have reverted to his shy teenage self with the presence of his mum and dad. He grins sheepishly as I walk them into the front room, just in time to see my mother hurrying in from the kitchen, drying her hands on a tea towel. Unfortunately, she's forgotten to remove her rather realistic 'bikini' apron – a present from my dad last Christmas – and for a moment, Mrs Patel doesn't know where to look. Our parents haven't really met before, apart from a brief hello during the occasional meal at the

Indian Queen, but after a few glasses of wine, they're chatting like old friends. It's not until we get onto dessert that the subject of my love life comes up, and to my embarrassment – and Ash's great amusement – I have to specify the kind of woman I'd ideally be looking for. And then, before I can stop them, my mum and dad decide to entertain the Patels with detailed tales of most of my previous relationships.

Eventually, and to my great relief, Mr Patel clears his throat. 'I think, Ben,' he says, holding out his glass for a refill from the bottle of red wine my father's proffering, 'the problem is that you've been approaching this in the wrong way. You're effectively trying to pick these women up from the street.'

'Well, that's not exactly how I'd put it,' I protest, before Mr Patel holds his hand up.

'Just hear me out,' he continues. 'We'd known Priti's family for ages, for example. So we knew we wouldn't be in for any surprises. That she was from good stock, as it were. And of course, she and Ashif had met before.'

'When we were five, Dad,' interrupts Ash.

'That's right,' says Mrs Patel, fondly. 'The two of you used to run around naked together in the garden. I think I've still got the photos somewhere.'

'Photos which better not make an appearance at the wedding, Mum,' warns Ash. As I make a mental note to ask Mrs Patel for copies for the stag night, Ash frowns. 'I didn't really remember her, though.'

'No, but your father and I knew you got on as children, didn't we, Sanjay?' she continues.

Mr Patel nods. 'And let's face it, we're all just big children, really,' he observes.

Some more childish than others, I think, looking across the table at my dad.

'So, let me get this straight,' says my mum. 'Ideally, what we have to do is find a girl from a family we know. Someone who maybe Ben knows too, but hasn't looked at in that way before.'

I help myself to some more wine. 'But who's seen me naked, obviously.'

'When I was *five*,' huffs Ash.

'Well, ideally, yes,' says Mrs Patel. 'A friend of the family, perhaps?'

'I've had an idea,' says my mother, before disappearing off into the next room, then coming back a few moments later with an armful of photo albums, which she hands round to everyone except me. 'All we have to do is look through these, find photos of Ben when he was younger, and then . . .'

I get up and follow her round the table, taking them back from everyone. 'Mum, I don't think Mrs Patel meant it quite as literally as that.'

'Why not?' interrupts Mr Patel. 'In fact, it's a splendid idea. I'm sure we can go through these in no time.'

'Great idea,' agrees my dad. 'I'll fetch the brandy.'

But by the time we've finished off most of the bottle, and what's left of my self-esteem thanks to my various embarrassing baby photos, we're none the wiser. Most of the families that we used to know have either moved, or we don't keep in contact with them apart from the odd Christmas card, and those that we're still in touch with don't have daughters. Or eligible ones, at least. My mum sighs loudly, then collects up the albums. 'Well, that was a fat lot of good,' she says, dumping them in a pile on the coffee table.

'No one at all?' asks Mr Patel.

My dad racks his brain for a moment or two. 'I'm afraid not. At least, not anyone who isn't married already,' he adds, looking accusingly across the table at me.

'Great,' I say, staring hopelessly up at the ceiling. It looks like this whole project is going to fail at the first hurdle, simply because my mum and dad aren't sociable enough.

My mum pats me on the back of the hand. 'There, there, Ben. I'm sure we'll think of something.'

'Yes,' agrees Mr Patel. 'And, anyway, given the unique nature of the situation, I think we're going to have to restrict the search to a local level. So maybe we should be less, well, specific.'

'Exactly.' Mrs Patel smiles. 'There must be other people you've met more recently. Friends or acquaintances, perhaps?'

'There's work colleagues, of course,' suggests Mr Patel. 'You need to spread the net as wide as possible. You too, Ben. Put it about that you're looking for a bride. Ask everyone you know. See whether they've got a sister.'

'Good idea,' says my dad, picking up the brandy bottle. 'So, Sanjay, does *Ash*?'

'Does Ash what?' says Mr Patel.

My dad empties the last of the brandy into Ash's glass. 'Have a sister.'

As everyone laughs except for his parents, Ash clears his throat. 'I do.'

I look across the table at him. 'Do what?'

'Have a sister.'

Mr and Mrs Patel suddenly look a little uncomfortable. 'I'm sure Alan was joking,' says Mr Patel.

'Not at all,' says my dad. 'What's she like?'

'Just Ben's type,' says Ash mischievously. 'Do it, Ben. Marry *her*. We'd be brothers.'

As I wonder firstly what Ash thinks my type actually is, and secondly why I've never heard of this sister before, Mrs Patel clears her throat loudly. 'Ashif,' she says, sternly, 'we're here to help Ben find a wife. Not our daughter find a husband.'

My dad picks up the brandy bottle again and tries to refill his glass, before remembering that it's empty. 'You haven't got anyone else lined up for her, have you?'

Ash's parents exchange awkward glances, before Ash's dad shifts uncomfortably in his chair. 'Well, no, but . . .'

'Great,' says my dad. 'So we could kill two birds with one stone, so to speak. Excellent.' He reaches across the table for the last remaining bottle of red wine, and unscrews the top. 'This calls for a celebration.'

'Exactly,' says Ash, mischievously, although by the looks on his parents' faces, a celebration is the last thing on their minds.

'So. How shall we fix them up?' continues my dad, warming to the task.

Mr Patel puts a hand over the top of his wine glass to stop my dad filling it up. 'I don't think that's such a good idea.'

'Why ever not?' asks my mum, defensively. 'What's wrong with Ben?'

'Well, the fact that he can't find himself a girlfriend, for one thing,' protests Mrs Patel.

'Just like Ashif, in fact,' says my mum.

Mr Patel looks at her. 'Pardon?'

'Ashif didn't have a girlfriend, did he? Not until you introduced him to Priti. And there's nothing wrong with him, is there?'

'Of course not,' says Mrs Patel.

My mum smiles. 'So in that case, there's nothing wrong with Ben, is there?'

As all heads swivel towards me, I stare at my plate.

'It's just . . .' Mr Patel sighs. 'It's nothing to do with Ben. Our daughter's just not . . .'

'Suitable,' says Mrs Patel.

I can tell my mum's about to ask why not, so I tap the side of my glass a couple of times with my knife. 'Shall we just move on? I think we were at "work colleagues", or something?'

'Yes,' says Mr Patel, holding his empty glass out towards my dad, relieved that I've changed the subject. 'Of course.'

As he explains how my mum and dad should plan their approach, the awkwardness gradually lifts from the table. And by the time we're on to coffee, along with the box of After Eights my mum's been saving since Christmas, my parents seem to be even more enthusiastic about the project.

'So, what's the next step?' asks my dad. 'Once we've identified a potential target, and Ben's been out with them. Assuming he's not scared them off, of course.'

I ignore the insult. 'Target? You've been reading too many of those SAS novels.'

'Sorry, son.' My dad grins. 'Once we've found someone for you to marry, I meant.'

'Well, then you have to meet the family, of course,' says Mr Patel.

My mum frowns. 'Why? What have they got to do with it?'

'Everything,' interrupts Ash. 'In fact, normally, we'd do it the other way round. You know, meet the parents first.'

I look at him incredulously. 'Why on earth would you want to do that? I mean, it's not them you're marrying, is it?'

Ash grins. 'You'd be surprised. Do you know what the difference is between outlaws and in-laws?'

I shrug. 'What?'

'Outlaws are *wanted*.' He laughs at his own joke, then stops when he sees that no one else is joining in. 'I'm serious, though. Making sure you get on with her parents is really important. Because if you think about it, you're going to be seeing an awful lot of them.'

'Plus,' says Mr Patel, 'they're going to be paying for the wedding, don't forget.'

'But . . .' I wonder how I can explain. 'What *we* do,' I say, more than a little conscious of not wanting to sound too racist, 'is actually the complete opposite. In fact, I'd probably leave meeting her folks until the last possible minute. And certainly not until I'd ensured that the two of us were compatible in the first place.'

Ash smiles. 'Maybe so. But it does have its value. I mean, there's the "is she going to turn out like her mother?" angle, for one thing. Like it or not, it's a pretty good indicator. And you can tell from the way they interact how good their family values are.'

I shake my head, then get up and walk round to where my mum and dad are sitting. 'It's her meeting my parents I'm more worried about,' I say, putting an arm around each of their shoulders and giving them a squeeze.

As my mum and dad start to protest, Ash's dad laughs. 'Good point. But you know how the date itself can be like a job interview? Well, if it's marriage you're after, then think of it more as a company merger. The coming together of two families. And while it's not crucial that they really get on, it's important that each one knows what the other is bringing to the table.'

'Like a holiday home,' says my mum hopefully. 'Or a boat.'

Chapter 11

When I meet Ash for a beer the following evening, he's surprisingly upbeat, and while I assume that's about my chances, it could just be because the big screen in the corner of the pub is showing tonight's cup match, and his team are two–nil up.

'So, that went well, then?' I say, as Ash puts a beer on the table in front of me without taking his eyes from the game, and then sits down, nearly missing his chair. 'Last night, I mean.'

'Could have been worse. At least your mum and dad have got a good idea about how to go about it now.'

'Yes, but there's a long way to go in between knowing how to go about it, and actually finding me someone suitable. You know, who I might actually *like*.'

He grins. 'Like my sister.'

'Yeah. Sorry about that.'

'S'all right. It was worth it just to see their faces. But tell me something, Ben, before you rush headlong into this. Why do you want to get married so badly?'

Ash takes a mouthful of lager. 'I mean, want it badly. Not to do it badly.'

'Well . . .' I pick my own glass up and take a long drink, primarily to give myself some thinking time, but also because I don't want to sound like a real saddo by admitting that one of the main reasons is simply because I'm lonely. 'For a start, most of my other friends are already married. Now even the likes of you are doing it. And before me.' And while I mean this half-jokingly, it is actually true. I do feel like I'm being left behind, because most of my friends *are* married. Some of them even have kids. And both of these factors are reasons for them to have less space in their lives for single old me, which would probably explain why I never see them any more. And I can't ignore the fact that there's a big part of me that's worried that unless I do it too – and soon – I can see a lifetime of TV dinners for one stretching out before me.

'So, you're doing it because "it's what people do", are you?'

'Well, partly . . .'

'Baa.'

'I'm sorry. Is that Indian for something?'

Ash turns round to face me, and shakes his head. 'Ben, for the million-and-oneth time, there's no "Indian" for anything. It could be Gujarati, or Urdu, or Hindi, but technically . . .'

I hold my hand up. 'Okay, Ash. I get your point. So what was the stupid noise for?'

'I was being a sheep. Or rather, you are.'

'What are you talking about?'

'You saying you want to get married because every-one else is. There's got to be another reason.'

'Sorry. Perhaps I wasn't being clear. I want to get married because I want to do what, traditionally, every-one else does when they get to my age. Find a wife. Settle down. Start a family.'

'And you have to get married to do all that?' says Ash, turning his attention back to the football. 'Apart from the "wife" part, obviously.'

'Well, yes.'

'Why?'

'Because . . .' I think hurriedly, trying to find an alternative answer to the 'it's what people do, isn't it' one. And fail. 'Because that's how you go about it.'

'Not necessarily.'

'What do you mean?'

'Well, what does actually being married mean to you?'

I think for a second. 'Well, it's the commitment thing, isn't it? Saying legally, and in front of people, that the two of you are entering into this institution where you're going to make a go of it. Life together, that is.'

Ash winces at a particularly bad tackle. 'And you can't make a go of it without actually saying "I do" in front of a group of people, most of whom you don't know?'

'Look who's talking.'

'Point taken. But it's more of the done thing with my lot. I mean, there's no way I could get away with it without actually marrying Priti. But I'm just interested why you put so much store by the actual wedding thing.'

'Well . . .' I'm just about to try to answer, when Ash realizes he's left his packet of crisps on the bar, and walks back over to get them.

'All I'm saying,' he says, sitting back down again while simultaneously pulling open his packet of McCoy's, 'is that for you, marriage isn't the only way. Let's face it, you can see it in a negative way too.'

'How so?'

Ash shrugs. 'Asking someone to marry you is a bit like saying "okay, we get on well together, and I suspect we might have a future together, so marry me, because that way legally you're not allowed to leave me." You want to demonstrate your commitment to someone, buy a house with them. Have a child with them. Agree to not look at other women. And you can do all that without actually forcing them to handcuff themselves to you.'

'Ash, it's not a handcuff. It's a gesture. A statement. Because as a man, you're saying that you're giving up, well, all other women, to make a commitment to this one. And as a woman, you're saying that "I believe you're a good enough man to support me and have a family with." So it's a statement, in public, that the two of you really rate the person you're with. And you want that to be recognized.'

'So you do it for other people?'

'No. Well yes. Partly.'

Ash sighs. 'But shouldn't you be doing it for yourself? Not to show everyone else you're crazy about each other, or to say "hands off". Because that's what a wedding ring is, isn't it? A badge to say you're unavailable, or taken.'

'Tell me that's not one of the reasons you're so keen to settle down with Priti?'

'I could, but it would be a lie,' admits Ash. 'But also because I've always known I'd get married, and had an idea of how that was going to happen, and so when Priti came along, well, I knew she was it almost before I'd even met her. But you, you're saying "I want to get married, so find me a wife, but she must measure up to my check-list, which I've worked out from all the failed relationships I've had before."'

'So I've got standards. What's wrong with that?'

'Just that you're going to be looking for something that you might not be able to find. Most people's ideal woman is just that – an ideal. She doesn't really exist. So if you keep holding out for her, you're going to end up disappointed. Not to mention disappointing the poor girls that your mum and dad send your way.'

'Are you telling me this isn't going to work?'

'No. But all I'm saying is, you can't lead any of these girls up the garden path, Ben. Anyone you meet this way is going to expect you to want to marry them. Not just try them out for a while.'

'Like I normally do?'

'I didn't say that.'

'Well, I won't. Not if I go into this with my eyes open.

I *do* want to be with someone for ever. And, sadly, the way things stand, this looks like the best way to ensure that happens.'

Ash rolls his eyes. 'Fine. As long as you know what you're doing.'

'I do,' I say, hoping that when I finally get to say those words, I actually, er, do.

'Good,' says Ash, moving his chair round to get a better view of the game. 'Lecture over.'

We sip our beer in silence for a few moments, and then I can't help asking, 'So, what's she like then?'

'Who?'

'You know full well who. Your sister.'

'Meera?' Ash grins. 'She's all right, I guess.'

'And do you, you know, think she might be interested? In me.'

He shakes his head. 'Nah.'

'Why not?' I ask, a little offended.

'Well, the fact you're missing two legs, for a start.'

'Huh?' I start to look under the table to check, then stop myself, hoping Ash hasn't seen me.

'The only thing she's interested in is horses.'

'Horses?'

He turns his gaze away from the football for a second. 'She's thirteen, Ben.'

'Ah.' I feel a sudden twinge of guilt. 'No wonder your parents were shocked.'

'Quite. Although not quite as shocked as when my mum found out she was having her in the first place.'

'I must have sounded like some kind of pervert.'

'Well, you would have, if not for the fact that . . . No. Never mind.'

I frown across the top of my glass at him. 'What.'

'I've got two.'

'Two what?'

'Sisters.'

'That's a relief. Unless the other one's three, or something.'

'Thirty-three, actually.'

'Oh. Right. And what's *her* name?' I ask, when Ash doesn't volunteer any further information.

'Why?' says Ash, suspiciously.

'No reason.' As he turns his attention back to the football, I realize that I should let it drop. But now, of course, I'm intrigued, and so can't help but ask. 'Is she single?'

Ash puts his glass down and folds his arms. 'Are you seriously asking me if I can set you up with my sister?'

'No. Of course not.' I avoid Ash's gaze, and stare at the screen in the corner, where a load of overpaid footballers seem to be spending more time kicking each other than the ball, then acting as if they've been shot when they get the slightest tap on the ankle themselves. 'Unless she's really good-looking, of course.'

'Ha ha,' he says sarcastically.

I mentally count to ten. 'So, what *is* she like?'

'Huh?' says Ash, engrossed in some goalmouth action. 'Who?'

'You know. Your sister.'

Ash puts his beer down, and turns his chair round to face me. 'Ben, for Christ's sake . . .'

'Sorry, mate. But I'm just trying to explore all my opportunities, you know. I mean, we've not known each other that long, but we get on well, don't we? So do our parents. So given what your dad was talking about last night, that sounds like a pretty good basis to me to investigate things further. Unless . . .'

'Unless what?'

'Unless she looks like a female version of you, of course.'

'Very funny,' says Ash, pretending to scratch his nose while giving me the finger. 'She's quite striking looking, actually.'

'Striking? As in "stunning"? Or just "striking"?'

'What's the difference?'

I think about this for a second. 'She's stunning,' I say, nodding towards the bikini-clad model on the faded KP peanuts poster behind the bar. 'Whereas you could describe the Elephant Man as striking.'

'Ah.' Ash laughs. 'The first one, then.'

'Oh. Right. Great. And, er, what does she do?'

'Well, I'll tell you what she doesn't do. And that's go out with my friends.'

'Why not?'

Ash looks me up and down. 'Where do you want me to start?'

'Fair point. I suppose your parents have got someone in mind for her anyway?'

Ash sighs, realizing that he's not going to get an un-interrupted chance to watch the match. 'No, actually. She's always been the rebel of the family.'

'Is that why your mum and dad were so defensive last night?'

'Don't think badly about my parents, Ben. They're not that strict. It's just that they've got these expecta-tions, that's all. They're not rules, just hopes. And every parent hopes their child will do the best for themselves, and so anything they can do to help out . . .' Ash stops talking, as if he's considering how much information to share. 'My sister just doesn't believe in doing things the traditional way, that's all. And I might not either, if Priti and I didn't get along so well. Trust me, it's not some iron-rule society where people are forced to do things against their will. My mum and dad just worry about her, that's all.'

'She sounds like she can look after herself.'

Ash nods. 'She can. And that's part of the problem. They still see her as their little girl. So it's a shock to them that she isn't any more.'

'So,' I swallow hard, 'you wouldn't mind if I asked her out?'

'Mind?' Ash lets out a short laugh, which I don't quite know how to interpret. 'Be my guest. Although I wouldn't tell her about this find-me-a-bride mission that you're embarking on.'

'Why not?'

Ash makes a face. 'She doesn't really believe in marriage.'

'Why ever not?'

'Because she's already been married. And it didn't work out.'

'Because of the, you know, *arrangement* thing?'

Ash laughs. 'Nah. Because her husband turned out to be gay.'

'What?'

He nods. 'Yup. And his parents were just trying to cover it all up, by getting him married off. Trouble was, she was a little too clever for them.'

'How did she find out?'

'Well, apart from anything else, the not sleeping together was getting to be a problem. But it's put her off for life.'

'What – marriage? Men? Or marrying gay men?'

Ash grins. 'All three. Besides, she'd run a mile if my parents even gave her the slightest hint that she was being set up again.'

'Ah. Okay. Forget I asked.'

'I will,' says Ash, turning back to the match.

I stare at the back of his head for a few moments, and then can't help myself. 'And why haven't I met her before?'

Ash shrugs. 'She's only just moved back down from London. Something about there being better opportunities in her line of work down here, I think she said.'

'So, come on. What does she do? For a living, I mean.'

Ash looks at me for a moment, then sighs loudly. 'Okay. She sells drugs.'

'Sells *drugs*?'

'Yes,' says Ash. 'Which my parents weren't best pleased about, because they'd always wanted her to be a doctor, which kind of started off her whole rebellious streak. They were really happy when she agreed to give the arranged marriage thing a go, but given what happened ... Well, let's just say that relations have been a little bit cooler between them since then.'

'Understandably. Hence the reason your folks were so sensitive when I mentioned her.'

Ash nods. 'Or they might just have assumed you actually meant Meera. No, I think they're just letting her make her own way. And just hoping that whoever she ends up with won't be too embarrassing for the family.'

'Okay. Fair enough. I'll steer clear then.'

'Thanks.'

'Don't mention it.' I shake my head. 'I still can't believe your sister's a drug dealer.'

'Yes.' Ash grins. 'Or rather, a "pharmacist", to give it its proper title.'

'A pharmacist?' I say, trying to ignore the sudden, uneasy feeling in my stomach. 'And what did you say her name was?'

'I didn't,' says Ash. 'But it's Seema.'

Bollocks. Just my luck. Although thinking about it, the Seema I 'met' wasn't called Patel. It's the slimmest of lifelines, but one I'm determined to hang on to with both hands. 'So, when you say she's a pharmacist, is this in a shop?'

Ash sighs. 'Boots,' he says, without turning round to look at me.

'Pardon?'

'You'll find Seema in Boots.'

'What sort?' I ask, hoping he's describing Seema's preferred footwear, rather than her place of work. 'Football? Wellington? Thigh-high leather ones?'

'Ben, please, this is my sister we're talking about. Boots the chemists, obviously.'

'Oh. Right,' I say, the lifeline slipping from my fingers. 'So that would be the Boots on the High Street, or the one in the shopping centre?'

'The High Street,' says Ash, reaching into his pocket and removing his mobile phone, then flicking through to the 'camera' option. 'This is her,' he says, handing it over to me.

I take the phone and peer nervously at the screen, waiting for the photo to load, and when it does, while it's a face that for some reason looks familiar, at least it's not from the other day. Although Ash was right – she certainly is stunning. '*This* is your sister?'

'What's wrong with her?' says Ash defensively.

'Nothing at all. In fact, I meant to say "this is *your* sister?". She's gorgeous.'

'Bugger off.'

I stare at the photo again in disbelief. 'But, Ash . . .'

'What?'

'Why is she topless?'

'Pardon? Oh, sorry.' Ash takes the phone and presses a couple of buttons before handing it back to me. 'That's Halle Berry. She's my new screensaver. *This* is Seema.'

'Thanks,' I say, taking the phone back, and then my stomach does a little flip. It's another face I recognize, although not, sadly, from the movies. 'And you're sure she's your sister?'

Ash gives me a look that's in keeping with the dumbness of the question I've just asked. 'Yes. She got the looks in the family. Unfortunately.'

'And the brains, judging by what she does for a living.'

'Yes, well, if she's got any brains, then she'll keep away from you,' he says, turning back towards the television.

'But you wouldn't mind if one day I did happen to, you know, ask her out? If all this find-me-a-bride stuff doesn't come to anything, of course.'

'It's a free country,' says Ash. 'Although I warn you – she'll eat you alive.'

But as I leave Ash to watch the rest of the match in peace, I start to think that might not be such a bad way to go.

Chapter 12

Nothing much happens for the next few days. I don't hear anything from my mum and dad, so I assume they're 'getting on with it', whatever 'it' is, and besides I'm not expecting immediate results. I've got a couple of commissions to be getting on with anyway, which keeps me busy, and keeps my mind off what they might be up to as well. I'm still way too embarrassed to even think about going to talk to Seema after our earlier encounter, and in fact keep completely away from the High Street to minimize my chances of bumping into her. As attractive as she is, I don't want my parents to be going to all this trouble for nothing, and besides there's a part of me that's intrigued to see what they come up with.

But one of the things Ash's parents did say I needed to start doing, and the earlier the better, was put the word around, which is what I do. Although I'm guessing they didn't mean telling the likes of Terry what I'm up to when I get to my art class this evening. And especially when there's still ten minutes to go before the others are due to arrive.

'Smile,' he says, pulling his phone out of his pocket and pointing the camera at me.

'What's that for?'

'It's a "before" picture,' smirks Terry. 'Because you certainly won't be smiling once some woman's got her claws into you. Besides, you're not ready to get married.'

'What do you mean?' I say, more than a little hurt.

'Financially, for one thing.'

'What are you talking about?'

'You need to wait until you've got at least two houses.'

'But women aren't that materialistic. At least, not the kind of women I want to meet.'

'I'm not talking about meeting them,' says Terry, staring at me earnestly from behind his easel. 'But you'll need the two houses for when you get divorced. That way, you won't be homeless when you have to hand over one of them.'

I laugh, but then stop suddenly, as it's clear Terry's not joking. 'Anyone ever told you you're a little bit cynical?'

Terry shakes his head. 'I'm just playing devil's advocate here. Mug's game, marriage. And it's the same the whole world over.'

'That's not true,' I say, recalling something I'd watched on the Discovery channel the other day. 'In fact, in certain Polynesian societies they even have more than one wife. Why would they do that if it was so bad?'

'At the same time?' Terry looks horrified. 'Nah, Ben,

when it comes to marriage, I'm of the Oscar Wilde school of thought.'

'Which is?' I have to ask, when Terry doesn't answer.

'You know – something along the lines of bigamy being one wife too many, and marriage being the same thing.'

'Yes, but he was, I mean . . .' I stop talking, not really wanting to be caught debating the merits of Oscar Wilde's sexuality with Terry in case Lizzie suddenly walks in. 'Wrong.'

Terry sniffs. 'Not at all. Realistic, more like.'

'It can't be that bad?'

He nods. 'Trust me – as someone who's tried it twice, oh yes it is. You wait until you run out of excuses not to marry them, rather than leaping into it like you're doing.'

'But . . . I *want* a wife.'

Terry shakes his head slowly. 'We all want a wife, Benny boy. It's what they turn into – and bring with them – that we don't bargain for. Because before you know it, you're saddled with a family and a life that you didn't bargain for, and the minute you object, she takes them with her, plus your house, your car, and half your money . . .' He pauses for breath. 'And you tell me how that's fair?'

'But . . .' I stop talking myself, because how do I explain that surely that's part of the bargain? 'Having the family comes with the territory, doesn't it? You know that if a woman agrees to marry you, then by way of compensation, she's going to want to have kids. And therefore it's the price you pay for getting that commitment out of her in the first place.'

'Yeah, but just you wait till she starts producing. Then you either do exactly as she says, or she's off. I'll tell you,' continues Terry, 'there should be some insurance against it.'

'There is. They're called condoms.'

'No. I mean the whole divorce thing. Look at me now – assuming I ever manage to meet another woman who I'd even contemplate spending the rest of my life with, would I ever get married again? No way!'

'Really?' I'd always thought Terry and his wives were blissfully happy. Up until they divorced him, that is.

'I just couldn't afford it, financially or emotionally. Nah, the way I see it, marriage is a concept invented by lawyers as a way of earning extra money. Nothing else.'

'That's rubbish.'

'Not at all,' says Terry. 'Look at all these same-sex marriages nowadays. Who's the happiest about it all? Not the gay couples themselves, but the lawyers, because they know that give it a couple of years, there'll be a whole new set of customers banging on their doors.' He shakes his head. 'Like I say, mug's game. Whatever team you play for.'

'I'm sorry, Terry. But I'm determined to go through with it.'

'Well, at least get yourself a satnav first.'

'A satnav?'

He nods. 'It'll give you some idea of what marriage is like – a woman's voice telling you where to go and what to do all the time.'

'Very funny, Terry,' I say sarcastically, although I can't hide my smile. 'But it is what I want.'

Terry sighs. 'Well, in that case, may divorce be with you. But do you want some advice?'

I don't want to offend him by saying 'no'. 'Go on, then.'

He leans in towards me and lowers his voice conspiratorially. 'You know the secret to a long and happy marriage?'

I shrug. 'Tell me.'

'Have a short and unhappy one first.'

I look at him in horror. 'What?'

'I'm serious. Think of it like school.'

'Like school?'

'You show up for a few years, learn something, then it's time to leave.'

'What are you talking about?'

'They're called "starter marriages". You know, like a starter home. Sort of gets you on the marriage ladder. Although the irony is, you end up losing your *actual* home. But it's a small price to pay, in the long run.'

'Huh?'

Terry beckons for me to sit down. 'You know when you buy your first place, it's a means to an end, isn't it? I mean, you're not planning to live there for the rest of your life, are you? But it teaches you how to go about

the buying process, all about DIY, and more importantly, what to avoid when you buy your next one.'

I look at him incredulously. 'So, you're saying I should
just marry any old person, wait for it to go wrong, and
then learn from my mistakes?'

Terry nods sagely. 'And you won't have to wait
long, because whoever you marry, it just will. In fact,
everything you do will be so wrong, you'll actually think
you're doing it on purpose.'

'But . . . that's ridiculous.'

'Is it?' Terry sighs. 'Look at the marriage statistics.
Divorces are one in two, right. And at the same time,
your second marriage is likely, on average, to last twice
as long as your first – even though at the time your first
will feel like it's never going to end. Proves my point.'

'That's not going to be me, though, Terry. I mean,
I've had enough relationships to be able to tell, surely.'

He laughs. For quite a while. 'Afraid not, Ben.
Because marriage – that's a different thing entirely. And
sadly the only way to experience it is to actually go
through with it. I mean, I'm not a bad person, am I?'

I look him up and down. 'I suppose not.'

'Thanks. But to talk to either of my ex-wives, you'd
think I was the devil incarnate. Because that's what
marriage does to people. Makes them lose all sense of
perspective. I tell you, forget their birthday once, call
'em by the wrong name in bed, or even sleep with their
best friend, and they rank it as a crime up there with
murder.'

'Surely that's not true.'

'Trust me,' says Terry. 'Or let me put it another way. If you went for a job, and someone said there was a fifty–fifty chance of you getting sacked within a couple of years, *and* you'd have to pay out a lot of money when you left, would you take it?'

'That would depend on the job.'

'Okay. Say you were buying a house,' says Terry, evidently warming to his task, 'and you knew there was an equal chance of it falling down. Would you still go ahead with it, knowing how expensive it's going to be?'

'Well, probably not,' I say, glancing at the slow-moving clock on the wall, and starting to feel a little depressed.

'And that's my point,' says Terry triumphantly. 'It's exactly the same with marriage. And yet, everyone always goes into it all starry-eyed, thinking "I'm not going to fail" or "we'll be different", and of course they're more often than not wrong. Because it's an inevitability.'

'But surely the only way to go into it is with starry-eyed optimism, because what's the alternative? Start off thinking it's going to go wrong, and then not being surprised when that happens?'

'Why not?' says Terry. 'That way, you're not going to end up disappointed, are you?'

'But that doesn't make any sense.'

'Nor does marriage,' says Terry. 'Given those odds.'

'But that's why a proposal of marriage is such a big

deal, isn't it? Because it's a statement from you saying "Hey, I know it's tough out there, and that marriage is tricky, but I really think that you and me can make a go of it". And in a way, the worse the statistics are, the bigger a compliment it is, because you're saying to someone "I know it's bad, but I want to give it a go. With you. Together we can make our way through this minefield."'

'Yeah, but men and women see it differently, don't they?'

My head is starting to hurt. 'Do they?'

'Of course they do,' says Terry, patiently. 'We propose, thinking we're doing the woman a favour. You know, of all the women I'm beating off with a shitty stick, you're the one I want to make a commitment to, blah blah blah. But they in fact see it more rationally. Can this person support me while I do what I'm biologically programmed to do, and if so, am I prepared to keep letting them have sex with me in return? It starts out as a trade-off, but what actually happens is that we end up doing all the compromising, and yet they make us feel like they are. And that's hardly a win–win situation, is it?'

I put my head in my hands. 'Are you trying to put me off?'

Terry grins. 'Not at all. I love a good wedding, me. Just not my own. I simply want to make sure you're going into this with your eyes wide open. Because so many people do the exact opposite.'

'I'm sorry, Terry. It's just that what you're saying kind of takes the fun out of it.'

'Sticking a ring on her finger will take care of that, Ben, don't you worry.' Terry smiles wistfully. 'All I'm saying is, just don't expect wonders. Because the only wonder you'll get is wondering why you went through with it in the first place.'

'But my parents seem happy enough.'

'And congratulations to them. They're two of the lucky ones. But don't forget, they're from a different generation. Trust me, before long, marriage will be a thing of the past.'

I'm starting to wish that this conversation was a thing of the past, and wondering how to change the subject, when fortunately the others arrive, somewhat cutting short Terry's rant, but even so, it's been enough to put me in a mood which lasts long after class finishes. And while Terry's observations are more than a little confusing, if there's one thing I'm sure of, it's that I'm determined to be one of the lucky ones. To have my cake and eat it. To *not* feel like I'm compromising, or getting married to someone because I have to, rather than because I want to.

It's just gone nine o'clock by the time I get home, and I can't be bothered to make myself any dinner, so just help myself to a beer from the fridge, pop open a packet of Pringles, and slump down in front of the TV. There's an old episode of the Simpsons playing – the one where Homer's at home, looking after the kids – and even though I'm laughing, I can't help wondering whether there's a lesson for me here too.

Because where Homer's lucky is that he's pretty oblivious, or rather, resigned, to his fate. He knows that life doesn't get any better than this – or rather, *his* won't get any better – until the kids are off his hands. So what does he do? He just gets on with it, and numbs any pain he feels with beer and food, making himself comfortable.

Is their quality of life amazing? Obviously not, given the demands that having a family places upon them. And yet, do they ever talk about splitting up, or ask for their money back, because it's not quite what it said on the packet? Of course not. Because that's life, isn't it? One long cycle of birth, marriage, and death. And in between, you have kids, and try and bring them up as best you can, which seems to me – at least, the way Homer does it – to be like hanging precariously on to the lead of a big dog that you can't quite keep under control.

Because it's all about a balance, isn't it? If you know that the price of staying with the woman you love is to do a job you might not have chosen for the next eighteen years, simply because you have to fund these kids who you didn't particularly plan for, and who occasionally cause you more trouble than happiness, then all you can do is make it as good as possible. I suppose it's like being in prison – if you're not going to plan an escape, then you might as well make the best of your 'stay', and make your cell as comfortable as possible.

Maybe I shouldn't take the Simpsons as role models. And am I being naive to think that I'll be able to do it differently? Possibly. But is it worth it in the end? Probably. Although it's ironic. You get married because you want to spend your life with one person, and, in reality, these other little people come along and actually prevent you and the person you married spending quality time together, because suddenly your focus is on them, rather than each other.

And yet when I look at my parents, it's all paid off. They might not say it so often, but I know they're proud of me, and take such pleasure in my achievements. Every time I tell my dad I've sold a painting, it's like he's seen me ride my bike without stabilizers for the first time. And now that I've left home, they have a good time together, too, perhaps because they feel that they've earned it. And as my dad often says to me, when you've really worked hard for something, then it means a lot more to you when you finally get it.

Maybe that's it. Maybe the secret to a long and happy marriage – despite what Terry says – is to work at it. I mean, you can't expect to get married and just have a great time together from day one. It's like serving an apprenticeship, I guess – although one that lasts longer than most other training schemes.

And that's another reason why I'm desperate to get on with it. Because I realize that the sooner I get started, the sooner I'll qualify, and that's when life really begins. Because while admittedly it can be fun being young, free, and single, there comes a time when you think 'here we go again', and in truth I reached that point a long time ago. Which is why I'm determined that I'm going to make it work with whoever it is I meet.

Look at Ash, for example. He can't possibly be *sure* that Priti's the one for him – he doesn't know her well enough – and neither can Priti, yet they're both going for it. And the fact that they're both so positive about where they want to be – rather than what they want the other person to be – means that they're more likely to make a success of it. And as long as you're both pulling in the same direction, then surely you'll get there in the end?

I turn my attention back to the TV, where despite everything that's happened, the family are together. A unit. Solid. Homer loves Marge, and Marge loves Homer, perhaps *because* of everything that's happened. And if someone like Homer can find love, then there's hope for me yet.

Chapter 13

However, as determined as I am to make it work with the right, er, *candidate*, there still has to be some fancying going on. I mean, think of the process: I have to see a girl, and find her attractive due to some mysterious combination of – admittedly superficial – characteristics. She then has to look at me and the same thing has to occur. And all that has to happen *before* one of us crosses the distance between us to make that first, tentative contact, where we open our mouths and actually *say* something to each other.

Trouble is, I'm not a hundred per cent sure I can rely on my mum and dad's aesthetic judgement. To that end, I spend most of the morning downloading a selection of images and video clips from the Internet, which I burn onto a CD, then take it round to my parents' house. Ignoring the usual exaggerated comments about it being too early for lunch, I set the laptop up on the coffee table, and instruct them both to sit down on the sofa.

'What's this?' asks my mum, thrusting a mug of tea

into my hand as soon as I've inserted the disk. 'Your holiday snaps?'

'I don't have any holiday snaps. Because I haven't been on holiday. Because I don't have anyone to go with. And even if I had been on my own, I'm hardly likely to take lots of photos of myself, am I?'

'Calm down, Ben,' she says. 'It's no wonder you can't get yourself a girlfriend if this is your attitude.'

As my dad shushes her, I start the slideshow playing, but after the first couple of pictures have loaded, my mum reaches over and snaps the screen shut.

'What are you doing?' This comes from my dad, who's obviously been enjoying it more than my mother has.

'I don't want to watch one of your blue movies.'

I have to fight the urge not to smile at my mum's quaint expression. 'It's not a "blue movie", Mum. It's a collection of pictures of the kind of women I find attractive. It's to help you pick someone for me. So you've got an idea of the kind of women I fancy.'

My mum laughs. 'This is Margate, Ben. Where are we going to find women who look like this? Certainly not feeding pound coins into the slot machines at the amusement arcade.'

'Besides,' says my dad, 'you've got to be realistic, haven't you?'

'I beg your pardon?'

He nods towards the laptop. 'Well, you wanting us to find you women like that. They're not real.'

'Yes, they are. Well, mostly.'

'No, they're not. Real people have beer bellies,' he says, patting his stomach, 'or fat backsides, or sticky-out ears, or bad teeth. And they find love too.'

'Are you saying I've got more chance with someone who's, well, deformed?'

'Not at all. But let's face it, you're hardly Marlon Brando, are you?'

'Who?'

My dad rolls his eyes. 'Okay, Bruce Willis, then. Although you do have more hair than him, admittedly.'

'A lot more,' says my mum, patting the top of my head proudly.

I smooth my hair back down. 'What are you trying to say, exactly?'

'Just that . . .' My dad shifts uncomfortably in his seat. I mean, you're not bad-looking. Not at all. But you might have to face facts and realize that you can't exactly pick and choose, can you?'

'What?'

'And besides,' continues my dad obliviously, 'marriage isn't all about looks.'

'Thank you very much, Alan!' says my mum, storming off into the kitchen.

My dad glares at me. 'You see what you've done now?' he says, leaping up off the sofa to chase after her. 'I mean, obviously I was lucky with your mum,' he continues, leading her back into the room, 'in that she was the most beautiful woman I'd ever seen, although mind you, that was probably because the Internet didn't exist then. But, anyway, my point is that marriage is about lots of other things. How well you get on as friends. And whether you're compatible. You know, in the bedroom department.'

'Dad, don't start that again, please . . .'

'All I'm saying is, there are other qualities that you should look for in a wife. Qualities that may not be apparent, or seem important, on first meeting them. And that's why you shouldn't be too hung up on this looks thing. Because looks fade. Though, not in your mum's case, obviously,' he adds, although given the expression on her face, a little too late for her liking.

'But . . .' I know my dad is trying to help. Trying to give me the benefit of his years of experience, while trying to avoid digging himself into a bigger hole with my mum. But the trouble is, even though I want to settle down, or even just want a girlfriend who I feel I can perhaps have a future with, as opposed to one where I'm just waiting for the inevitable day when she dumps me, I still want some kind of spark when I first see them. I open up the laptop again. 'Will you please just look at these? So I know we're at least in the same book, if not exactly on the same page.'

My dad clicks the screen shut, although I notice he doesn't give me the disk back. 'No need, son.'

'Why not?'

'Well, we've been busy, your mum and me.'

Uh-oh. 'Really? How busy, exactly?'

'Well, we've been asking around, as per Mr and Mrs Patel's instructions, and we've had quite a few responses. So we've drawn up a shortlist.'

For the first time, I notice the plastic A4 folder on the dining table. 'A shortlist?'

'That's right,' says my dad, sounding rather pleased with himself. 'Here.' He hands over what look like three CVs, all neatly typed on A4 sheets of paper, then watches as I scan through them quickly before putting them down on the table.

'Er . . .'

'What's the matter?'

'Is this it?'

'What do you mean?'

'Well, I don't want to sound ungrateful, but there are only three.'

My dad bristles slightly. 'Well, given the fact that you'd specified women of a certain age, not divorced, no kids, *and* not looking like the back end of a bus, that really didn't leave us a huge field to choose from. Primarily because most women answering that description seem to have been snapped up already.'

'Not surprisingly,' adds my mother, before heading back into the kitchen.

'And then there were the ones who weren't interested in you, despite my best efforts at – what is it you say – bigging you up? Which just left, well, these.'

'So, it's not really a shortlist, is it?' I say ungratefully.

'Do you want to see them or not?' snaps my dad.

'Okay, okay.' I fan the three sheets of paper out on the table, frowning as I turn each one over.

'What's the matter now?'

'It's just, well, there aren't any photos.'

He gives me a look I remember seeing a lot when I was growing up whenever I'd done something particularly stupid. 'Weren't you listening earlier? Looks aren't important.'

'So, you'd have been attracted to Mum even if she was a minger?'

My dad stares vacantly at me, possibly because he's trying to work out what the word 'minger' means, then lowers his voice. 'What I actually mean is, they're not the most important thing. Not where long-term happiness is concerned.'

'I can still hear you, you know,' calls my mum from the kitchen.

As my dad makes the 'now I'm in trouble' face, I shake my head. 'Well, I'm afraid they are to me.'

'Okay, then. In that case, let's just view this as a little experiment. Have a look at these women on paper first. See which one seems the most . . . Interesting. And then you can look at their photos, and see if that changes your mind.'

'Fine.' I turn my attention back to the sheets of A4 on the table, pleased that there are actually photos, but wondering how I can explain to my dad that *of course* it's going to make a difference. Unless they're identical triplets, then I can't help but be influenced by how they look, *because that's how it works*. And while I accept that women might not quite think in exactly the same way, and they might believe that certain other things, like financial security – in which case, I'm screwed – might be more important when settling down, that's because their needs are different. Whereas we need someone we're attracted to. Someone we want to sleep with. Because that's how we work. And whatever my dad says, I'm afraid that's one of the irrefutable facts of life.

I'm working out how exactly to phrase this without getting another lecture when my dad hands me a biro. 'Here.'

'What's this for?'

'So you can rank them. Write a one, two, or three on their details. You know, in the order in which you like them.'

'With "one" being the highest, right?'

'What do you think?' he says, although it sounds more like 'Don't be so stupid'.

I grudgingly take the pen from him, and stare at the details in front of me. As far as I'm concerned, they're pretty much identical, and the harder I look at them, the more I fail to spot a difference between them. Girl A works in a bank – so what? If she was a pole dancer, then maybe that would make a difference. And girl C has an art GCSE. I'm an artist. Is that supposed to mean that we're compatible, and will live happily ever after?

After a couple of minutes of pretending to consider them all carefully, I write my preferences – somewhat randomly, it has to be said – on each piece of paper.

'Here,' I say, handing them back to my dad.

'Great.' He reaches inside the folder, and removes a brown envelope, from which he produces three Polaroid photos. 'Now, tell me what you think.'

I take the pictures and study them carefully, feeling a little like I'm looking at mug shots in a police station, but relieved to see that they're all fairly good-looking. My dad's not the best photographer in the world, and to be honest, given the age of the camera and the film, and quite possibly the age of the photographer, all of them look a little out-of-focus. Plus, they're all just head shots, and if I'm being completely sexist, I need a little more to go on than that.

'Go on then,' he says, nodding towards where I've left the pen. 'Mark away.'

With a sigh, I pick up the biro, and place the photos face-up on the table, side by side. My dad's carefully marked each one with an 'X', 'Y', and 'Z', so as not to give any clues away as to which one matches their résumés, but to be honest I've already forgotten most of the stuff I've read anyway. Let's face it, when you're browsing through the profiles on a dating website, it's only after you've decided the girl in the photo is attractive that you consider reading what she's written in her profile, and even then, unless she's put 'axe-murderer' down in the 'occupation' section you're unlikely to discount her – and even then, if she's got big tits, you might not. Which is why I need to hear my dad's description. Some enthusiasm about each of them. Because that's how sales pitches work. And what's this if it's not just one big sales pitch?

I turn my attention back to the photos. All three girls are attractive, in their own way. None of them appear to be nutters, from what I can tell from their pictures. Would I notice them at a bar, and be sufficiently motivated to go over to them, talk to them, buy them a drink even? It's hard to tell given my dad's lack of ability with the camera. And at the same time, I feel sorry for them too. The humiliation of having to go through an 'interview' with my dad, and then have your photo taken, knowing there's a 2 in 3 chance you'll be rejected ... What does that say about them? And, more importantly, what does it say about me if I do reject them?

In the end, I mark 'X' number one because she's smiling, 'Z' comes second because even though she's not smiling as much, she's got nice long blonde hair, and 'Y' gets last place because, well, she's not smiling, and her hair isn't as long. And if that's not a good set of criteria for choosing someone to spend the rest of my life with, I tell myself, sarcastically, I don't know what is.

'Well done,' says my dad, as if he's congratulating me on finishing an exam. 'Now, let's see how your results compare.'

'I can hardly wait,' I say, as enthusiastically as I can muster.

He reaches into his inside jacket pocket and removes

a piece of paper, and for a moment, I think he's going to announce 'and the winner is . . .'

'Well, that's interesting,' he says, checking my answers against his list. 'You've ranked them in completely the opposite order. What were the chances of that?'

Well, seeing as I chose them completely randomly, fairly high, I would have thought. 'That's incredible,' I say flatly. 'So, where do we go from here?'

My dad considers this for a second. 'Well, as we suspected, there's not a clear winner. So maybe you should meet them all.'

I look up sharply, and glance nervously towards the door. 'They're not all *here*, are they?'

My dad laughs. 'Not exactly. But they all live locally.'

'And they're very keen to meet you,' says my mum, carrying a plate of sandwiches in from the kitchen.

And although for some reason that last fact sets the alarm bells ringing, I don't see that I've got any choice. 'So what should I do? Call them all and arrange a drink one evening? Separately, of course.'

'No need,' says my dad. 'It's all arranged.'

'What? When for?'

My mum and dad exchange glances. 'Well, tomorrow, Monday, and Tuesday,' says my dad.

'What?' I splutter, more than a little shocked that my dad feels he can manage my social calendar on my behalf. 'How did you know I wasn't busy?'

As my mum and dad don't reply, I let out a long sigh. 'Just tell me where and what time.'

Chapter 14

It's Sunday evening, and as I check my reflection nervously in my hallway mirror, I suddenly realize that I've never been on a blind date before. This seems slightly strange to me, at twenty-nine years of age, but then again, I've never asked anyone to set me up before, and I have to admit, it's more than a little exciting. I'm also intrigued as to the kind of woman my dad would pick, rather than pick up, for me.

'You all ready, then?' says Ash, who's come round to give me a pep talk.

'I think so.'

'Got everything?'

'Yup. Er . . . Such as?'

'Money. Mobile phone. Condoms.'

I frown at him. 'What do I need condoms for?'

'You know – for when you . . . I mean, if it goes well, and she asks you back to her place.'

'I know the mechanics, Ash. But are you really expecting me to consider marrying someone who'll sleep with me on the first date?'

Ash grins. 'If I were you, I'd consider marrying the first person who was prepared to sleep with you at all.'

'Which is what you're doing, right?'

'Very funny.'

'So, did you and Priti get intimate?' I say, picking up my car keys from the table. 'On the first date?'

'Yeah, right. With about a thousand members of my family there. Besides, what's that got to do with anything?' he says, blushing slightly.

'Nothing. I was just . . .' I look at him, and realization dawns. 'Don't tell me you haven't, yet?'

'Of course I have,' he says, blushing furiously now. 'Just, er, not with Priti.'

'What?'

'Don't look so surprised. It's just the way things are. And she was only here for one weekend, after all.'

'But you are planning to, right? I mean, before the wedding.'

Ash stares at his shoes. 'Well, we've not talked about it.'

I look at him incredulously. 'Ash, you can't seriously be planning to marry a woman you've never slept with?'

He smiles awkwardly. 'Why not? People used to do it all the time. Besides, you can tell, can't you?'

'Tell what?'

'You know – if you're compatible. Sexually, I mean.'

'Yes, you can, Ash,' I say, putting an arm round his shoulders. 'But only usually by actually having sex.'

He shrugs me off. 'Stop going on about it. It's not such a big deal.'

'Yes, it is! This is someone you're going to be having sex with for the rest of your life. What if it's awful?'

'It won't be awful,' protests Ash. 'And, anyway, it's kind of . . . exciting.'

'Exciting? But think of the wedding night,' I say. 'The pressure. I'm not sure I'd be able to perform. I mean, you've been waiting for it for ages, and suddenly – and I mean "suddenly" – bang! It's all over. What's Priti going to feel?'

'Satisfied, hopefully. Besides, you've obviously never been to an Indian wedding. By the time the evening comes, you're too tired to do anything, let alone have sex.'

'But don't you think you ought to, well, give it a go beforehand? Just in case?'

Ash stands there for a second or two, considering all the possibilities that 'just in case' might actually mean. 'Nah. We'll be okay. Besides, when? I don't think we're allowed to be on our own between now and the big day.'

I stare at Ash, amazed at his naive optimism. 'I could never marry someone I hadn't slept with. It's like buying a car you haven't test driven.'

Ash shrugs. 'Yeah, but as long as it's got an MOT, not too many former owners. No – bad example. Say you buy a . . .'

'House?' I suggest, remembering my conversation with Terry the other day.

'Exactly,' says Ash. 'A house. You don't get to spend the night there before you make your final decision, do you? And yet most people live in houses for years that they've bought without sleeping with first. I mean, in.'

'Yes, but that doesn't mean they're still not spooked by strange noises in the night. Or, find out afterwards that the rooms are too small. Or too big.'

'We are still talking about houses, right?'

'Of course.'

'Don't you think you're putting a little too much importance on the physical side?' says Ash. 'I mean, how long does sex actually last?'

I think about this for a moment or two. 'I dunno. You mean including the actual foreplay part, or just, you know, penetration? Because I'm thinking maybe fifteen minutes . . .'

Ash makes a face. 'Thanks for sharing. I meant in *years*. Do your parents still have sex, for example?'

I shudder. 'God, I hope not. As far as I'm concerned, they did it the once, I came along, then never again, and that's how I like to think of it.'

Ash smirks. 'All I'm saying is, there's lots of other aspects to marriage too. You're going to be spending a lot more time talking to her across the kitchen table than you are taking her over it. So think about your priorities.'

'You sound just like my dad. But I like sex. And dare I say, I like to think that I'm good at it. And it's something that I want to keep doing for a very long time. So I'd need to know.'

'Well, in that case,' continues Ash, obviously keen to move the conversation back on to me, 'what's wrong with someone who's prepared to sleep with you on the first date? I mean, it could just be because the chemistry's so strong that she fancies the pants off you – hard as that is to believe – and that you can't resist each other.'

I puff my cheeks out in thought. 'I don't know. I guess I'd just need them to show a little restraint. You know. A little decorum.'

'I'm getting the faintest whiff of double standards,' says Ash. 'On the one hand, you're saying that you need someone to be sexually compatible with, and on the other, you're saying that if you meet someone and sparks fly from the off, you're going to think bad of her if she wants to jump your bones the first time you see her.'

'Well, yes,' I say, realizing for the first time that perhaps it does sound a little absurd. 'Maybe. I don't know.'

Ash shakes his head. 'This, my friend, is your problem. You're too specific.'

'I'm not. I just want . . .'

Ash holds his hand up to silence me. 'Yes, you are. You've got such a preconceived idea of what this perfect woman should be like that you've managed to convince yourself that anyone who deviates even slightly from it isn't going to cut the mustard.'

'What does that mean – "cut the mustard"? I mean, surely mustard doesn't need cutting . . .'

'Stop changing the subject, Ben. This is something you need to sort out. And fast. Otherwise all of this work your mum and dad are putting in isn't going to amount to anything.'

'Sorry, Ash. Yes. You're right. I'll try and be a bit more open-minded.'

'Good. Now, what's this first one called?'

'Lisa,' I say, handing him the crib sheet my dad's prepared for me, with Lisa's photograph paperclipped to the back.

'Not bad,' says Ash, handing me back the Polaroid, then scanning quickly through her details. 'Although the "hobbies" thing might worry me a little.'

'Hobbies?' I can't help but laugh at my dad's quaint description. 'Who says "hobbies" any more? And why? What's she put?'

'Well, "tennis", which is a good thing, because you like tennis.'

'Thanks, Ash. That hadn't occurred to me.'

'And "shopping", which maybe isn't so good.'

'It could be worse. After all, for some of the women I've gone out with, shopping has been more of a profession than a hobby.'

'Yes, but it's the next item that's a little, well, strange.'

I take the page back from him, and scan through it until I find the appropriate section. '*Cats*. What's wrong with that?'

Ash clears his throat. 'A little strange to mention that as a hobby, don't you think?'

I fold the piece of paper in quarters and slip it into my shirt pocket. 'It's probably just the way my dad asked the question.'

'Suit yourself,' says Ash. 'But don't say I didn't warn you. And remember. Relax. Be natural. And don't forget, you're the one in charge here. She has to see that you mean business. You're committed. And ready to settle down.'

'Okay, Ash. I know what I'm doing. I have been out with women before, you know?'

'And look where that's got you,' he says, following me out through the front door.

Chapter 15

When I get to The Cottage, Lisa's already waiting, nursing a glass of white wine at a table in the corner. It's a pleasant surprise that she actually looks better than her picture, and I find myself hoping that she feels the same way about me.

'I see you've brought my résumé,' says Lisa, pointing to the piece of paper sticking out of my pocket, which unfortunately has the word 'Lisa' clearly visible on it.

'What – this?' I crumple it into a ball, and drop it into the ashtray.

'What does it say?' she asks, picking it up and smoothing it out on the table.

'Oh, nothing. Just some facts and figures my dad jotted down. Where you work, what you did at school, and, er, the fact that you like cats.'

'Oh yes. Doesn't everybody?' says Lisa, in a tone that dares me to disagree with her.

'Of course,' I say. In truth, I hate the things, but Lisa is rather attractive.

'Although Mike — that's my previous boyfriend — suddenly developed an allergy.'

'To you?'

'No, to cats.' She smiles. 'So I had to get rid of him.'

'Your cat?' I say, making a mental note to tell Ash his fears were unfounded.

'No,' says Lisa, as if I've just accused her of the most heinous crime imaginable. 'Mike.'

I'm pretty sure she's joking, but something about the look on her face makes me decide not to ask any further, so instead I ask her about her job, and then she asks me about what I do, and she listens intently, and as the evening progresses, we seem to be getting on really well. Lisa appears to be at the same stage in life that I am, and to be honest, by the time she asks me to walk her home, I've forgotten all about Ash's warning. Until, that is, we get back to her place.

It's the smell that gets me at first — mainly because the house is pitch black as we walk inside — and I'm about to ask Lisa whether there's a problem with her drains, when I stop myself, as it's hardly the most silver-tongued thing to say. But then, when I feel something brush past my ankle, it's all I can do not to scream out like a girl.

'What was that?'

'What was what?' says Lisa, leading me by the hand along the dark hallway and into the lounge.

'Something just brushed past my leg.'

Lisa laughs. 'Oh, they're just being friendly.'

I'm a little alarmed at her choice of the word 'they'. 'Who are?'

When Lisa flicks the light on, I get my answer, and my first instinct is to jump in the air and grab for the lampshade, because the room is full of cats. What looks like hundreds of them, in fact, on the sofa, lying on the carpet, walking along one of the bookshelves, and even climbing up the curtains. And though the actual number's probably nearer twenty, that's still nineteen more than most normal people should have.

'My cats,' she says, rather unnecessarily.

Oh my God. This isn't a hobby. It's an obsession. 'Do you, like, run a cattery, or something?' I say, wanting her to answer 'yes', and to say that these don't all belong to her. But instead, Lisa just laughs.

'No. I get them all through my work with SNIP.'

I almost don't want to ask. 'SNIP?'

'Yes. It's a charity I've set up. "Stop Neutering Innocent Pets". Isn't it awful how when some people get a pet, the first thing they do is have its bits cut off. I mean, how would you like it?'

'Er, not at all.'

'Poor babies.' Lisa smiles affectionately down at the mewing felines as if they're her children. 'I mean, it's treating them like . . .'

'Animals?'

'Exactly,' says Lisa, unaware of the irony.

'So what does SNIP actually do?' I ask, although I've got a fair idea of what the answer's going to be.

'Well, we give homes to cats who are about to be neutered. Don't we?' she says, addressing one of the flea-bitten creatures, then picking it up off the armchair and giving it a huge kiss on the lips. That is, if cats *have* lips. 'Like little Monty here.'

'Is that, you know, hygienic?'

'Oh yes. Don't worry. Cats can't normally catch anything from us humans.'

'No, I meant the other way . . . Never mind,' I say, trying to surreptitiously kick a couple of the more mobile ones who have decided to rub themselves against my shins. 'I thought that these charities normally gave them to other people's homes. Not their own.'

'We do,' says Lisa, putting Monty back down on the chair. 'But occasionally one comes into us that I just can't resist.'

'Oh.' More than occasionally, it seems to me. 'Right.'

Lisa nods towards the sofa. 'Do you want to sit down?'

My first answer should be 'Where?', given that each of the cushions seems to be already occupied by something furry. Plus, I'm wearing my best jeans, and don't want to spend the next few days trying to remove all the cat hairs. 'That's okay,' I say, looking at my watch. 'I'd better be going soon, anyway. I mean, it is our first date, and all that.' And quite possibly our last.

'Are you sure I can't tempt you to stay?'

'I'd better not,' I say, edging backwards slowly, as Lisa advances towards me. She's obviously after a kiss, but as attractive as she is, I can't quite bring myself to put my mouth where little Monty has just had his furry gob. The only escape route that appears to be feline-free is round behind the sofa, but as I start to head that way, I hear a crunch, then possibly the worst smell I've ever experienced starts to permeate in through my nostrils.

'Ben,' says Lisa, although a little too late. 'Not there . . .'

I look down in horror, to discover that I seem to be walking through the world's largest cat litter tray. And although that in itself might not have been a problem, because cats usually bury their, er, business, it is actually about twenty litter trays arranged into a rectangle to make one big one, and what I've done is step on the edge of a couple of them, thus catapulting the grit – and what was obviously underneath it – onto my jeans, and even into my shoes.

I start to panic, feeling like I've blundered into a mine-field, and can't quite work out where to step next. At least I won't have to worry about fending Lisa off, I suppose, imagining that the smell must be doing that already. But when I look up, she seems quite unperturbed by the whole thing.

'Here,' she says, shooing a couple of cats out of the way, before kneeling on the sofa, and reaching over to unbuckle my belt. 'Let's get you out of those trousers.'

For a moment, it doesn't occur to me that she might just be wanting to help me with my predicament, rather than trying to take the evening to the next level. 'No, that's okay,' I say, staggering backwards to get out of range of her hands, which somehow have already managed to unzip my fly, then stepping in another of the trays with a soggy crunch. By now, the stench is making me retch, and yet Lisa seems oblivious to it.

As I finally reach dry carpet, my jeans around my ankles, I hear a voice from the sofa. 'Is it just me,' says Lisa, my belt in her hands, and a strange look on her face, 'or is this a real turn-on?'

'Er . . .' Yes, it *is* just you, I want to shout. In fact, I doubt I could get a hard-on if Michelle Pfeiffer walked into the room wearing her Catwoman outfit. And that's an image that's never failed to work for me in the past.

'Come on,' she says, starting to undo her blouse.

'I can't. I . . .' What on earth do I say? It's obvious that Lisa's serious, and that she wants us to have sex right here – and in front of all these cats. And as attractive as she is, who knows what they'll do? I don't want to risk a sudden swipe of sharp-nailed claw just as I'm reaching the crucial moment, and besides, I smell bad. 'I stink.'

'You can't be that bad,' she says.

'No, not at sex. I mean . . . I just can't.'

I glance across towards the door, wondering whether I should make a run for it, but I'm too worried about leaving a trail of cat poo on Lisa's carpet. Assuming it is a carpet, and not just a large rug that she's spun from the hair of these animals.

'Why not?'

It's a fair question, I suppose. What excuse can a man *ever* make for not having sex? I mean, women can use anything – from the standard 'time of the month', to having a headache, but we men can always perform. Just not when we're covered in cat excrement. And then, out of the blue, it strikes me. 'I haven't got anything to, you know, put on,' I say, suddenly inspired by my encounter with Seema the other day, and the large unopened box of condoms on my bedside table.

'That's okay,' says Lisa matter-of-factly. 'I've got some upstairs. Shall I go and fetch them?'

I don't like to tell her that the only thing I want to wear in this house is a flea-collar. But at least it'll give me a way out. 'Er, okay.'

'Great,' says Lisa, jumping up off the sofa. 'Back in a sex.' She laughs. 'I mean, sec.'

As Lisa disappears upstairs, I hurriedly pull my trousers back up and make my escape, struggling to close the front door behind me without letting any of the furry little buggers escape. But it's not until I'm walking back home, trying hard to ignore the pungent odour that's coming from my shoes, that I remember I've forgotten my belt. For a moment, I consider going back and trying to find it, but chances are, it's somewhere under that huge pile of cats on the sofa, and the thought of fighting my way through them, let alone trying to fight Lisa off, is more than I can bear.

This is why I hate dating. And much as I'd like to blame my dad for his lack of 'research', I can't.

Because in reality, if it wasn't for me, I wouldn't be in this mess.

Chapter 16

It's the following evening, and following several long, hot showers and a trip to the shops for a new pair of trainers and a belt, I'm in the pub – again – sitting opposite a girl called Dawn. She's the daughter of Barbara and Martin, two of my mum's friends who own the pound shop next door to You've Been Framed, and while she's not exactly the kind of girl I'd look twice at in a club, she's actually quite pretty in a girl-next-door way. Although I suppose that description really depends on whether your neighbours are Mr and Mrs Moss and their daughter Kate. Or not.

But so far, it seems to be going fairly well. I haven't offended her or spilled my drink, and we even seem to have some things in common, like a preference for *Coronation Street* over *EastEnders*, and an addiction to cheese and onion crisps, which is good, because it means we can share a packet without worrying about crisp-breath if there's any kissing later. And one particularly positive piece of news is that she's only got the one cat – a fact I checked up on approximately thirty seconds after she sat down.

While she laughs at my – admittedly bad – jokes, she seems a little shy, which I realize is perhaps understandable given the nature of how we've met, and although she's dressed a little primly, her cardigan buttoned up firmly over her not inconsiderable chest – as the evening goes on, I can see how I might fancy her. The only problem is, the more I flirt, the less Dawn seems to be responding. Every time I say something with the mildest of double entendres, she stares nervously down at the table, and if I were a body language expert – which admittedly I'm not, given the amount of times I've misread signals in the past – if it wasn't for the fact that she's still here, I'd be worried that tonight was going rapidly downhill.

But maybe this is how it works. Okay, so the lust thing isn't there, but it might grow into something more serious. Besides, Dawn doesn't know me from Adam, and simply might not fancy me. And who knows what her relationship history is? Maybe she's been hurt in the past – and by someone like me – so she might be reluctant to show any signs of interest until she's sure. Or, at least sure that I'm interested in her.

By eleven o'clock, she's still nursing the same white wine I bought her at the start of the evening, although that could be because when I answered 'large' to the barman's question, he produced a glass the size of a small bucket and filled it with the best part of the bottle. I'm on my third pint, and desperate to go to the toilet, but given Dawn's apparent lack of enthusiasm, I'm worried that I can't get up to go in case she's not here when I get back.

Normally I'd think that a couple of drinks would loosen us both up, but by the looks of Dawn, an earthquake wouldn't even do the trick. But if what she's doing is playing hard to get, then it's working, because quite frankly I'd cut off my own arm if I thought it would provoke a response. Regretfully, I realize that sometimes it's much easier when you're in a club, and both out that evening for the same reason. Here? Well, I'm starting to wonder why she agreed to meet me, especially when – and just as I'm running out of things to talk about – Dawn looks at the clock on the wall and announces she has to leave.

'I'll walk you home,' I say, desperate to prolong the evening, hoping that she'll say yes, or at least give me some sign that maybe it's gone better than average.

Dawn picks up her wine glass and drains the rest of the contents – a pretty impressive feat seeing as there's still about a third of a bottle in there – then gives me the faintest of smiles. 'If you like.'

We walk up the High Street in near silence, and as we reach the corner of her road, I desperately try to think what I can do to get some sort of reaction. At this stage, and especially after her 'if you like', I don't know whether I'm expected to kiss her goodnight, or shake her by the hand, although given how reserved she's been physically, I'm not sure whether even that would be inappropriate.

'Well, this is me,' she says, nodding towards a small cottage at the end of the row of houses.

'Are you sure?' I say. 'Looks like a house to me.'

Dawn looks at me strangely, either not getting, or more likely, not finding funny my admittedly poor attempt at humour. And while I know that this should be a sign for me to say 'thank you' and 'goodnight', whether it's through sheer macho pride, or complete desperation, I'm sure that I want a second date out of her – if only to prove to myself that this one hasn't been a complete disaster. But just as I'm wondering whether I've got the nerve to ask to see her again, and am preparing myself for the inevitable rejection, she smiles – and it's almost her first proper smile of the evening.

'Do you want to come in?'

I stare open-mouthed at her for a moment, not quite believing that this has happened against the run of play. And do I want to come in for what? Normally someone adds the words 'for a coffee' to the end of that sentence, even though coffee might be the last thing on their mind. When I don't answer immediately, Dawn looks a little offended, and I have to think on my feet.

'Of course. I mean, that would be nice. For a coffee, or something.'

'A coffee.' She fishes in her handbag for her keys, an amused expression playing across her face. 'Or something. Sure.'

As she leads me up the garden path – which I'm hoping isn't a metaphor – I wonder whether perhaps it's the wine finally kicking in. To be honest, I'm wishing I hadn't had those three pints myself, as I'm desperate for the toilet, and as Dawn leads me into the lounge, I start to ask if I can use her bathroom, but before I can get the words out she jumps on me – literally – and the two of us crash down on the sofa in a heap. And while the sudden presence of her tongue down my throat and her hand inside my jeans isn't completely unwelcome, the weight of her pressing on my bladder is.

'Hold on,' I say, breaking away breathlessly. 'I really need to use your bathroom.'

Dawn looks up from where she's unbuttoning her cardigan to reveal the briefest of lacy black bras, which seems to be defying the laws of physics given what it's managing to keep contained. 'Up the stairs,' she pants. 'First door on the right. And don't be too long.'

I jump up from the sofa and make my way awkwardly up the stairs, although that's as much down to my hard-on as the three pints I've had, and make it into the bathroom with a sigh of relief. Who'd have thought that quiet, church-mouse Dawn would turn out to be like, well, *this*? It's a bit like jumping behind the wheel of a Ford Mondeo, and finding that it drives like a racing car.

Of course, the problem is, I'm so turned on by this unexpected turn of events that I can't get my hard-on to go down, which of course makes it impossible to pee –

except vertically upwards, that is – and I'm not sure the bathroom's big enough for me to stand far enough back from the toilet to make a suitable arc. Plus, Dawn's bathroom has carpet on the floor, and my aim's not that good. Especially after three pints.

As the pain in my bladder gets worse, I start to panic. I could go in the bath, I suppose, but then I'd have to run the tap, and that might seem a little suspicious. And there's no way I can have sex like this. If only I could think of something to calm things down. But what?

Suddenly, there's a scratching sound on the outside of the bathroom door. For a second, I think it might be Dawn, but unless she's on all fours in the hallway – or has unusually long toenails – it can't be.

I open it a crack, and a mangy-looking cat walks in, pads across the bath mat, then rubs itself against my leg. With a shudder, I get a sudden flashback to the events at Lisa's house last night, and I'm just about to shoo it out, when thankfully I start to feel the first subsidence in my groin.

After a couple of minutes, and with a sigh of pleasure, I relieve myself, and I've just flushed – and scratched the cat affectionately under its chin – when there's a knock on the door.

'Everything okay?' asks Dawn.

'Yes,' I reply, 'I'll be out in a moment or two.'

'I'll be waiting,' comes the reply. 'In the bedroom.'

I look down at the cat, noticing for the first time that

it's black, and as it stares back up at me, think that maybe, just maybe, this could be my lucky night.

Or maybe not, as sadly my previous assessment of 'fifteen minutes' when Ash asked me 'How long does sex last?' proves to be way out. In fact, it's 4 a.m. before I finally manage to extricate myself from the tangle of limbs and make my way downstairs, nearly tripping over the damn cat in the process. I've had to leave one of my shoes in Dawn's bedroom because I couldn't find it, and didn't want to turn the light on and risk waking her, and therefore initiating another session. Mind you, given how enthusiastically she ripped my clothes off me and threw them around the room, it's a miracle that I've managed to find so much of the rest of what I was wearing.

As I tiptoe along the hallway, I don't know whether to be happy or sad. Yes, I've had sex, but it's been so energetic, so frantic, so demanding, and so *painful*, that there's not a part of my body that doesn't hurt. And I mean not one part.

I'm a little hurt emotionally, too. Because towards the end of the third – or it could have been the fourth – time, by which point I was just grateful that I could still go through the motions, Dawn had called out 'Oh, Brian', and I'd been too polite – and knackered – to point out her mistake. When I'd made a joke of it afterwards she'd laughed, and explained that Brian was her boyfriend, and although I'd sat up suddenly, worried he might come round and catch us, she'd told me not to worry – he doesn't get out for another four months – before rolling over and starting to snore noisily before I could ask any more.

I feel guilty about leaving like this, of course, and think about writing Dawn a 'thank you' note, but don't want Brian to find it – and then come and find me – so just let myself quietly out of the front door. But as I walk home in my socks, carrying my other shoe in my hand to avoid an awkward limp, I find myself bemused by the evening's events. Ignoring the fact that she already seems to have a boyfriend, could I ever marry someone like that? To know that the sex was always going to be that . . . Intense. Physical. And – convict-boyfriend aside – dangerous? Probably not – I wouldn't make it to forty. Let's face it, if I want a ride that scary, I can always go the amusement park on the seafront. And who wants to go there every night?

As to how I'm going to explain it to my parents, I'm not so sure. I've already given them a report on my disastrous date with Lisa, which for some reason they seemed to think was my fault, so this time I need to come up with something that'll put the blame on Dawn. Unfortunately, I don't get a lot of time to think about it, given the first thing my dad says to me is 'How was she?' when the two of them call round at my studio on their way to Aldi the following morning.

'Er . . . Okay.'

'You got on, then?'

'Oh yes,' I say, stopping short of adding 'so did she. Several times.'

'Do I need to buy a hat?' says my mum, as we sip the tea that she's brought round in a Thermos flask.

Maybe I do, I think to myself, if I see Dawn again, but it would be a crash helmet. 'I don't think so.'

'Why ever not?' My mum sounds a little disappointed.

For a moment, I wonder what to say, and then realize that unless I start providing my parents with honest feedback, things aren't going to get any better. 'She was a bit, well, rough.'

'Rubbish,' says my mum. 'I've known her mum and dad for ages. And they're lovely people.'

'No, Mum.' I take a deep breath. 'Rough in bed. With me.'

As my mum doesn't quite know where to look, my dad folds his arms. 'Don't tell me you slept with her?' he says sternly. 'And on the first date?'

'I didn't have a choice, Dad,' I say, giving him an edited version of the previous evening's events. 'Besides, it would have been rude to say no.'

He picks his tea up, and blows on the top. 'Fair enough.'

'You're sure she wasn't just trying to impress you?' says my mum.

I shake my head. 'Impress? No. Asphyxiate, maybe.'

'So what am I going to say when I see her mum and dad again?' she says anxiously. 'I mean, they'll be at the tennis club this weekend.'

'I don't know. Just tell them it's me, or something. Or tell them I'm not into threesomes,' I say, explaining the other thing it would have been useful to know before yesterday evening.

My dad purses his lips. 'You know, I've always thought that family were a bit funny. Remember that Christmas drinks party of theirs we went to, and there was that big bowl on the dining table, and when I asked what it was for, Martin smiled and said that it was so we could all throw our car keys in it.'

'That's a good idea,' says my mum. 'Some people are always losing their keys.'

'That's not what he meant, Sue.' My dad sighs. 'I bet they're the kind of parents who walk around the house naked. It's no wonder she's turned out like that.'

'Turned out like what?' I say, feeling the need to leap to Dawn's defence. 'I mean, what she did was hardly illegal, was it? It's just a different way of doing things.'

'Doing it, don't you mean?' says my mum, still a little shocked. 'And can you imagine conceiving a child that way? The poor thing's bound to come out traumatized.'

My dad puts a consoling arm around my shoulders, which makes me wince as it's the exact spot where Dawn's scratched me. 'So, you're not seeing her again, then, son?'

'Oh, yes,' I say. 'Tonight, in fact. To discuss our engagement.'

My mother almost drops her tea. 'But . . .'

'Ha.' I get up and help myself to a custard cream from

the Tupperware container on the windowsill. 'You should have seen your faces.'

My dad grins. 'Well done, son. Very funny.'

'Yes, well. If you could do your research a little better next time?'

'We're sorry, Ben,' says my mum. 'We had no way of checking that kind of thing.'

'I'm sure you didn't,' I say, popping the rest of the biscuit into my mouth.

My dad clears his throat, then pulls his notebook out of his coat pocket. 'So, neither of them?' he says, crossing their names off his list.

'Nope. Sorry.'

My parents exchange glances. 'And you're sure it wasn't . . .' My dad clears his throat. 'You?'

'As sure as I can be.'

He sighs. 'Well, you better hope this evening goes a little better. She's our favourite, this one.'

'*Your* favourite, Alan,' says my mum.

'Well, it couldn't go much worse, Dad,' I say, in an attempt to reassure myself as much as them.

My dad smiles grimly back at me. 'There's such a thing as tempting fate, son.'

Chapter 17

Sarah's thirty, and although I've never dated an older woman before – even if it's only by a few months – I'm possibly a little more excited than I should be. She's one of Dad's colleagues at school – the science teacher, in fact – and so I've had to listen to the same joke from my dad time and time again about whether there'll be any chemistry between the two of us this evening.

Not surprisingly, given the previous two dates, I'm a little apprehensive, even though my dad actually knows Sarah, and, in fact, I'm wondering whether I do too, because the more I look at her photograph, which of course I've brought with me so I can recognize her, the more she seems familiar. But she's not unattractive, and according to my dad, when he suggested she and I go out for a date she was certainly 'up for it', to use his words. Whether she's 'up for it' in the sense I'd mean, we'll just have to wait and see, although of course, given my experience last night with Dawn, I'm not sure I am.

We've arranged to meet at The Cottage at seven o'clock, and I'm just about to leave my flat when my phone goes. It's my dad, ringing to check up on me. Again. He's calling from his mobile, and I'm having a little difficulty hearing him, as there's a strange echo in the background.

'Now, don't mess it up,' he says, sounding more nervous than me. 'I've got to work with her, remember.'

'Mess it up? How am I going to do that?'

'You know.' My dad sighs. 'Get drunk. Or bore her. Or try any funny business.'

I feel myself blushing, even though I'm on the phone. 'I won't, Dad.'

'What are you wearing?'

'Jeans and a shirt. Why?'

'Jeans?' I can hear the exasperation in my dad's voice. 'Have you never heard the term "dress to impress"?'

'Dad, it's not like that any more.'

'More's the pity. At least look like you're making an effort. Put a tie on or something.'

'Dad, ties . . .' I stop talking, realizing that this is one argument I won't win. 'Okay. And there's nothing wrong with her, right?'

'Of course not,' says my dad, a little offended. 'She's very nice. In fact, if I was twenty years younger . . .'

'. . . and not married to Mum.'

'Quite,' says my dad. 'You have a good time, now. And don't do anything I wouldn't do.'

'I won't,' I say, grimacing at the thought of what that might mean.

But in the end, my fears are unfounded, as Sarah and

I get on fine. After an initial embarrassed few minutes, when we both joke about what we're doing here, we find out that, actually, we've got rather a lot in common. And more than that, there's a strange sense of *déjà vu* about Sarah. A kind of comfort, like I've known her all my life. And by the end of the evening, I'm starting to think that even after a couple of false starts, maybe there's some merit in this approach, and that I might just owe my parents a big thank you. Which I'll give them during my speech on the big day, of course.

It's getting late, and I'm planning to offer to walk her home, so I excuse myself to go to the toilet to avoid a repetition of last night's bladder problem, and I'm standing at the urinal, when a familiar voice surprises me.

'How's it going, son?'

I wheel around in shock, nearly peeing on my shoes in the process, to see my dad – wearing one of my old baseball caps and a pair of dark glasses – peering over the top of one of the cubicles. 'Jesus, Dad, you scared me. What are you doing here? And what's with the outfit?'

He emerges from the cubicle, then checks his reflection in the mirror. 'I didn't want to be recognized, did I?' he says, walking over to the urinal next to me and unzipping his trousers. As he feels around in front of him to try to locate the wall, I realize that he can't see where he's aiming, and so move one urinal to my left.

'Take the sunglasses off. At least in here. You look like one of the Village People. Which is not a good thing in a gents' toilet for a number of reasons.'

'Sorry,' he says, removing his Ray-Bans. 'You're right. Sarah's hardly likely to follow you in here, is she?'

'I should hope not. And what are you doing here, again?'

My dad nods towards the urinal. 'I had to go. The old prostate's not what it used to be.'

'No. Here in the pub.'

He shrugs. 'We just thought we'd come along and see how you were doing.'

'We? Mum's here?' I zip myself up and peer around the toilets anxiously, but if Mum's the old man washing his hands at the sink, then it's a hell of a disguise.

'I've left her at the bar. So she can keep an eye on Sarah. See if she's interested or not.'

'How's she going to tell that?'

'Well, if she leaves while you're in here, for one thing.' My dad laughs. 'Plus, we've been making some notes. How much she yawns. Her body language. And your mum's out there checking to see if she falls asleep, or if she calls someone else to get them to rescue her. Plus . . .'

'Plus?'

'Well, we wanted to check up on you, too. See that you're doing everything right. Nothing that'll scare her off, or anything. After all, we don't want to go to all this trouble if you're not going to pull your weight.'

I open my mouth, then close it again, not sure exactly where to start. 'Dad, I . . . I don't need you checking up on me. I can have a normal evening with a woman without her thinking I'm a madman, you know?'

'Yes, but I thought you might benefit from some tips from your old man. I know a few things about the art of seduction, don't forget. I mean, when your mother and I first met . . .'

The old guy at the basin has finished washing his hands, and is quite obviously listening in to our conversation. 'Dad, just take Mum and go home, will you? But let me leave first. Sarah's already going to be thinking I've got a bladder problem.'

My dad shrugs, zips his trousers back up, and replaces his dark glasses. 'Suit yourself.'

I hurry out of the Gents and get back to the table, taking advantage of the fact that Sarah appears to be sending a text message to scan the room, and eventually spot my mother, wearing a badly fitting blonde wig, sat at the bar. And it's then that it hits me. The reason that something about Sarah feels so familiar is because she's a younger version of my mum. Everything about her, from her mannerisms to the way she smiles, even the tone of her voice. And it's especially noticeable given my mum's disguise.

So this is why my dad picked her. And of course, it makes sense. He's looking for someone for me who reminds him of Mum, because subconsciously or otherwise, that's who *he'd* choose. And while I can see where he's coming from, at the same time that's the *last* thing I want – although thinking about it, someone who reminds me of him might possibly be worse.

As I sit back down, Sarah puts her phone away, and looks at her watch. 'Well, thank you for a lovely evening,' she says. 'But I have to go. After all, it is a school night.'

'Yes. Of course. Especially with you being a teacher, and all that.'

As I realize I've made just about the dumbest observation possible, Sarah smiles. 'It's been fun.'

'Yes,' I say. 'Yes, it has.'

'So . . .'

Ah. What on earth can I say now – *Yes, it has been fun, and if I hadn't suddenly realized that you looked, acted, and even sounded just like my mother, then I'm sure I'd be asking you out again, and we'd possibly end up having a lot more fun, some of it even of the horizontal variety?* Because the way it stands at the moment, I don't think I'd ever be able to give her anything more than a peck on the cheek.

'So?'

'Walk me to my car?'

'Er . . . Sure.'

As we stroll along the pavement, it's a little chilly, and Sarah doesn't have a jacket, so I offer to lend her mine, which she accepts gratefully, but as we near her car, I start to get increasingly nervous. Of course, given that she's invited me to accompany her the twenty yards down the High Street to where she's parked, she's going to expect a kiss goodbye. And judging by the fact that she's walking slowly, occasionally brushing against me, she's going to want a proper kiss.

I try to look at her objectively. Apart from her face, her body's different, and so that's what I try to concentrate on, although of course thinking about my mum's body in comparison is even more of a passion dampener. But as Sarah stops by a silver Ford Focus and turns round to face me, it's obvious what she's expecting.

It's not like kissing your mother, I tell myself, as I lean in towards her. *I can do this. You're not my mum,* I repeat, under my breath. *You're not my mum.* 'You're not my mum.'

'Pardon?' says Sarah, taking a step back from me.

Bollocks. I've said it out loud. 'I said, um, "It was fun."'

'No, you didn't,' says Sarah angrily. 'You said "You're not my mum." What's that supposed to mean?'

'Nothing.'

'What are you? Some kind of pervert?'

As Sarah stares at me, then fumbles in her bag for her car keys, I realize that's probably a rhetorical question, and wonder whether I can still salvage the evening, but I'd be an idiot if I couldn't work out what the complete change in body language means.

'Well, I'll, er, call you.'

'Don't bother,' she says, jumping into her car, and slamming the door behind her. 'Weirdo.'

I watch Sarah as she screeches off down the road, still wearing my jacket, then stand there for a few moments, gazing at the empty space where her car's just been, before sighing loudly, and starting the walk back home.

As I reach the corner of my street, I'm startled by a voice behind me.

'How did it go, son?' says my dad, still wearing his dark glasses. 'Marks out of ten?'

'Yes, Ben. Any "spark"?' asks my mother. Fortunately she's removed her blonde wig, strands of which I can see protruding from her handbag, as if she's smuggling a small animal in there.

'Er . . .' What do I say? How do I tell my dad where he went wrong, without insulting my mum? 'No. Not really.'

My dad's face falls. 'Really? Why not?'

'She, I mean, I . . .' I stare at my shoes. 'Just not compatible, I guess.'

'Never mind,' says my mum, patting my cheek affectionately. 'And you haven't heard from either of the other two?'

'Nope,' I say, making for my front door, my mum and dad trailing up the path behind me. 'Although given the manner in which each of the dates ended, maybe that's not so surprising.'

My mum and dad follow me wordlessly into my flat, and then, as we get into the front room, my dad reaches into his jacket pocket and removes a piece of paper. 'Here.'

I stare at the folded sheet of A4, which looks suspiciously like another one of the CVs I had to choose from the other day. 'What's this?'

'Just read it, son,' he says, handing it to me.

I slump down on the sofa and scan through the details disinterestedly, then perk up a little, because at first glance, this one looks pretty good. Better, perhaps, than all of the other three. No apparent flaws, a good career, and under 'hobbies' she's listed 'the gym', which can't be bad. 'She looks . . .'

'Perfect?' suggests my dad.

'Well, yes. What's her name? And more importantly, when can I meet her?'

My mum smiles as she walks into the kitchen. 'You already have,' she says, filling the kettle up and switching it on.

'Huh?' I think quickly, wondering whether there's some long-lost distant cousin I used to frolic with in my paddling pool. But if there is, I've obviously forgotten her.

'It's *Amy*,' says my dad.

I drop the piece of paper as if it's radioactive. 'You haven't spoken to her, have you? About this, I mean.'

'Of course not,' says my dad. 'We just wanted to make a point.'

'Which was?'

My mum clears her throat. 'It's just that, well, your father and I, we think you might be being a little . . .'

'Fussy,' says my dad, picking up the biscuit tin from the coffee table and helping himself to a HobNob.

'What do you mean, fussy?'

My mum reaches across to take the biscuit from my dad, and puts it back into the tin. 'You want everything "just so". From day one. And if you don't like it, you think nothing of just moving on.'

'That's not true.'

'Yes, it is.' My dad nods towards the coffee table, where I've deposited my mobile phone. 'Look at that, for example,' he says, picking up the shiny iPhone. 'What was wrong with your old model?'

'Well, nothing. I just fancied—'

'A new one. Exactly.' My dad puts it back on the table. 'And sometimes that prevents you from sticking with something you've already got that's quite frankly good enough. Because you always think the next one will be better.'

I know what he's talking about. And it's not phones. 'Well, that's because it can be a little … scary. Not knowing if what you've got is actually what you want.'

My mum pats my arm sympathetically. 'Remember when you left college, Ben. And you decided to go inter-railing?'

Anything to avoid starting my accountancy training, I seem to remember. 'Er, what about it?'

'And you met that lad on the ferry, and ended up travelling round Europe with him, and having a great time. What was his name again?'

'Mike. So?'

'Well, think of marriage like that,' she says, heading back into the kitchen to make the tea.

'I should just pick up a stranger on a boat?'

'No.' My dad gives me his usual long-suffering smile.

'See it as a journey, where the two of you have just met, and you're embarking on a long voyage together. You don't know anything about each other, so it's exciting, and a challenge, but, ultimately, it's one of life's great experiences.'

I don't like to remind him that while Mike and I did have a great time for most of the trip, we ended up falling out when we got to Berlin, and one night he stole the last of my money and left me without anywhere to sleep. Which is the way most marriages go, according to Terry. 'Yes, but . . .'

'No buts, son. Eventually you've just got to bite the bullet. Make your choice. Pick someone you think you've got a decent chance of making a go of it with, and set off on your journey. Sure, you're going to have to make compromises on the way, maybe even change your itinerary. But remember, it's all about the journey. Not the destination.'

I hate it when my dad gets all philosophical, and it's at times like these that I want to tell him that it's not fair for him to lecture me. From what I can tell, he and mum were head-over-heels in love when they decided to get married, which must have made it a no-brainer. And while that's an inspiration for me, it's also a burden. Because it's made me realize that that's what I want too.

My dad smiles at me. 'Ben,' he continues, 'the most important thing in life is to be happy. And having a good woman at your side . . .' He nods towards the kitchen, where my mum's struggling to locate three clean mugs.

'Well, most men don't know it, or perhaps don't want to admit it, but it's the thing that makes you happiest in the world. Plus, if I didn't have your mum, I wouldn't have you. And I'd have hated to have missed out on either of those two things.'

For a moment, I can't make eye contact. We've never been the best family at talking about our emotions, and to hear my dad making such a heartfelt statement, well, I just don't know how to respond, so instead I get up and start pacing around the lounge.

'But that puts more pressure on me to make it suc- ceed. Because say Amy and I had got married, and it didn't work out? I couldn't leave her then, could I? Because of you two.'

My dad shakes his head. 'And that's precisely my point. All relationships go through tough times. Even your mum and me have had our share of disagreements.'

'No, we haven't, Alan,' calls my mum from the kitchen, trying to inject some humour into the situation.

'And if you're married, what you do is simple. You deal with them. Because what's the alternative? Live with a simmering resentment that means you end up hating the other person? And let's face it, most arguments are simply differences of opinion. Whereas if you're just going out with someone and the same thing happens, you see it as the worst thing in the world, and' – he points to my mobile phone – 'decide to move on.'

The worst thing about what he's saying is, it's all true. When I think back to all of my past relationships, the minute we've started to argue, I've kind of assumed that that was it – the relationship was on its way out, and it was only a matter of time before we'd split up, so of course, we always did. And when I remember the level of some of the arguments that had been the beginning of the end, I'm more than a little embarrassed: What DVD to rent. How to load the dishwasher properly. Even the merits of McDonald's versus Burger King. Because I always saw them as symptomatic of the bigger picture, when in actual fact, they were simply differences. And thinking about it, who wants to be with someone who's exactly the same as them? Suddenly, what my dad is saying starts to make sense. Because when you're 'coupled' together as man and wife, or even with a baby, you don't have the choice but to try to work through your problems, or find a solution. And any fool can see that that's a better situation to be in than just thinking 'next'.

'But none of them have been, well, right, in the first place. And I don't just mean the women you've been lining me up with. I mean them all. Including Amy.'

'Well, maybe it *is* you, then,' suggests my dad.

'What do you mean by that?'

'Maybe you pick the wrong kind of women. Not enough of a challenge. Too easy.'

I think I know which context he means 'easy' in, and it's probably not the same definition that I'd use. 'How do you mean?'

'Well, women want to be wooed.'

'They can be as rude as they like, as far as I'm concerned. Although maybe Dawn was a bit over the top . . .'

'No, "wooed", Ben. Romanced. Like I did with your mother. Rather than just a sure thing placed in front of you. And the fact that you can't be bothered, or don't care when you split up with them, proves that you didn't really want them in the first place, maybe because they just weren't enough of a challenge.'

'Dad, I . . .' I hold my hands up, trying to put off a story I've probably heard a hundred times before, but it's too late, as my dad's already in full swing.

'When I first met your mother, I mean, she didn't want to know. But then, gradually, I wore her down . . .'

'And I still find him wearing today,' interrupts my mum from the kitchen.

'But I worked at it, and in the end, when I finally got her, I appreciated her much more, than if she'd been . . .'

'Easy?'

'Exactly.'

I start to mentally count elephants, betting that he'll come out with his 'moped' story before ten seconds have passed. And sure enough, even though he must know I've heard it a thousand times before, by the time I've counted three of the long-nosed mammals, he's already launching into the old familiar tale.

'I mean, you remember when we bought you that moped for your sixteenth birthday?'

'And I'd had it for two weeks when you decided to

show off by pulling a wheelie on it in front of Mum, and ended up crashing into the back wall of the garage.'

As my mum walks back into the lounge carrying three mugs and a carton of milk, my dad reddens a little. 'Yes, but what did that teach you?'

'Never to let you ride it again, for a start, if I wanted to look after it.'

'But you didn't, did you? In fact, you hardly ever cleaned it, or had it serviced. It's a wonder it lasted for as long as it did.'

I know what he's talking about, of course. He's alluding to the fact that I might just be the same where relationships are concerned. Once I've actually got the 'bike', if the getting it hasn't required much of an effort, I might not take care of it. Which is why it lets me down. Or, more accurately, won't let me ride it any more.

'And yet, when you wanted your first car,' continues my dad, 'it was different, wasn't it? We could have bought you one, of course, but instead we decided to teach you the value of hard work. So you went and got that job at the local swimming baths, and worked every weekend, and saved, and saved, and eventually you got enough money to buy one. And you loved that car. Every weekend, you'd be out there, polishing the bodywork, checking the oil with your dipstick . . .'

'Okay, Dad. I get the point,' I say, trying to ignore the imagery.

'Do you?'

'Yes. You're saying that I don't put the work into my relationships. So it's no wonder they go wrong.'

'Not only that. I'm saying that perhaps you're also choosing the wrong kind of cars. And then, when they go wrong, you can't be bothered to fix them, and so you just get any old one to replace it, instead of going for the model you really want. Like I did with your mother.'

'Really?' That comes from my mum, not me.

'Of course,' he says, pinching her affectionately on the backside as she leans over him to put the teapot on the table, before heading off to use the bathroom. He waits until she's shut the door, then lowers his voice. 'I mean, when I first saw her, I fell hook, line, and sinker. At least, I assumed that's what it was. But after a while, you realize that what you thought was love is actually lust. And while the symptoms may be the same, the cause is something totally different.'

'Are you going somewhere with this?'

He nods. 'My point is this. I'd been out with lots of girls before your mother. Hundreds, even. I don't mind telling you, when I was your age, people used to call me . . .'

'Dad, please.'

'Yes, sorry,' he says, snapping out of his reverie. 'The point is, these other women, they were fun, and all that. But when I met your mother, I knew she was different.'

'No fun, you mean?'

He ignores me. 'And I think maybe that's the problem

you've been having. None of the girls you've met has been like your mum.'

Apart from Sarah this evening, I feel like saying. 'How do you mean?'

'I mean that somehow, you've just known they weren't right.'

I think about what he's said for a second or two. 'Subconsciously, you mean? So while we may have connected on a physical level, the emotional side of things just wasn't right?'

'Stop complicating it with all this New Age rubbish.' My dad thumps himself on the chest. 'Here, I mean. In your heart. I mean, I still get butterflies every time I see your mum across a crowded room.'

'Only because you're worried she'll see what you're up to.'

'And that's why you've not worked hard to keep them,' he continues. 'Because as far as you've been concerned, they haven't been keepers.'

I frown. 'But why? I mean, what's been wrong with them?'

'God knows. Maybe nothing. Maybe it is you. Or maybe you're just not at that point yet.'

'What're you two talking about?' says my mum, walking back into the room.

'Cars,' says my dad quickly.

My mother looks at me reproachfully as she pours the tea. 'Ben,' she scolds. 'You're not thinking of changing yours again, I hope?'

'Well, Dad and I were just talking it over.'

She walks over to where my dad's sitting, resting an affectionate hand on his shoulder as she hands him his mug. 'Why can't you be more like your father? He's been happy with the same one for years?'

And as I watch my dad sip his tea contentedly, I can't help but ask myself exactly the same question.

Chapter 18

I don't hear much from my parents for the rest of the week, which is actually a good thing, because to be honest, even though I don't seem to be any closer to finding a bride, let alone a date for Ash's forthcoming engagement party, I could do with a rest after what's been an eventful few days. Plus, the cost of replacing the various items of clothing I seem to be losing is starting to add up.

I don't see anything of Ash either, although that's because he's gone up to Scotland to visit Priti for a few days, which is even better, because it gives me a chance to get on with some work, rather than wasting my time chasing more of his duff leads.

By Saturday lunchtime, I'm feeling somewhat recovered, and I'm walking along the High Street when I spot Hope – the girl I went out with before Amy – heading towards me. Hope is probably the most inappropriately named person I know, because she always struck me as the world's most pessimistic, glass-half-empty, it'll-all-end-in-tears person. Though to give her some credit, when it came to our relationship, she was spot on.

I glance left and right quickly, but it's too late to hide, and unless I want to dart into Boots and risk bumping into Seema again, I'm going to have to brazen it out. Besides, by the look of Hope's suddenly stern expression, she's already seen me.

'Ben,' she says curtly, as we draw near each other.

'Hope. Hi.' I think about leaning in and kissing her on the cheek, but I'm never quite sure about ex-girlfriend etiquette. She dumped me, after all, so am I even allowed to make the smallest of physical gestures towards her? And this always strikes me as ridiculous. Here's someone who used to let me, well, I won't go into detail, and then suddenly, after a word from them, *everything's* off limits, as if splitting up with them puts you in a worse situation from where you started. And, *because* she dumped me, I can tell that Hope is worried about even letting me kiss her on the cheek, as if I might take that as some sort of encouragement that she wants me back. Mind you, when I started going out with Amy, Hope used to cross the street to avoid me, so I suppose the simple fact that she's remained on the same bit of pavement must mean that the ice is melting a little bit. 'How have you been?'

'Oh, you know.' Hope is one of those people you should not ask that question, because she usually tells you, and in great detail. But fortunately not today. 'Getting by.'

'Good. That's nice to hear. Well, lovely to see you.' I start to walk off, but she blocks my path.

'Not so fast, Ben. I had an interesting conversation with your dad the other day.'

'What?'

'Your dad,' says Hope. 'He phoned me.'

For a second, this doesn't compute. 'My dad? Phoned you? How?'

'By picking up his telephone and dialling my number, I imagine.'

'No, not how . . . I mean, where did he get your number?' And yet, as soon as I say this, I realize exactly how. And why my dad asked to borrow my mobile phone the other day, under the pretext of wanting to get a new one himself.

She sighs. 'I don't know, Ben. But he was asking some rather strange questions.'

'Really?' I feel my face start to drain of colour. 'What, er, kind of questions?'

'Just about you and me, really. Why I dumped you. In the end, he seemed quite surprised why you wouldn't want to make more of an effort, seeing as . . .'

'I'm sorry. My dad phoned you to ask you why you dumped me?'

Hope nods. 'Yes. It was quite funny really. We were chatting about our relationship for ages.'

'Ages? And, er, what did you tell him?' Hope and I had a rather active sex life, a lot of which revolved around her preference for bondage – which wasn't something I really shared.

She rolls her eyes. 'Don't worry. Just about the way

you behaved when we were going out. That kind of
stuff. Nothing too personal.'

'Nothing too personal? How can any of that kind of
stuff not be too personal?'

Hope puts a hand on my arm, then removes it quickly,
as if she's suddenly worried that I might be overcome
with passion as a result. 'He seemed very concerned
about you, Ben. We all are.'

'What? Why? And who are "we all"?'

'Oh yes. He's spoken to Melissa too, apparently. And
Louisa. And Holly.'

As Hope reels off a list of my most recent ex-
girlfriends as if they're members of some kind of club, I
curse under my breath. I *knew* I should have deleted
their numbers from my phone. 'But . . .'

'And like I said, we had a good old chat. And I think
the conclusion we came to − all of us, that is − was that
you're too much of a commitment-phobe to ever get
married.'

'What? Me? Rubbish.'

Hope looks at me. 'You are. You just won't admit
it. The minute anyone asks you to get serious, you blow
more hot and cold than a broken hairdryer. And let's
face it, that was pretty much the reason you and I split
up.'

'No it wasn't.'

'Yes it was,' she says, accusingly. 'You said so yourself.'

I'm about to open my mouth and let her have it with
both barrels. Tell her that no, the actual reason we split

up was because she was a borderline manic depress-
ive, and that I was worried about telling her that and
making her even more depressed, and in fact I'd only
accidentally started the 'Where is this relationship going?'
conversation by telling her I felt uneasy about being
tied down. I'd meant in bed, whereas she'd thought I'd
meant to her, and to be honest, when I realized she was
prepared to dump me over it, it seemed like a pretty good
get-out opportunity.

'Hope, that's . . .' I sigh, then decide to lie. After all,
I want to spare her feelings, plus I'm conscious how
much rope she's got at home. 'You're right. I'm sorry. It
wasn't you, it was me.'

Hope smiles – a rare occurrence. 'That's exactly what
your dad said,' she says, almost skipping off down the
High Street.

Twenty minutes later, I'm confronting him across the
kitchen table.

'How could you?'

'I just thought it might be helpful,' he says sheepishly.

'How could trawling through a list of my embittered
exes possibly be helpful? They're hardly going to be
objective, are they?'

'Okay,' says my dad, folding his arms. 'Look at it
another way. What was it about these girls that stopped
you proposing to them?'

'What, apart from the fact that they all dumped me
before I could?'

He exhales loudly. 'Yes, Ben. Apart from that. And

remember, they might have simply have dumped you because you didn't get around to proposing to them.'

'Huh?'

'Well, they weren't getting any younger, were they? And what with you dithering . . .'

For a moment, I can't quite believe what I'm hearing. 'So, you're saying that because I didn't propose to them, they went and did the completely opposite thing and dumped me? That's a bit extreme, isn't it? I mean, talk about cutting off your nose to spite your face. And why on earth didn't they just propose to me instead?'

My dad looks at me as if I've just asked the most obvious of questions. 'Because it doesn't work like that, does it? Women proposing is like the Olympics.'

'What – if it happens to you, you deserve a medal?'

'No. I mean women are only allowed to propose once every four years. In a leap year, or something. It's the law.'

'Yes, well, that's not very fair, is it?' I say, not sure that it's a legal thing. 'I mean, what happened to equal opportunities? Burning your bra, and all that?'

He grins. 'Your mother burned her bra once. Not on purpose, mind. We were having this candlelit dinner, and things got a bit out of hand, and . . .'

'Dad, please!'

'Sorry, son. All I'm wondering, is why you never got down on one knee. That's all.'

I shrug. 'But that's the other thing. Why do we have to go down on one knee when we do it? Because it's the "begging" position. And that can't be right, surely?'

My dad raises both eyebrows. 'Why not? After all, it's the biggest question we can ever ask of someone. Because what we're saying to that person is "This is me. And can you consider spending the rest of your life with someone like me . . ." Well, not someone like me. I mean actually me. Or you, if you see what I . . .'

'I get the point, Dad.'

'Anyway in those few seconds, we're laying ourselves bare, asking if they think we're worthy. And that's tough to do.'

'But isn't it a bit unfair? Asking someone all that – putting them on the spot like that? Out of the blue.'

'Aha,' says my dad. 'But that's just it. You're not putting them on the spot at all. Because every single woman, pretty much from the moment you met them, has already had that discussion with herself about you. And she knows exactly what her answer will be.'

'What? Why?'

'Because while we men initially look at women just to have some fun, and then eventually decide whether we want to get married to them or not, women look at us as whether we're worthy of marrying from day one. And in most cases won't have anything to do with us in the first place unless we are.'

'Well, at least that's a good sign, then, surely? I mean, if I can get women to go out with me, and stay going out with me, then that must mean they think I've got potential. And if I've got potential, then I can work on that. Now if I could only work out what it is that's wrong with me . . .'

'That's the thing,' interrupts my dad. 'There's probably nothing wrong with you. But in your mind, there's obviously been something wrong with them, which is why you've never found yourself interested enough to actually make it more permanent. And I don't mean that there's actually something wrong with them – like a club foot, or something – although that Louisa girl did have a rather strange . . .'

'Dad!'

'But just that they're not right, for you. Or so you thought.'

I stare at him helplessly. 'But how do you know? When they are, I mean?'

My dad shrugs. 'You just do, son.'

'But I can't accept that out of all the women I've gone out with, none of them has been right. Why haven't I been able to choose one?'

He smiles at me. 'It's the same as when you were five.'

'When I was five? What has that got to do with it?'

'We used to give you your pocket money, then take you down to the sweetshop on the corner. You'd stand there for ages, trying to make a choice between the CurlyWurlys and the Sherbet Fountains. Sometimes we had to threaten to take you home empty-handed before you'd actually decide what to buy.'

'Yes, well, that's because there was so much to choose

from. And you've got to choose correctly, haven't you? After all, you can't have everything.'

He laughs. 'You'd have bought the whole shop if you'd had enough money. Well, all except for those little pink shrimp-shaped ones. You never liked those. I remember, your gran bought you a bag of them once and you cried your little eyes out.'

'Dad, as fun as this trip down memory lane is, is there actually a point to your story?'

My dad sighs. 'You're still that kid in the sweetshop, which is why you're still having the same trouble. And you know what? Sometimes, you've just got to make a choice. Because there's going to be a time when you go back to that shop, and it's going to be closed. Or running out of stock. And the last thing you want to be left with is a jar of pink shrimps.'

'Yes, well, it was important. To get the right ones, I mean.'

He folds his arms. 'The irony was, you'd go back the next week – every week, in fact – and you'd still be none the wiser, and that's when it was just for sweets; something that was only supposed to last you a few days. This?' He looks at me earnestly. 'This is for life, son. And you're too worried that you'll get it wrong. Which is why it's even harder for you to choose.'

'But that's my problem. Because there's even more choice nowadays – in everything.' I stare up at the ceiling, wondering how I can get my dad to understand how difficult it is for my generation, and how the modern world is more of a sweetshop than ever, wanting him to understand that I haven't been 'fussy', then have an idea.

'Come on,' I say, picking up my car keys. 'I'll show you what I mean.'

Chapter 19

So this is what I'm reduced to on a Saturday afternoon. Taking my dad clothes shopping. I only hope no one I know sees us, but then I suppose I could pretend I'm doing one of those 'care in the community' charity programmes – as long as he doesn't open his mouth. But then again, given the amount of rubbish he's been spouting over the last few weeks, maybe it's better if he does.

'So, where are we going?' he asks, as I point the car towards Westwood Cross, the shopping centre just outside town.

'Westwood.'

'Cross?'

'No. Just a lot on my mind.'

It's my father's favourite joke, so I indulge him. The fact that he still giggles at it given the number of times he's heard it actually makes me laugh too.

'It's quite exciting, isn't it?' he says, sticking his head out of the car window like a dog being driven to the park.

'What?'

'You and me. Going shopping together. For a pair of jeans.'

'Dad, if we were mother and daughter and I was ten years old, then maybe. In reality, it's quite sad. We should be going to the football instead, not bonding over men's fashion.'

'Rubbish,' he says. 'It's a significant moment, this. The handing over of the baton, from father to son. Suddenly, the tables are turned. You're giving me advice.' He swallows hard, then turns and stares out through the windscreen. 'It's quite touching, really.'

'Oh, please.' I roll my eyes, then flip the indicator to take us into the car park, deciding not to tell him that what he regards as a significant father–son event, I see as a few steps away from me choosing his retirement home.

'So, which shop?' he asks, as I pull into the first available space.

'For jeans? Depends whether you want to look your age or not.'

'M&S?'

I point at the shop in front of where we're parked. 'I was thinking more along the lines of H&M.'

My dad peers at the garish window display. 'Won't that be a bit . . . young? For me, I mean?'

'Well, seeing as there's no middle ground . . .'

He nudges me. 'Pity there's not a shop called S&M, eh?'

I look at him as we get out of the car, wondering if he knows what he's just said. 'Quite.'

As we walk into the shop, my dad winces at the music. 'A little loud, isn't it?'

'Just turn your hearing aid down. You'll be okay.'

He looks at me for a second. 'Point taken,' he says, before starting to jig a little to the beat, so much so that a couple of shop assistants stop what they're doing and point at him.

'Dad, please. We're not out clubbing now, so try not to embarrass me,' I say, having to stop myself from adding the word 'again'.

'Sorry, son,' he says, before doing exactly that by marching straight into the *women's* section.

I wave him back over. 'This side, please.'

'Sorry,' he says, adopting a serious face, then picking up a chequered trilby hat, and walking towards one of the mirrors.

I grab it from him before he can try it on, then lead him over to the jeans section, and stand him in front of the display. 'Any that take your fancy?' I say, nodding towards the table.

He stares at the various piles of different styles as if wondering where to start, then walks slowly around the display, selecting various pairs, then holding them up to the light, and even on a few occasions, fingering the material. 'What about these?' he says, handing me the pair he's chosen.

I take them from him, and examine the label. 'No good. Boot cut,' I say, putting them back on the pile.

'What's wrong with that?'

'Do you have any boots?'

'Well, wellies, obviously.'

I glance at my watch, realizing that this might take some time, but then again I've got nowhere else to be. 'Try again. Remember, these are supposed to be a fashion statement, not something to replace your gardening pair.'

'Okay. A statement.' My dad frowns, then circles the table again, obviously bewildered by the number of styles on offer. Several times, he reaches out a hand as if to pick up a particular pair, then recoils, as if they're hot.

I tap the face of my watch. 'Get a move on, will you?'

My dad looks up desperately. 'It's difficult. There's too much choice. I can't make a decision.'

'And why is that?'

He shrugs. 'I don't know. I just can't tell what will suit me.'

'Aha.'

For the first time, I think he understands my problem. Because there *is* too much choice. Back in his day, you pretty much married the first girl that let you put your hand up her jumper, but nowadays most people lose their virginity before they lose their milk teeth, and by the time you leave college, you've probably had more partners than your parents have had in their entire lifetime – unless your dad's Mick Jagger, of course.

'Well, maybe I should try some on for size.'

'Which ones?'

My dad looks at me helplessly. 'You choose.'

'Here,' I say, walking round the table, and pointing to a pair with 'Original' written on them. 'What's your size?'

My dad pats his stomach. 'Thirty-four,' he says, sounding a little wheezy from the effort of holding it in.

'Really?'

'Yes, really.'

'Here you go,' I say, handing him the appropriate pair, then pointing him towards the changing rooms at the far end of the shop. 'Go and try them on.'

I watch him go, then turn round and flick absent-mindedly through some shirts on the rail behind me, but a few moments later, feel a tap on my shoulder. Not surprisingly, it's my dad.

'What's the matter? Didn't they fit?'

'No. It's the changing rooms.'

'What's wrong with them?'

'They're, you know, *mixed*.'

'So?'

'Someone might see me. You know, one of my pupils.'

'You get your own cubicle once you're in there, Dad. It's not like at school.'

'Oh. Good,' he says, heading back towards the changing rooms. But two minutes later, he's back, looking slightly red-faced.

'What's the matter now? Weren't they any good?'

He looks suspiciously at the pair of jeans he's carrying. 'No. They seem to be faulty.'

I take the jeans from him and examine them. They look all right to me. 'What's wrong with them?'

'Well, the label says thirty-four, but they feel much smaller than that.'

I just about manage to stop myself from grinning. 'Maybe you'd better try another pair, then,' I say, rifling through the pile and pulling out some others.

'And maybe a pair of thirty-sixes,' says my dad sheepishly. 'Just in case.'

I hand him the bigger pair as well, then stroll round the store as I wait for him to try them on, although I've hardly had time to look at anything before he's striding along the aisle towards me. 'How do they look?' he says, in a voice a little too loud for my liking.

I have to admit, they're not bad. 'Fine.'

'They don't make my bum look big?'

'That question would assume that I'm going to look at your bum. Which of course I'm not.'

'That's not very fair, is it, son?' he says, admiring his reflection in the mirror. 'Considering that I had to wipe yours when you were growing up.'

'Thanks, Dad. That makes me feel much better. Anyway, they'll do. You can take them off now.'

'Great. Will do,' he says.

'In the changing rooms, Dad.'

Five minutes later, he's back, carrying his intended purchase proudly. 'Ta-da,' he says, holding them up against his legs, and doing a little dance.

'Let's just pay for them and get out of here, shall we?'

'Good idea,' he says, still wincing a little at the music. 'How much are they?'

I peer at the label. 'Nineteen ninety-nine.'

'For a pair of jeans?' My dad does a double take. 'You're joking.'

'Too expensive?'

'Too cheap.' He looks suspiciously around the store. 'Are you sure they're any good?'

'But that's the thing I've been trying to tell you, Dad. They're not *meant* to last.'

He stares at the jeans he's holding, then looks down at his existing pair – the ones he's had for the last ten years – and I can see that he's finally beginning to understand.

Chapter 20

It's Sunday afternoon, and I've just been back into H&M to return my dad's jeans on my mother's instructions – while they didn't make his bum look big, apparently hers now does by comparison – when I remember that I need to get some deodorant. I'm a strong believer in the Lynx effect, or more specifically the effect of not wearing any, and so without a second thought I head into Boots, find my favourite variety, Africa – although if this is what Africa actually smells like I'd be very surprised – and queue up to pay. And I've just reached the till when a familiar voice startles me.

'That was quick.'

I look up from where I've been checking the year on a particularly shiny pound coin to see Seema smiling at me. Oh *no*. 'I'm sorry?'

'And impressive, if I may say so? Especially with – what was it – a groin strain. How is that now?'

'Er . . .' In truth, while I didn't have one before, I am limping a little after my night with Dawn. 'Fine. Thank you.'

'Even so, getting through a packet of that size so quickly,' continues Seema, her eyes wide in mock admiration. 'I had no idea.'

'Oh, you mean the condoms? No, I, um, haven't started them yet. I need to buy this.' I hold the deodorant out towards her, then stop talking, wondering what on earth I'm doing debating my level of condom use, then feel even more embarrassed, because now I've just implied that without the deodorant, I've been too smelly to sleep with anyone.

Seema smiles at me again. 'Well, at least you're intending to practise safe sex, I suppose.'

'Of course,' I say, trying hard to regain my composure. 'Always do.'

'Pleased to hear it.' She takes the deodorant from me, and scans it through the till. 'That's one pound eighty-nine, please. And you're sure you don't want to get another . . .'

'No,' I say, a little snappily. 'Thank you. I told you, I haven't even opened the box yet.'

'I meant that these were on three-for-two,' she says, holding the deodorant up. 'No need to bite my head off.'

'Sorry,' I say, suddenly feeling guilty. 'I was just a little embarrassed. And you surprised me. What are you doing here?'

Seema glances down at her uniform, and taps the Boots badge on her lapel. 'I work here, remember? Or did you think I'd just put on a white coat last time so I could steal your money?'

'No, I mean in this branch. I thought you worked in the one on the High Street.'

'I do, normally. But I'm locum today.'

'Ah.' I nod, but I've got no idea what 'locum' actually means, so I have to ask. 'Is that, er, Indian for something?'

Seema laughs. 'There's no "Indian" for anything. It could be . . .'

'. . . Gujarati. I know. Or Urdu, or Hindi.'

'Not bad,' says Seema. 'I'd say you're not as stupid as you look, but then again, you possibly don't know what "locum" means. Unless you were being funny?'

'That's right,' I say, leaving Seema to work out which of her two observations I'm talking about. 'You just threw me a little. I mean, you're very pretty, and . . .' I can't stop myself from blushing. Do people still call each other pretty nowadays, or is it one of these feminist taboos that seem to have been designed to catch us men out, like automatically buying a woman a half-pint, when most of the girls I've met can down a whole one quicker than me?

'You're not so bad yourself. And loving the cool hairstyle,' says Seema, looking a little self-conscious herself, before narrowing her eyes and peering up at me. 'Have we met before?'

'What, apart from the other day, when I was buying the . . . I don't know,' I say. And then, because I can't help myself, I blurt out, 'I'm Ash's mate. Ben. I mean, Ash is my agent. And friend.'

'Ash?' Seema frowns at me. 'My brother Ash?'

'Yes.'

This admission is obviously a mistake, because Seema's smile suddenly disappears. 'How do you know who I am? Are you here to check up on me?'

'No. Of course not. I just . . .' I stop talking again, because while I did just come in here to buy some deodorant, there is a big part of me that wanted to run into her again. 'He mentioned he had a sister who worked in Boots, that's all. And I noticed the, you know . . .' I point towards her name badge, then realize that it doesn't actually have 'Patel' written on it, which leaves me pointing at her chest instead. 'Family resemblance,' I say, weakly, although thinking about it, Ash's man-boobs are almost the same size as Seema's, er, women's ones.

'Oh,' says Seema, her voice softening. 'Sorry. I just get a bit paranoid sometimes.' She narrows her eyes at me again, as if remembering something. 'You're the artist, aren't you? The one who gave up being an accountant to pursue his dream.'

'Er, yes,' I say, not sure if she's being sarcastic, or disdainful. 'How do you know that?'

'I remember Ash telling me about you. You're his favourite client.'

'Ash's only . . .' I'm about to add the word 'client', but I don't want to jeopardize the positive light I suddenly seem to find myself in, or be disparaging about Ash. '. . . being kind.'

'Not at all,' says Seema. 'And good for you. It takes a lot of guts to do things differently.'

'Oh. Right. Thanks,' I say, wondering if Seema recognizes a kindred spirit. But when she doesn't say anything further, I don't know what to do next, so just hold my hand out towards her. To my surprise, she takes hold of it and shakes it firmly. 'Nice to meet you, Ben.'

'And you. But I was actually trying to give you my money,' I say, nodding towards the deodorant on the counter.

'Oh.' Seema laughs, and takes the two pound coins I'm holding. '*Déjà vu.*'

I point to the deodorant. 'Really? I thought it was called "Africa".'

It's a lame attempt at a joke, but it's obviously so lame that it doesn't even manage to limp into Seema's view. I stand there a little awkwardly as she rings the transaction through the till, then hands me my change, along with the deodorant, which she's slipped into a child's-size carrier bag.

'Listen,' says Seema. 'Do you still have them? The condoms, I mean.'

'Er, yes,' I say, not quite sure what she's getting at.

'You don't have them with you, I suppose?'

I want to ask her whether I'm the kind of guy who looks like he carries a jumbo box of condoms around with him, but then again, I don't want her answer to be 'yes'. Or 'no', for that matter.

'No. Why?'

'Just that I'll give you a refund, if you like. Seeing as I sort of bullied you into buying them. We don't usually take those kind of items back, although to be honest, we don't normally need to.'

'Oh. Right. Of course. A refund.'

Seema raises one eyebrow. 'What did you think I meant?'

'Well, *that*, obviously.'

She glances behind me, where an old lady is struggling with a family-size packet of toilet rolls that looks like it might last longer than she will. 'So, if you want to bring them in some time . . .'

Not for the first time where Seema's concerned, I don't know how to respond. While 'bring that box of condoms in for a refund' isn't the greatest hint that she might want to see me again, I've had worse come-ons in my time. And managed to get relationships lasting months out of them too.

Then again, maybe I'm kidding myself. Let's face it, the offer of a refund on some condoms might mean exactly that. In fact, it may actually be that she feels so sorry for me that she doesn't think I'm ever going to get through a packet of condoms that size – and that's hardly a good position to ask someone out from. And to top it all, I remember one crucial thing that Ash said – about Seema not wanting to get married again – and realize that that's the biggest problem of all. Because I do. And if Seema really doesn't, then of course I shouldn't even think about asking her out. I suppose if she did say yes, then in time I could try to convince her that getting married to me would be different, but by the sounds of it, that's a pretty big obstacle to overcome. I mean, if someone's actually stated that they're against something, it's a little stupid to try to turn them around.

As the old lady behind me finally manages to wrestle the packet of Andrex up onto the counter, I snap back to reality.

'That's okay,' I say, reluctantly. 'I might hang on to them. Just in case.'

Seema smiles warmly at me, and it's a smile that makes me feel a little light-headed. 'Suit yourself. Although if you change your mind, you know where I'm at.'

But as I walk outside and get into my car, I'm not sure I can say the same about myself.

Chapter 21

It's the following morning, and the newly back Ash and I are discussing progress over a coffee in Mr Bean.

'*None* of them?'

'Don't you start.' I stir my coffee miserably. 'And I think my parents are starting to run out of friends' daughters. Or eligible ones, at least.'

'Why don't you go, you know, older.'

I look across the table at him. 'Older? Older how?'

Ash hesitates. 'Just . . . Older. They're bound to be a little more . . .'

'Desperate?'

'Ready to settle down, I was going to say. But now you mention it.'

'Thanks very much. Besides, they should be ready to settle down at *my* age.'

He shrugs. 'Ah, but older women are the new thing, aren't they?'

'Are they?'

'Yeah. You want to find yourself a MILF. A cougar.'

He rips open a sachet of sweetener and pours the contents into his mug. 'A sugar mummy.'

'What?'

Ash picks his coffee up and takes a sip, grimacing at the taste, before adding a sachet of sugar. 'Seriously, I was reading about it the other day.'

I don't like to ask him where. 'Yes, but I don't want someone past it. What if we want to have kids?'

'She might have them already.'

'But they won't be mine and hers. And what if she dies before me?'

'I'm not talking about marrying your gran, am I? Think about it. Women on average live around five or six years longer than men, so find yourself one five or six years older than you are and you'll both pop off together. Bingo.'

'Is that where you're suggesting I'll meet her?'

'Very funny.'

'But she might be, you know, wrinkly.'

'In her mid-thirties?' Ash shakes his head. 'Doubtful. Besides, there's even loads of fit women over forty. Just look at that lot from *Desperate Housewives* – they don't look that desperate, do they? And the sex . . .' Ash licks his lips. 'They know what they're doing, by that age. And anyhow, they can have it all done nowadays, can't they?'

'Have what done?'

'Everything. Lifted, smoothed out. Even tightened, apparently. You know. Their *lady bits*.'

'And how would you know this, exactly? Anyway, I'm worried they'll be a little, well, bitter.'

'What? Down there?' Ash points to his groin, then catches sight of my expression. 'Oh, that wasn't what you meant, was it?'

'*No*, Ash. Plus let's face it, anyone mid-thirties who hasn't settled down, well, there's going to be something wrong with them, isn't there?'

Ash takes a mouthful of coffee, then shakes his head. 'Not necessarily. Say you stay single for the next five years. Will there be something wrong with you?'

'I might start to worry that there was, yes.'

'Well, it's simple, then. Find yourself someone in their mid-thirties who's just got divorced, and in you swoop to pick up the pieces.'

'I'm just not sure I want someone who's already been married, that's all.'

'Why on earth not? I mean, it's not like buying a car, is it? Because even at your age, everyone you meet is going to have at least a few miles on the clock. And it's not as if they lose value the second they're driven out of the showroom.'

'It's just, well, having been married is different, isn't it? I mean, they've already made that commitment to spend the rest of their life with someone, thrown their lot in with them, and for whatever reason, it hasn't worked out. And here they are again, going through the same motions with someone else. And the trouble with that is they're going to carry some baggage with them, so everything you do, everything you say, is going to be judged relative to their previous partner. And I don't want to go into something like that, where I'm constantly being compared to someone else – someone I don't know. I want it to be for me. Fresh. Discovering things together, not someone waiting for me to make the same mistakes that their previous partner made, and her thinking the fact I occasionally forget to take the rubbish out means it's never going to last.'

'It wouldn't be like that, surely?'

'With all due respect, Ash, how would you know? Take you and Priti. The second that you actually tie the knot you're both heading into uncharted territory. Neither of you have been there, so it's a journey of discovery for the both of you. Feeling your way.'

Ash sniggers. 'I'm particularly looking forward to that bit.'

'I'm serious. It's going to be exciting. And any mistakes you make, you're going to make together, and they're going to be new mistakes. Mistakes that both of you make. And not ones that have a whole load of significance attached to them.'

'You could turn that round,' says Ash. 'Look at it in a positive light.'

'How do you mean?'

'Well, say this woman has had a terrible marriage. She's divorced, and been scarred by the whole experience. Doesn't have a lot of faith in men.'

'Is this someone you know? Because they're not sounding all that attractive.'

He makes a face. 'No, I'm speaking hypothetically. But say she's been through all that, and she's still prepared to get married. And to you. That must mean that she has a real belief in marriage being a good thing, and that you're the kind of person she can make it work with. Which is a compliment.'

'Maybe . . .'

'All I'm saying is, people get divorced for any number of reasons, especially when they're our age. And perhaps the main reason is because they know they've made a mistake, and are desperate to meet someone and try again . . .'

'. . . before it's too late?' I exhale loudly. 'But there's another thing. Someone who hasn't been married before is evidently in no rush, which means she's probably not rushing into it with me. But someone who has, and to use your phrase, is "desperate" to make it happen again . . . I don't want someone desperate. Because then you might find you're both making allowances, or compromising, just to make it work.'

Ash rolls his eyes. 'But don't you see? That's what it's all about. When people talk about the "C" word, and how most people, men in particular, are afraid of it, they don't mean "commitment". They mean "compromise". Because fundamentally we're all selfish, and compromising is the last thing we want to do. Or feel that we have to do.'

I stare moodily into my cappuccino. 'Maybe I'm just being too naive, then. Because I kind of thought that when I met "the one", I wouldn't have to compromise.'

'Nope,' says Ash. 'It's more a case of not feeling like you're compromising. And there is a difference.'

'Says the man about to marry the perfect woman.'

Ash grins. 'Okay. I may have lucked out with Priti, I admit. But there's a lot of compromises I'm making.'

'Such as?'

Ash thinks for a moment. And then another moment. 'Well, I don't get to sleep with anyone else, for example,' he says, eventually.

'Yeah, right. Because you were really fighting them off before she came along.'

'That's not the point,' splutters Ash. 'Although true.'

I put my coffee down on the table. 'Ash, you don't realize how lucky you've been, firstly to meet someone who you're crazy about, secondly because she evidently feels the same way about you, and thirdly because someone else did all the spade work to get the two of you together.'

Ash shrugs. 'Maybe so. But all I'm saying is, don't blindly discount any of these avenues of opportunity. Because you never know when you're going to meet her. Or where. Or what she's going to be like.'

'Even if she's a divorcee.'

Ash sighs. 'Ben, just because someone's been divorced, it doesn't mean there's anything wrong with them. They might have been the ones doing the divorcing, don't forget.'

'Maybe,' I say, unconvinced.

'Have you ever dated one?'

'No.'

'Well, how do you know what they're like, then? I mean, you hadn't had a proper curry until you met me. And now you love the stuff.'

'That's hardly the same.'

'All right. Well, say you'd never had sex before. Would you want to do it your first time with a virgin? Or someone who knew what she was doing.'

'Ah,' I say, gesturing towards him with my teaspoon. 'There are advantages to doing something with someone who hasn't done it before, particularly if neither of you know what you're doing, because then, neither of you know if you're doing anything wrong.'

'Or right,' points out Ash. 'Which is why it might not be such a bad idea. If you really want this marriage to work, why not marry someone who's done it already? Because she'll sure as hell not want it to fail a second time. Plus, it means she'll only marry you if she thinks it can work with you from the outset.'

'You think?'

'Definitely,' says Ash.

'But what if they turn out to be like Amy? You know, wanting me to be someone I'm not?'

Ash swallows the last of his coffee. 'There's an old wedding joke, where the bride tries to remember what she has to do on the day – walk up the aisle, stand at the altar, and sing a hymn. Trouble is, when she gets there, and whispers this to herself, what the groom hears is "aisle", "altar", "hymn" and he's off like a shot. Well, they'll know they can't do that this time around. So you're bound to have a better shot.'

As I smile at Ash's joke, I have to admit, it sounds like a plan. 'But where on earth can I meet these women? After all, there's hardly a directory listing the recent divorcees, is there?'

'Yes, there is.'

'There is?'

'The Internet.'

'What – I should just Google "divorced women" and see what comes up?'

'No. Try one of those dating websites. You have to put your status on there. Apparently.'

'And won't that seem a little creepy? Me targeting divorced women on the Internet?'

Ash shakes his head. 'Not at all. After all, anyone looking to have their portrait painted in Margate can use Google to find you,' he says, referring to the website he's in the process of setting up for me. 'Just treat this like that.'

As I stare at Ash across the table, it occurs to me that this might just work. I'm a decent guy, so if I appear all nice, trustworthy, and ready to commit, then I might be the perfect antidote to their cynicism, and it'll be me who's beating them off with a stick – assuming they ever want to get married again. 'But, what site do I choose? There's hundreds of them.'

'Sign up with them all,' he says excitedly. Or rather, the ones where you can search on "divorced". That way you can be a bit more . . .'

'Cynical?'

'Targeted.'

'I don't know. It just feels a bit . . .'

'What?'

'Wrong.'

'Why?'

'I don't know.' I lean heavily back in my chair. 'Possibly because I'm looking for love. Not a car.'

'No,' says Ash. 'You're looking for a wife. And I'm afraid those two things are a little different.'

'You mean "love" and "a wife", not "love" and "a car", I take it?'

'What do you think?' he says, gazing adoringly out of the window at his BMW.

'Yes, but, Internet dating . . .'

Ash shrugs. 'So? Everyone's doing it nowadays.'

'Everyone's also fiddling their tax returns. It doesn't make it right, does it? I mean, where's the romance? How do I tell people that we met?'

Ash smiles. 'What would you tell them if you'd met in a bar? It's hardly romantic, and yet you're prepared to take that approach. Trust me, in ten years' time, there's more people going to be saying they've met their partners this way than any other. And besides – what's more embarrassing? Saying that your parents found you a woman because you couldn't find one of your own?'

'What – like yours did?'

'Aha,' says Ash. 'But then again, I always expected them to.'

I have to admit, he's got a point – particularly on the 'divorced women' angle. And I'm just wondering whether that might include a certain divorced woman who works in Boots when my mobile rings, although I'm momentarily puzzled when the name 'Kerry' appears on the screen.

'Oh no,' I say, putting the phone down on the table as my memory finally kicks in.

'Aren't you going to answer that?'

'Not on your life,' I say. 'It's the girl my dad spoke to at Tramps. Although I don't know how she got my number.'

'She might be nice.'

'I'm sure she is, Ash,' I say, as the phone thankfully stops ringing. 'But I didn't fancy her, so what's the point? I mean, you need a spark, don't you?'

'You do,' he says, as it starts ringing again. 'Do you want me to answer it? Get rid of her for you?'

'No. Just ignore it. I don't want to be nasty.'

Ash raises one eyebrow, then darts his hand out and picks my mobile up. 'Ben's phone,' he says, grinning across the table at me. 'Yes, he is. Just one second.'

'What? No!' I wave the phone away, but he thrusts it into my hand.

'Just talk to her.'

I stare daggers across at him, then hit the 'speaker-phone' button, and put it down on the table. 'Er . . . Hello?'

'Hi, Ben,' says the voice on the other end. 'It's Kerry.'

'Hi,' I say. Then, when she doesn't say anything else, 'What can I do for you?'

'I'm just returning your call,' says Kerry.

I frown across the table at Ash. 'My call?'

'Yes,' she says. 'You left me a message the other day. And I wasn't going to call you back, seeing as you left it so long to phone *me*, but you sounded insistent.'

'I left you a message? What did I say?'

'Can't you remember?' she says crossly.

'I'm sorry, Kerry. My dad's been . . .' I stop talking, not quite sure how to explain what my dad's been up to.

'Oh, of course, Ben,' she says, suddenly concerned, and obviously jumping to the wrong conclusion. 'You must have a lot on your plate, what with your dad being, you know, terminal. You apologized for not being in touch sooner, said you'd still love to take me out, and wondered whether I was interested. And I wouldn't be, if not for the fact that your dad's dying.'

Great. A sympathy date. I roll my eyes at Ash, who's struggling not to laugh. 'And did I say anything else?'

'Not really,' says Kerry. 'But you sounded funny.'

'Funny how?'

'Well, your voice sounded different, for one thing. A bit muffled. As if you'd been crying.'

Or been holding a handkerchief over the receiver, more likely. 'Listen, Kerry. I'm sure you're lovely, but I'm afraid it wasn't me who called you the other day. It was my dad, pretending to be me. And I'm sorry. It won't happen again.'

'Why? Is he . . . Dead?' asks Kerry, hesitantly.

'Yes,' I say, ending the call, then dialling my dad's number. 'Yes, he is.'

Chapter 22

It's Tuesday afternoon, and I'm back in Mr Bean, drinking a cappuccino while waiting for my dad, who for some reason has told me to meet him here. He's late, and I'm just about to call him to find out where he is when I notice a woman standing next to me.

'Excuse me,' she says. 'Are you Ben?'

I look up to see a dark-haired girl, about my age, standing next to my table, holding a cup of coffee in one hand, and a laptop bag in the other. She's not someone I recognize, but then that's probably not surprising, seeing as she's had to ask who I am. 'Er, yes.'

'I'm Amanda. I work for the *Gazette*?'

I'm not sure exactly how I'm supposed to respond to that. *And?* seems a little too rude, and *Congratulations* seems a little too, well, cheeky. 'Oh. Right.'

'I thought I recognized you,' she says.

'Recognized me?'

'You know, having seen your pictures. On the Internet.'

'My pictures?' I have to think quickly, then realize

she must be referring to my new website. Finally, Ash has done something right, although he seems to have neglected to tell me it's actually up and running. And while I'd rather refer to them as my 'paintings', I don't want to appear anal. 'Oh. Of course.'

Amanda nods towards the empty chair opposite. 'May I?'

'Be my guest,' I say, noticing for the first time how attractive she is. 'So, you liked my, er, pictures?'

Amanda sits down, pulls a tape recorder out of her bag, which she puts down on the table in between us, and then smiles at me. 'Oh yes. Although I have to say, you look younger than I was expecting.'

'Thanks,' I say, warming to her immediately. Not only has she seen my work, but evidently it looks like it was painted by someone a lot more mature. Which I can only take as a compliment.

Amanda taps the tape recorder with her fingernail. 'You don't mind if I record this?'

'Help yourself,' I say, thinking what a stroke of luck this is. Ash has been trying to get the local paper to do a piece on me for ages. Plus, it'll fill the time until my dad gets here.

'So,' says Amanda, pressing the 'record' button, then taking a sip of her coffee, 'you must feel quite chuffed.'

'How do you mean?'

'You know. Having such a lot of fans.'

I find myself blushing slightly. 'Well, I don't know if I've got that many.'

'Don't be modest,' says Amanda. 'I've seen the pictures, and some of them are lovely. It must be difficult, though, deciding which ones to go with. How do you choose? From them all, I mean.'

I think about this for a second or two, not remembering how many of my paintings Ash was planning to put up on the site. 'Well, normally I just have them up against the wall of my studio.'

Amanda looks at me strangely. 'Against the wall?'

'Oh yes. That's the best way to tell what they'll be like. And then, once I've mounted them, I get my dealer to come round and tell me what he thinks.'

'Your *dealer*?'

I nod. 'That's right. After all, he gets a piece of each one too.'

Amanda shifts uncomfortably in her seat. 'Really? And how many of them have you, well, *done*?'

'I've done them all,' I say proudly.

Amanda looks shocked. 'All forty-seven?'

I sit back in my chair, more than a little impressed at both my evident output, as well as Ash's uploading efforts. 'Well, I can sometimes knock them up pretty quickly. Especially if someone pays for me to do them.'

Amanda frowns across the table at me. 'I'm sorry. You're expecting them to *pay*?'

'Well, how else do you think I make my living?' I say, taking a sip of my coffee. 'My studio might be in an old charity shop, but I don't actually *do* them for charity, you know.'

At that, Amanda's whole attitude seems to change. 'I see,' she says, pressing the 'stop' button on the tape recorder crossly.

I put my cup down nervously. 'Is, er, something the matter?'

'Sorry, Ben,' she says, glaring across the table at me, before picking up her bag, 'I think I've made a mistake.'

'But . . . What did I say?'

'Nothing. I just hadn't expected you to be so cynical, that's all.'

'Cynical? Wait a minute. How is it cynical to make money out of a talent that you have?'

'And arrogant as well,' says Amanda. 'Well, I wish I could say it's been a pleasure.'

'But . . . Don't you want to see my work? Or I could do you? This afternoon, if you like. And for free? It won't take long.'

'I'm sure it won't,' says Amanda, standing up suddenly and emptying the rest of her coffee over my head. 'I know there are some weirdos on the Internet, but using Facebook to, well, sell your *services*?' she says, before making for the door.

'Facebook?' I stare at her retreating figure in surprise, cappuccino running down past my ears. 'I'm an artist. I don't do Facebook,' I say, then realize just how pretentious that sounds. 'I mean, I don't use a computer much. And, anyway, even if I did, what's wrong with using the Internet to sell a few paintings?'

Amanda stops in her tracks, then wheels round to face me. 'A few *paintings*?'

'Yes. I'm a painter.'

Amanda stares at me for a moment or two. 'You are Ben Grant, right?'

'Yes.'

'Six foot one, twelve-and-a-half stone?'

'Yes,' I say hesitantly, wondering where she's getting her information from.

She walks back over to the table. 'And you're looking to get married?'

'Well, er, yes I am,' I say, wondering how on earth she knows *that*. 'But what's that got to do with anything. And Facebook in particular?'

'You didn't send me a message asking me to meet you here this morning? To see if I was interested in doing a piece on you?'

'No. Why? What sort of piece?'

Amanda doesn't answer, but instead hands me a packet of Kleenex from her pocket. 'I think you might want to see this,' she says, slipping her laptop out of her bag, firing it up, tapping in a few details, then swivelling it round to face me.

I scan the page quickly, dabbing the coffee from my hair and face with a tissue as I do so. From what I can tell, it seems to be a Facebook group, and what's more it's a group dedicated to me. And while the picture of me at the top of it is worrying enough, the name of the group makes me wide-eyed in shock.

I'm Ben Grant – Marry Me I read. 'What is this?'

'You really have no idea, do you?'

'No!'

'Well, in that case,' says Amanda, sitting back down opposite me, 'I'd say someone's playing a joke on you.'

I scroll down the page in stunned silence. Beneath the personal details is a paragraph about my relationship history, and the fact that I'm looking for a bride. And Amanda's right – there are in fact forty-seven people who have joined, or 'become a fan', as the page says.

While reassuringly – at first glance, at least – most of them seem to be women, as I read on through I'm a little mystified as to who's set this up. That is, until I click on the 'photo gallery', and understand there's only one place these pictures could have come from.

'Excuse me a moment, will you?' I say, my voice faltering slightly, then pull my mobile out of my pocket and dial the familiar number. After a couple of rings, my dad answers.

'Hello, son.'

'Hi, Dad. See if you can guess where I am?'

There's a few seconds of silence, and then, 'Bali?'

I stare at the phone, wondering why on earth that would be my dad's first guess, before putting it back to my ear. 'No, I'm in a cafe waiting for you, but someone else has turned up instead. And they've just shown me a certain Facebook page.'

There's another pause, longer this time, before my

dad's voice comes back on the line. 'It's rather good, isn't it?'

'Good? Just what were you hoping to achieve? Apart from making me a laughing stock, obviously.'

'Don't be like that, son. I think it's flattering that all those women are interested in you.'

'They're not "interested" in me, Dad. They've probably just signed up to make fun of me.'

'Don't be so negative. There's a few nice ones on there. Why don't we invite some of them round? Have a big party, maybe, and you can choose . . .'

'Dad, please,' I say, imagining him running some kind of *X-Factor* audition process. 'Don't you remember anything that Ash's parents said? What if some of them are gold-diggers?'

'Have you got any gold?'

'Well, no, but . . .'

'So what have you got to lose?'

I stare at the phone in disbelief. 'You'll be suggesting I get myself one of these mail-order brides next.'

'You can do that?' he says.

'Just delete it, please.'

'Oh.' My dad sounds a little hurt. 'What does your lady friend think? Amanda, isn't it?' he says, the rustle of paper in the background suggesting he's consulting his notes.

'She's not my lady friend, Dad. And even if she was, I'd be surprised if she ever spoke to me again after your little stunt.'

'Does she still want to do a story about you? It might help, you know. Widen the net a little.'

'Dad, I don't want to marry someone who's responded to a story they've read about me in the local paper.'

'Why not? You never know. They might be nice.'

'Or an axe-murderer.'

He laughs. 'Listen, son. You never know whether that special person is going to be the next person you bump into in the street. All I was trying to do was increase the odds of that happening.'

'Yes, but if I'd wanted to place an advert in the paper, I'd have done it myself. This whole scheme isn't about that. It's about trying to meet someone suitable. Not trying to meet anyone, and hoping they might turn out to be suitable.'

'Why not just give a few of them a go?'

'Because . . .' I sigh loudly down the phone. 'I'm tired of giving girls a go, and then having them tell me where to go. I want someone who I've a better chance of having a long term future with. Not someone who's responded to a piece in the bloody *Gazette*. No offence, Amanda,' I add, looking up at her.

'None taken,' she mouths back at me.

'But don't you see,' says my dad. 'That's why this is a good plan. Because the reason they might respond is because they're looking for someone for the same reason. And surely that's the biggest hurdle?'

'For the last time, I don't want my face splashed all over the papers. I'll be a laughing stock.'

'Well, why not at least stay and have a coffee with her.'

'We've already shared one,' I say, wiping a splash of cappuccino off the end of my nose.

'That's my boy. And have you asked her if she's single?'

'Goodbye, Dad.'

I put the phone back in my pocket, and look up to where Amanda is gathering her things together again, although a little less angrily this time.

'Let me guess. Your dad's idea?'

'One of many,' I say, shaking my head slowly, which only serves to drip more coffee on my shirt. 'I'm so sorry.'

'He's trying to get you married off?'

'Yes. Well, no. I mean, I want to get married, and he's trying to help.' I smile pathetically at her. 'Pretty tragic, huh?'

'Not at all.'

'Yes, but . . . Facebook?'

'At least it's original. I mean, it got *me* here, didn't it?'

'You don't think it smacks of . . . desperation?'

Amanda smiles. 'Not really. Internet dating is all the thing nowadays. I've even been on a couple of dates myself, with guys I met on there. Mind you,' she says, checking herself, 'they turned out to be losers.'

'You see?' I say. 'That's my point. The kind of people who have to resort to this kind of thing *are* losers.'

'Thanks very much.'

'No,' I say, quickly. 'Not you. And not most women. But the guys who can't meet anyone normally.'

'Nor can us girls,' says Amanda, slipping her laptop back into her bag. 'Sometimes.'

'Tell me. Why would someone as, well, *attractive* as you look for dates online? I mean, I can't believe that men don't stop you in the street and ask you out.'

'You'd be surprised,' says Amanda, blushing a little. 'Besides, it's probably our fault.'

'Women?'

'No,' laughs Amanda. 'The media.'

'How so?'

'You know – how women are portrayed nowadays as strong, independent, and how we don't need men nowadays, even if we want to have a baby, while in actual fact, for most of us the opposite is true. But the problem is that it's scaring you lot off. And that's the last thing we want.'

'But what is it you *do* want?'

'What everyone wants, Ben.'

'Which is?' I ask, feeling I'm on the verge of finding out something momentous.

Amanda looks at me levelly. 'To be loved,' she says, before standing up and making for the door.

And as I walk back to my studio later, I can't stop thinking about what she said. Because surely it's not just about being loved, but about being *in* love. It's a reciprocal thing, after all; you can't ever be in love with someone who doesn't feel the same way about you. And equally, sadly, just because someone says they love you, it doesn't mean you automatically love them back.

However much you wish you did.

Chapter 23

It's seven o'clock on Wednesday, and I'm just finishing up for the evening, having spent the afternoon trying – not very successfully – to make a portrait I've painted of someone's baby look more like a cute child and less like Winston Churchill when my mum and dad knock on the door.

'What do you want?' I say, still a bit mad with my dad over the Facebook/Kerry incidents.

'Your father's come round to apologize,' says my mum. 'Haven't you, Alan?'

'Er, yes. Sorry, son,' says my dad, frowning at the picture I've been working on. 'What's this one called – "We shall fight them on the beaches"?'

'It's actually a good likeness,' I say, showing them the photograph I've been working from. 'I'm just trying to make her look less like . . .'

'It's a *her*?' says my dad. 'Well, best of luck.'

I snatch the photo back. 'Was that all you wanted?'

'Actually, no,' he says. 'Are you hungry?'

'I might be,' I say, conscious that all I've had to eat all

day is a Snickers bar and a packet of peanuts. 'Why?'

'We thought we'd take you out to dinner this evening. You know, to make it up to you.'

'Really?'

'Really,' he says. 'Anywhere you like. You choose. And it's on us.'

'Well . . .' I look at the two of them suspiciously. 'Anywhere I like?'

'Sure,' says my dad.

'And you're paying?'

'Of course,' says my mum. 'Aren't you, Alan?'

'Well, there's that new Thai restaurant that's just opened up on the seafront. Why don't we go there?'

My mum and dad exchange glances. 'Not the Indian Queen?' asks my mum. 'I thought you loved it there.'

'I could really go a curry,' says my dad, rubbing his stomach exaggeratedly.

'Well, what about a Thai curry?'

'I'm not sure.' My dad makes a face. 'Aren't they a bit spicy?'

'Yes. I'd prefer Indian,' says my mum.

'But I thought you said anywhere *I* liked?'

'We did,' says my mum. 'But we thought you might fancy an Indian.'

If only you knew, I think. 'I do. But I'd quite like to try that Thai.'

My dad shrugs. 'Yes, but seeing as *we're* paying . . .'

Ten minutes later, we're walking into the Indian Queen, to be greeted at the door by Ash's dad. 'Well, if it isn't the Grants,' he says. 'What a pleasant surprise. Table for three, is it?'

'Yes, please, Sanjay,' says my dad, as if they're best friends now. 'For three.'

I follow the three of them into the dining room, trying to ignore the lack of 'sold' stickers on my paintings, when my dad suddenly stops in his tracks, causing my mum and me to bump into him. 'Look, Sue,' he announces, pointing to the large table in the corner, where a middle-aged couple are sitting. 'It's Tony and June.'

'Joan,' whispers my mum.

'Of course,' says my dad, walking over to their table, and beckoning for us to follow. 'Tony. How lovely to see you.'

'Alan,' says Tony, standing up awkwardly, and phrasing my dad's name like a question. 'Nice to meet, I mean, *see* you too. This is my wife . . .'

'Of course,' interrupts my dad. 'Nice to see you again, June.'

'Joan,' hisses my mum.

'I don't think you know Ben, my son,' says my dad, putting his hands on my shoulders and pushing me forwards, as if he's presenting me for an award. 'Ben did all the paintings you see up on the walls here.'

'And very nice they are too,' says Joan. 'We've been sitting here admiring them.'

'Thank you,' I say, shaking them both by the hand, then standing there awkwardly, as nobody seems to know what to say next.

Fortunately, Mr Patel coughs. 'I'm sorry, Alan. I've just checked the diary and we seem to be fully booked this evening.'

'I knew we should have reserved a table,' says my dad rather loudly. 'And I so fancied a curry. Didn't you, Sue?'

As my mum nods enthusiastically, I glance around the restaurant. Apart from Tony and Joan, there's no one else here. 'Oh well,' I say. 'Thais Are Us here we come.'

'Unless you'd like to join us,' suggests Tony suddenly. 'We're just waiting for our daughter, but I think this table will comfortably sit six people.'

'That'd be lovely,' says my dad, as if on cue. 'Why don't I sit next to June here . . .'

'Joan!' says my mum.

'And Sue, you sit opposite Tony. And Ben,' he says, pulling out a chair for me at the end of the table. 'You sit here, so you can keep Catherine company when she arrives.'

'Caroline,' says Joan.

I look down at the table. There are already six places set. 'Mum? Dad?' I say, deliberately not taking a seat. 'Can I have a word with you?'

'Sure, son,' says my dad.

'Outside?'

'What's wrong with here,' he asks nervously.

'Come on,' I say, marching them back into the reception area, leaving Tony and Joan sitting awkwardly at the table.

'What's going on?' I say, once we're out of earshot.

'What do you mean?' says my mum, as innocently as she can. Which isn't very.

'With Tony and Joan.'

'June,' says my dad.

'Whatever her name is. You've quite plainly never met them before.'

'Don't be ridiculous,' splutters my mum. 'They're old friends.'

'So where do you know them from, then?'

'The, er, bowls club,' says my mum, although unfortunately at exactly the same time as my dad says the word 'tennis'.

'Dad, the table's plainly laid for six people, the restaurant's obviously not fully booked, and Mr Patel's certainly not that good an actor. I recognize a set-up when I see one.'

My parents stare at each other accusingly, as if each thinks it's the other one's fault that I've seen through their brilliant plan. Eventually, my dad sighs.

'Okay, son. Guilty as charged.'

'Yes, Ben,' says my mum. 'We just thought this would be a good way for you to meet her.'

'Who?'

'Ca ...' My dad starts to say her name, then reaches into his pocket and pulls out what looks suspiciously like a printout from a Facebook page. '. . . roline.'

I scowl at the piece of paper, then at him. 'I thought I told you to delete that?'

'Yes, well, I've told you to do hundreds of things over the years, and you haven't paid much attention to me.'

'And so she's the best of the responses, is she?'

'Well, we hope so,' says my mum. 'Only . . .'

'. . . we haven't met her yet,' admits my dad.

'What? So what are Tony and Joan doing here? Or are they setting her up as well?'

'They responded on her behalf,' says my mum. 'Sounds like she's in the same boat you are. So we thought we'd see if we couldn't make something happen between the four of us. And this seemed like the best way.'

'What – tricking the two of us into some strange happy families dinner? No, that wouldn't have been awkward at all.'

'But she looks very nice,' says my dad, handing me the Facebook profile. 'On paper, at least.'

'I'm sorry, Mum, Dad, but I just can't,' I say, buttoning my coat up. 'Not like this. No matter how nice she is.'

'She works at the lap-dancing club on the seafront,' says my dad, desperately.

Against my better judgement, I snatch the profile from him, and scan quickly through her details. 'As a receptionist, Dad.'

'Made you look, though, son.'

I ignore his childishness. 'And besides, even if she was one of the performers, would you really want a lap-dancer as your daughter-in-law?'

'Well ...' For a moment, I can tell my dad has a dilemma as to what his answer should be.

'Of course not, Ben,' says my mum, answering for him. 'But why not stay and meet her anyway? You don't want to disappoint her.'

'Does she know I'm going to be here?'

My dad looks guiltily at his shoes. 'No.'

'Well, in that case, she won't be disappointed when I'm not, will she? Besides, I'd only end up disappointing her eventually.'

'How do you know that?' says my mum.

'Because I disappoint them all,' I say, making for the door.

'Don't go, son,' pleads my dad. 'At least stay and have something to eat.'

'No, Dad. Thanks. I'll see you both later.'

His face falls. 'But I thought you were hungry?'

And the truth is, I'm starving. But I'm beginning to suspect I'm going to have to make my own dinner.

Chapter 24

'How'd you get on with her?'

'Who?'

'You know,' Ash says, as we walk up the High Street towards The Cottage the following lunchtime. 'That woman who wanted you to paint a picture of her house.'

'Ash, she wanted me to *actually* paint her house.'

'Ah.'

We walk on in silence for a second or two, and then Ash clears his throat. 'But you're still doing it, right?'

'What do you think? And next time you have the great idea of printing me up some business cards, try putting 'artist' rather than 'painter' on them, please.'

'Sorry, Ben. But decorating can be quite lucrative ...'

'So can having a decent agent, apparently. Oh, and speaking of women,' I say, as we stroll past Boots, 'I bumped into your sister the other day.'

Ash looks at me suspiciously. 'Define "bumped into".'

I desperately try to keep the colour from my cheeks. 'I was buying some deodorant, and remembered you saying something about having a sister who worked in

Boots, and would you believe it I just happened to be in the queue at her till?'

'What sort of deodorant?'

'What has that got to do with it?'

'Because whatever it is, it can't quite mask the smell of bullshit that's wafting over me.'

'Scout's honour,' I say, holding my hand up and giving a little salute, unable to remember what the correct hand signal is supposed to be. I've already decided not to own up to the 'condom' saga. In truth, I've had the box sitting in my hallway for a couple of days now, but I haven't quite had the nerve to take it in for my refund. 'But why is she called "Mistry"?'

'It was her married name,' says Ash. 'And I don't think she's got around to changing it back yet. Or maybe it's her way of getting back at my parents. Who knows?'

'Oh. Right. Maybe she won't have to. Change it back, I mean.'

'Huh.'

'Well, if she's going to be changing it to "Grant", eventually . . .'

Ash stops walking, and looks at me pityingly. 'For Christ's sake, Ben, if you're going to ask her out, just ask her out. In fact, I've got an idea.'

'What?' I start to panic, thinking that Ash is going to drag me into Boots to confront her, but instead he just retrieves his mobile from his pocket.

'Relax,' he says, his fingers moving rapidly across the dial pad. 'I'm just going to give you her number. Or if you'd prefer, I'll text her yours. Leave the ball firmly in her court.'

'Don't you dare,' I say, getting my own phone out, and I'm just about to type Seema's number in when it rings.

'That was fast work,' says Ash, as I squint nervously at the screen, although I'm both relieved and a little disappointed when my dad's number appears.

For a moment, I consider not answering it. Even though I know his heart's in the right place, this whole find-me-a-bride thing just isn't working out as I hoped it might. My finger hovers over the red button, but I realize that would only delay the inevitable, and that at least this way, I don't have to pay for the call. But when I press 'accept', I can hardly hear him.

'Where are you?' I say, nudging the volume up on the handset. 'And why do you sound like you're whispering?'

'That's because I *am* whispering,' whispers my dad.

'Why?'

'I'm at the police station.'

'What?'

'I'm at the police station,' he repeats, a little louder this time.

'That's what I thought you said.' My dad is often down there talking about improvements to the neighbourhood watch scheme he runs. 'What are you doing? Next door's shed been broken into again?'

'Not quite,' he says. 'Your mum's been arrested.'

'What? When? What for?'

'Kerb crawling, or something.'

'Kerb crawling? Mum?'

'I don't have time to explain. Can you come down here?'

'Yeah. Sure.' I laugh, sure it's another one of his ruses. 'And don't tell me – there'll be a nice young police-woman there who's keen to take down my particulars.'

'It's not funny, son.'

Something about the tone of his voice makes me realize he's telling the truth. 'I'm on my way.'

I make my excuses to Ash, then hurry round to where I've left my car, and by the time I get down to the police station, my dad's on his second cup of coffee from the machine in the waiting room. As a result, he's pacing around so agitatedly that he's in danger of being arrested himself.

'Calm down,' I say, leading him towards the bench in the corner.

He glares at the door that leads to the holding cells. 'That's easy for you to say when your mother's in there, surrounded by rapists and murderers.'

'Dad, this is Margate. The busiest they get is the odd drunk tourist at the weekend. What happened?'

My dad points towards the stern-looking police-woman behind the 'enquiries' window, who seems to be doing a good job of ignoring us. 'You'd better ask her.'

'Okay. Stay here,' I say, getting up and walking over towards the far end of the room, then clearing my throat.

'Yes?' The policewoman doesn't even look up from her form-filling, where, worryingly, I can see my mum's name, along with the words 'kerb' and 'crawling'.

'I'm Ben. Ben Grant. And, er, she's my mother,' I say, nodding down at the form.

'Ah, yes. Mrs Grant. In for, what is it? Kerb crawling,' says the policewoman matter-of-factly, although it looks like she's trying to keep the smile off her face.

'She's not in any trouble, is she?'

'Well, perhaps. We found her propositioning a number of young girls. Working girls, to be specific.'

'What? My mum? There must be some mistake.'

'As I've been trying to tell them,' says my dad, who's suddenly appeared at my shoulder. 'She's a member of the bowls club.'

I glance round at him, wondering why he thinks that makes a difference. 'Sit down, Dad. Where was this?' I ask the policewoman.

She looks up briefly from her form-filling. 'Down on the industrial estate. Darwin Road.'

'But that's, well, a . . .'

The policewoman raises one eyebrow. 'A what, sir?'

'Well, you know, a red light district. Apparently.'

'Quite. And so what would your mother have been doing down there, exactly?'

'Exactly? Er . . .' It's a good question. And unless she was taking the long way round to Asda, I can't think of a plausible answer.

The policewoman puts down her pen. 'We just

happened to be doing a random drive through. Saw this woman acting suspiciously around the girls. And when we questioned her, she said . . .' She takes her notepad out of her pocket, licks her index finger, then flicks through a few pages until she finds the one she wants. '"I was only trying to find a girl for my son." And that would be you, I believe?' she adds, looking accusingly up at me. 'Ben, wasn't it?'

'Oh,' I say, as breezily as I can manage. 'Well, *that* I can explain.'

'Can you?'

'Er, yes,' I say, although whether I actually want to is another matter, but seeing as my mum wouldn't be here if it wasn't for me, I don't really have the choice. When I've finished, the policewoman looks me up and down.

'What a shame I'm not single myself,' she says, dryly. 'Otherwise I'd be first in the queue.'

'Really?' I look at her closely. Although her tightly clipped hair makes her look a little stern, she's actually quite pretty, in an authoritarian kind of way. And the uniform's definitely a turn-on.

'Oh yes. In fact, I'm surprised no one's snapped you up already. Particularly given the fact that your mum's reduced to finding you dates on Darwin Road.'

I'm just about to answer, although not particularly politely, when fortunately I'm interrupted by my father's loud 'Excuse me' from where he's sitting on the bench at the far end of the room. 'Are you charging her?'

The policewoman looks at him briefly, before going

back to her form. 'I've told you once already, Mr Grant. She'll probably get off with a caution.'

'Because if you're not charging her, then she's free to go, surely?' he says, appearing at my shoulder again. My dad never misses an episode of *The Bill*, and his knowledge of police procedures is probably second to none.

'As soon as I've finished filling this in.'

'Haven't you got something better to do? Any real criminals to catch?'

The policewoman puts her pen back down, and stares at my dad. 'Kerb crawling is a real crime, Mr Grant. Now I suggest you go and sit down and wait until I've finished.'

'Which will be when?'

'A lot longer if you keep interrupting me.'

I lead my dad back over to the coffee machine and buy him a cup of decaff, which he drinks in an anxious silence while we wait, although when my mum finally appears, he seems almost disappointed that she's not wearing handcuffs, or at least some of those plastic garden tie-things that they seem to use nowadays. In fact, given how relaxed she seems, you'd be forgiven for thinking she'd had a day out at a health spa.

'Sue,' says my dad, rushing over to meet her, and enveloping her in a huge hug. 'Are you okay?'

'Fine, thank you,' she says, brushing him off awkwardly.

'What were you doing? You know, *there*?' He says

this last bit in a whisper, conscious that the desk sergeant is watching from the window.

My mum shrugs. 'I was picking up some picture frames from the wholesalers, so I thought I'd take a short cut along Darwin Road. And when I saw all these girls hanging around on the pavement, I thought, well, one or two of them might be available.'

'Mum, they're all available. By the hour. They're ladies of the night,' I say, trying to phrase it in terms she'll understand.

She makes a face. 'How was I supposed to know that? It was lunchtime.'

'By the way they dressed, perhaps?'

She thinks about this for a second. 'I suppose some of those skirts were rather short for the time of year.'

'Well, we're just pleased to have you back,' says my dad, putting a protective arm around her shoulders, before leading her outside. 'Aren't we, son?'

As I follow them out of the building and along the street to where their car's parked, I can't help but look at the two of them fondly – by the way my dad is hanging on to her, you'd think he hadn't seen her for a five-year stretch.

'Listen,' says my mum, when we get to where my dad's parked the car. 'I've been doing some thinking. While I've been inside.'

I roll my eyes. My mum's actual time 'inside' has amounted to all of an hour and a half.

'What about?' asks my dad.

'This whole "find Ben a bride" thing. And the fact that despite our best efforts, we've not found a single woman who's been suitable.'

'Or even a married one,' jokes my dad.

'And I just feel, Ben,' she says, rubbing my arm in what I assume is supposed to be a comforting fashion, 'that you should think again about your back-up option.'

'Amy,' says my dad, somewhat unnecessarily.

'But I . . . I can't.'

'Why not?'

'Well, because I just don't think you should ever go back.'

'Sometimes you have to go backwards before you can move forwards,' says my dad cryptically.

When I get home later, the first thing I see is the huge unopened box of condoms, which seems to be rubbing my single status in my face. And it makes me think that maybe he's got a point.

Chapter 25

It's Friday lunchtime, and Ash and I are playing tennis at the courts on the seafront. We've long stopped keeping a tally as to who's won the most times – in fact, the only thing we both know is that whichever one of us you ask will think it's them. Despite his size, Ash is pretty skilful, and the only chance I've got of beating him is to try to run him around the court. Trouble is, because he's so handy with the racquet, that's not always so easy to do.

I love tennis. And it's not that I'm very good, rather that I can kind of lose myself in it. And although I often actually lose too, I don't care. As long as I've played a decent game, I'll remember it more for that stunning backhand winner I played in the second set, rather than the overall score.

But for some reason today, I don't hit any backhand winners, stunning or not, and Ash wipes the floor with me. And I don't know what the cause is, but I just feel a bit lethargic. Perhaps it's because I'm getting worn down by this whole process. Maybe it's that I don't feel I can ask my mum and dad to keep looking for me, particularly given my mum's brush with the law yesterday. Or maybe it's as simple as the weather, given that there's a light drizzle falling, which has the effect of slowing the tennis balls down a bit, thus giving Ash those valuable extra few milliseconds to get to what would otherwise be my winning shots. But whatever the reason, it can't prevent me from feeling a little depressed.

'What was up with you?' says Ash, shaking my hand across the net.

I shrug, and pick up one of the soggy yellow Dunlops. 'Who knows? Balls a bit heavy, perhaps.'

Ash puts his arm around my shoulders as we walk off the court. 'Well, you're bound to meet someone eventually.'

'No, the tennis balls . . .' I look up, and see that he's joking. 'Very funny.'

'Well, you'd better get your head together soon. It's nearly that time again.'

I can only assume he's talking about the club championships. Ash and I played together last year, and we lost in the first round. 'Don't remind me.'

'You are still up for it?'

I sigh. 'I don't know, Ash. Maybe I better just face it. Some people are good at doubles, some are better at singles. And I'm starting to worry that maybe I'm more of the latter.'

'You are still talking about the tennis, right?'

I walk over to where I've left my bag and slump in the

white plastic chair. 'What if it *is* me, Ash? I mean, when I think about all the relationships I've had that haven't worked, there's one common factor – yours truly.'

'Nah. You've got to be true to yourself,' says Ash, attempting to sit in the chair next to me, but giving up when he's unable to wedge himself in between the arms. 'And so if none of these women have been right, then, well, they're not right.'

I reach into my bag and extract two cans of Coke. 'Maybe some men are meant to be alone,' I say, handing one to Ash. 'Like Cliff Richard.'

'Or my weird uncle Raj, who we never talk about,' grins Ash, opening his can and taking a swig. 'But then again, that could be because of his prison record.'

'But what I don't get is, well, the difference between Cliff and your uncle Raj and me is that I desperately want to be with someone, one hundred per cent. I *want* the whole nine yards, the two point four children, the ...' I stop talking, having run out of numbers to make my point.

'The Hundred Years War?'

I pick up a tennis ball and throw it at Ash. 'So why have I never even come close to finding it?'

'Maybe because you're dating nutters?' he says, no doubt referring to my recent experience with Linda, which I've had to come clean about. 'Or maybe you're looking too hard.'

'How can you look too hard? Surely the harder you look, the more likely you are to find it?'

'Not necessarily.'

'How so?'

'Well, you might not be able to see the wood for the trees.'

'Huh? What do you mean by that?'

'Er . . . I'm not sure.'

'And besides, I haven't been looking too hard. If anything, quite the opposite. I mean, I waited around in almost all of those relationships to see if they'd turn into something more permanent, and they didn't.'

'Well, maybe that's your problem,' says Ash, leaning his racquet against the net and attempting a couple of half-hearted stretches.

'Thanks, Ash. You're being extremely helpful today.'

'All I'm saying is, perhaps this isn't something you can force.'

I take a mouthful of Coke, frowning at him over the top of the can. 'What are you talking about?'

'Maybe it just, you know, happens.'

'Just happens?'

'Yeah. Look at me and Priti. Now, I'd be the first to admit that I've been lucky there . . .'

'You're telling me.'

He ignores me. 'But it just kind of happened. You know – once we'd been put together, we both knew it was right. From day one. So for you to try to *make* it happen – maybe that's just the wrong approach.'

'You're saying that *now*?'

Ash grins, guiltily. 'Maybe.'

'But I can't wait, given the alternative.'

'Why not? And what's the alternative?'

'Nothing, Ash. The alternative is nothing. And I don't want nothing.'

And this is the problem, I realize, as Ash stares at me, trying to work out whether I've said something significant or I'm just using poor grammar. Because I'm worried the longer I wait, one of two things will happen. Either I'll leave it so late that I'll never meet anyone, and then I'll be even more lonely, or I'll start to get desperate, and so I'll end up compromising, and ultimately that'll make me even more unhappy.

'Well, maybe your focus is too much on the marriage aspect,' he says eventually.

'How so?'

'If you start looking at every single woman you meet with a view to getting down on one knee, it might just be a little . . . off putting. For them.'

'But that's what makes it so unfair. I thought that was what women wanted. When did it all change? I mean, read any of those bloody books that my dad used to force on us at school, and they're all about the same thing – women trying to find a husband. In fact, if Mister bloody Darcy and his mates are to be believed, they often proposed even before meeting the girl, or after just one dance at one of their fancy soirées they'd be chasing the dad the next morning to ask for the girl's hand in marriage. They wouldn't even consider 'walking out' with someone unless marriage was on the cards.

And yet now . . .' I stare up at the sky in frustration.

'Yes, but they actually had something to offer, don't forget. Money, a country house, an estate.'

'I've got an estate.'

'You've got an estate *car*, Ben. Besides, nowadays, we can't just swoop in, lay our cards on the table, and expect the woman to accept our opening offer. We have to start from a position of strength, and then slowly convince her that we're her best bet. And if you're not starting from a position of strength any more . . .'

'Why can't I just find someone who likes me for *me*?'

'You've already had someone like that, don't forget.'

'Yes, but that was a me that I'm not any more,' I say. 'If you see what I mean. And like I've told you a billion times, Amy just wasn't right.'

Ash picks up his bag and stuffs his racquet inside. 'Ben, maybe Amy wanting to marry you is about as right as you're going to get. Did you ever think about that?'

Chapter 26

Thanks to Ash's comment, I don't think about much else for the rest of the day, and when I get to my art class that evening, Terry asks how I'm getting on. And against my better judgement, I tell him.

'Your whole approach is wrong, Ben,' he says, when I've eventually finished. 'You shouldn't be getting married because you feel you should.'

'I shouldn't?'

'Nah. Do it because you're ready.'

'But . . . I feel that I should. Be ready, that is.'

'That's not the same thing.'

'But . . . I'm not getting any younger,' I say, trying to ignore how lame that actually sounds.

Terry shakes his head wistfully. 'Doesn't matter. Age, I mean.'

'How can you say that?'

'Simple.' Terry motions for me to sit down. 'Because what you have to realize is this. All men are like taxi drivers.'

'Taxi drivers?'

'When it comes to women, at least. And I should know.'

'Huh? I can guess the "pick them up" bit, but ... Charging them for a ride? They give you a tip? No – surely that'd be the other way round?'

Terry laughs. 'No, what I mean is that most men drive around all their lives picking up fares – or rather, girlfriends. Some they take for a short ride, some go on longer journeys, but inevitably, they drop them all off somewhere, without giving much thought to where it is they're going themselves. Then at some point in time, they suddenly decide that they're tired of driving around, so they simply turn off the "for hire" sign and go home – but with their passenger still on board. And whoever's in the back of the cab at that particular time is the one they marry.'

'So what does that mean? For me, I mean.'

'Simple. For men, it's all a matter of timing.' Terry stands up and walks over to the window to check on his cab. 'Some women get bored of being driven around aimlessly, or being stuck in traffic, never reaching their destination, so they stop the cab and get out early. Others who try and force the issue are chucked un-ceremoniously out of the back of the cab. The clever ones are those who hang in there quietly on the back seat, waiting for you to turn off your meter.'

'So what you're saying is, we never know *if* she's the one. It's more a case of *when*.'

Terry beams at me, as if I'm his star pupil. 'Exactly.'

I stare back at him. 'But that means if I split up with Amy, but I'm suddenly desperate to get married, then maybe I was too hasty. And if that's the case, then surely it's her I should be marrying.'

'Could be.'

'But how can I be sure Amy's the right one?'

'You can't,' says Terry. 'But the problem is, you're never going to know until afterwards anyway, so you might just as well go ahead with it.'

'Huh?'

'It's a leap of faith, isn't it?'

'Is it?'

'Yeah. Like when you do that team-building bollocks, and they make you close your eyes and fall over backwards, in the hope that the rest of your team will catch you.'

'But that's –' I try to find a better word than 'stupid', but fail – 'stupid.'

Terry shrugs. 'It's just the way it is.'

'But surely, if you're, you know, in love, then you're not taking that much of a risk?'

'Aha!'

'Aha what?'

'Well, it's just that love comes after marriage, doesn't it?'

'Does it?'

Terry perches on the corner of the windowsill and folds his arms. 'Oh yes. If you're lucky, that is. And remember, marriage alters people, particularly women.

So the girl you thought you knew and loved beforehand suddenly becomes a different person. They're not your girlfriend any more, they're your wife. And that's a change in status that makes people behave differently.'

'But I lived with Amy. For a few weeks, at least. So I've got a good idea of what she'd be like.'

'But not as husband and wife.'

'Why does that make a difference?'

Terry sighs. 'It just does. It's all to do with the ring on your finger, although it might as well be through your nose, given how much they think they can use it to control you.'

'So I won't really know her until we're married?'

'Oh no,' says Terry, bitterly. 'In actual fact, you never really know someone until they've left you. Because that's the time you find out how nasty, vindictive, and money-grabbing they really are.'

I have to admit, I'm a little confused. On the one hand, Terry is telling me that there's no possible way that I can prepare myself for marriage until I actually go ahead and take the plunge, and it's only after I've actually done it that I'll know whether I've made the right decision or not. And on the other hand, he's always painted such a bleak picture that it makes me wonder if it's the kind of thing I really want to be doing at all.

'Besides,' continues Terry. 'You're trying too hard.'

'What?'

'You're trying too hard. You should just let it happen.'

I look at him sceptically, wondering whether he and

Ash have been comparing notes. 'What are you talking about?'

'Your whole approach. It's no wonder you haven't had much luck.'

'Huh?'

'Speak to most people. Ask them how they met their partners. It's not from grilling every single person they meet to find out if they could be the one.'

'What makes you such an expert?'

Terry looks at me as if I'm an idiot. 'Hello? Married twice, don't forget.'

And divorced twice too, I feel like reminding him. 'Sorry, Terry. How does it happen, then?'

'Accidents. Coincidences. Most people say "I wasn't looking, and there she was". For example, I met my second wife when she was working on the checkout in Sainsbury's – and I had my first wife with me at the time, so I certainly wasn't looking. But the minute she smiled up at me and asked if I wanted a "bag for life", I just knew she was the one.' He grins. 'Although it turned out she was talking about herself, which is why we ended up getting divorced. But, seriously, it's all about accidents. And how do accidents happen? When you're not paying attention, or looking where you're going. Trust me, I know.'

I make a mental note not to use Terry's taxi service again. 'Yes, but accidents are mainly bad things, aren't they?'

He shrugs. 'Depends on your point of view. But I'm

serious. Stop focusing on this like it's the most important thing in the world, and I guarantee you'll meet someone sooner rather than later.'

'You'll guarantee it? What on earth does that mean?'

'You know, that you're bound to . . .'

'No, it doesn't. A guarantee suggests that if it doesn't work out, I'll get it fixed. Or some replacement. What're you going to do? Find me someone yourself if I take your advice and nothing happens?'

'Well, no, but . . .'

'Exactly,' I say, getting up and pacing around the classroom. 'And this is what I resent. People who've already won life's lottery by actually managing to meet someone who'll have you – and twice, in your case – getting all smug. And then you preach from this position of experience that this is the way to do it, or that's how not to. It's like saying, yes, all you need to do is pick these six numbers and you're guaranteed to be a winner. Well, I'm afraid life doesn't work like that. And more importantly love doesn't work like that either.'

Terry looks at me until he's sure I've finished, and even then has to check to make sure. 'You done?'

'Yes.' I sit back down. 'I think so. But I've been trying to let it happen naturally for most of my life, and it hasn't. Which is why I've been doing *this*.'

Terry smiles. 'But there's your problem. If you're *trying*, then it's never going to happen naturally, is it? I tell you, the minute you stop all this "find me a bride" rubbish, the next woman you see is probably going to be your perfect woman.'

'Really?' I walk over and peer out of the window myself, to see Lesbian Lizzie appear round the corner, and raise my eyebrows at Terry.

'Okay, maybe not the next person,' he says. 'But you take my point.'

'That I'm hardly going to find Pamela Anderson walking down Margate High Street?'

Terry laughs. 'And that's another of your problems.'

'What is?'

'Pamela Anderson. Would you really want to be married to her?'

'Too bloody right I would.'

'Terry looks at me in disgust. 'Have you ever heard of "the marrying kind"?'

'What are you talking about?'

'Well, there are those women who you'd like to, you know, get intimate with. And those who'll make good wives. And sometimes, one isn't the other.'

I lean heavily against the wall, and stare at the ceiling. 'Terry, please, don't confuse the issue further.'

'I'm sorry, Ben. But you need to know. Your expectations are just a little . . . unrealistic.'

It's not the first time I've been told this. *But why*, I always want to ask. So I do. 'Why?'

'Simple,' says Terry. 'If you're George Clooney, or Brad Pitt, then you can get the Pamela Andersons of this world. But you're not. You're Ben Grant. A struggling artist from Margate. And I'm afraid that nowadays that's not quite enough to cut it where Pammie's concerned. Or most women, to be honest.'

'So you're saying I should look past the physical?'

Terry nods, as if it's the most obvious thing in the world. 'Yes. Or stop being a struggling artist.'

'But if that's the case, then why can't they?' I say, ignoring Terry's second suggestion.

'Why can't they what?'

'Look past all that?'

Terry gives a wry smile. 'Because they've got the power, Ben. They're in charge. It's them who're selling, and we're the overanxious buyers.'

'Okay, okay. I get the picture.'

Terry shrugs. 'It's one of life's great unfairnesses, and the sooner you get used to it, the better.'

'But . . . that's not fair,' I say, winning the 'stating the bleeding obvious' prize.

Terry shrugs again. 'Welcome to the real world.'

'So let me get this straight. I'm never going to meet someone to settle down with, because currently I'm trying too hard.'

He nods. 'Yup.'

'Plus, my expectations are too unrealistic, and until I change them I'm going to end up being disappointed?'

'Pretty much.'

'But the minute I'm more realistic, and start targeting women who are more . . .'

'Appropriate.'

'. . . then I'm going to have a lot more luck? Especially if I stop actively targeting them.'

'Exactly,' says Terry.

I'm a little confused. 'But what about women? Why don't they have this problem? I mean, surely they all start out wanting Brad Pitt, and go through the same process we do?'

'Aha,' says Terry. 'But then the old biological clock starts ticking, and someone who previously might not make the grade becomes prime marriage material. And because women are a lot more practical than us blokes, they know that, and therefore are prepared to compromise a lot earlier.'

'Whereas we're too fickle.'

Terry nods. 'You want a babe. They just want babies. It's as simple as that.'

'Well, surely all I need to do is wait until Pamela Anderson gets that urge, and make sure I'm hanging around at the appropriate time, and . . . bingo.'

'You might be waiting a long time. Besides, doesn't she already have kids?'

'I was talking figuratively.'

'And she's got quite a figure.'

'You know what I mean, Terry. And besides, I'm just worried that unless I really fancy them, then I'm not going to be able to, you know, do it.'

'There's a reason why most married people keep the lights turned off during sex. It's so *they* don't get turned off. My ex wife? When we first got together, we were at it like rabbits, and whenever we were in bed I had to think of football just to stop myself from, you know, peaking too early. By the end of the marriage, all I had to do was think of her, and it had the same effect.'

'Not that. Marriage, I mean. Because it's an important part of it for me.'

'Well, maybe it *is* too early for you. Maybe you've still got some wild oats to sow. Trust me, even after all I've been through, if I had my time again, I'd still do exactly the same thing.'

That surprises me. 'What? Why?'

He considers this for a moment. 'I guess that's just one of life's great mysteries.'

And while it may be a mystery to Terry, unfortunately, things are becoming clearer for me.

Chapter 27

When I call round at my parents' house after class, my mum and dad are sitting watching *University Challenge*. As usual, my dad is waiting until one of the teams has answered correctly before nodding, and saying 'That's right', as if he knew the answer all along. Which given that he's an English teacher, and most of the questions seem to be about applied mathematics or particle physics, seems a little unlikely.

'Here,' I say, handing over the chilled bottle of champagne I've picked up on the way.

'What's this for?' says my mother.

'Are we celebrating something?' asks my dad, hopefully.

'I'm not,' I say. 'But you are.'

My mum looks at me uncomprehendingly. 'Pardon?'

'And they say romance is dead.' I point to the two cards on the mantelpiece. 'Happy anniversary?'

'Oh,' says my dad. 'Right. Thanks. But there was no need to buy champagne.'

'No need?' I head off into the kitchen, returning a few seconds later with three glasses. 'But it's a special one this year, isn't it?'

My dad looks uneasily across at my mum, as if he's worried he's forgotten some important date. 'Is it?'

I nod. 'Your thirtieth?'

My mum frowns. 'I don't think so.'

'Yes, it is,' says my dad quickly.

'It must be,' I say, peeling the foil off the top of the bottle. 'I'm going to be thirty next year. Which means this year is your thirtieth.' I smile at the two of them, and start to lever the cork out of the bottle. 'Unless there's something you're not telling me.'

My mum and dad exchange anxious glances. 'Alan?' says my mum.

I stop what I'm doing. 'What's going on?'

'Nothing,' says my dad, although he suddenly can't make eye contact with either of us.

'Is this anything to do with me?'

As my mum sits there silently, my dad reaches for the remote control, and switches off the television. *University Challenge* hasn't even finished, so I know it's going to be something serious. 'Well,' he says. 'Yes, and no.'

'What does *that* mean?'

'Listen, son.' My dad indicates for me to sit down on the sofa. 'There's something we haven't told you.'

Normally, I'd be taking the mickey out of a comment like that. But there's something about the expression on their faces that makes me think that this is important. I put the half-opened bottle down on the coffee table, and do as instructed. 'What?'

'Me and your mum. It's not quite our thirtieth anniversary today.'

'Yes, it is. I was born in nineteen eighty, which makes me twenty-nine. You were married in nineteen seventy-nine. That makes thirty years. And . . .'

'No, son,' says my dad. 'It's actually our twenty-ninth anniversary. Not thirtieth. We got married in nineteen eighty.'

'I don't understand,' I say, although I'm beginning to worry that I do. 'Please tell me I'm a year younger than I think I am.'

My mum and dad stare at each other, until she eventually breaks the silence. 'No, Ben. I'm afraid not.'

For a moment, I can't quite believe this. 'You mean, I was a b . . .'

'. . . lessing in disguise,' says my dad. 'And no, we were married when we had you.'

'Just,' says my mum. 'As you can probably guess from the wedding photographs.'

I look over to the mantelpiece, where there's a photo of my parents on their wedding day, and only now do I realize why it's just a head shot. 'But . . .'

My dad stands up and walks over to the mantelpiece. 'We'd only just met, your mum and I, and then she fell pregnant . . .'

'*Fell* pregnant? What on earth does that mean?'

'Well,' says my dad. 'I'm afraid one night we'd had a

little bit too much to drink, and I got a bit carried away. Your mum was a real looker in those days, and I'm afraid I couldn't control . . .' There's a loud bang, and my dad stops talking, because the champagne cork has decided to fire itself out of the bottle at that precise moment. 'Well, you get the picture.'

'Dad, *please*.' I shake my head in disbelief. 'So, I was an accident?'

'Yes. But a happy accident,' says my mum, fetching a cloth from the kitchen. 'We were both really pleased.'

'Eventually,' says my dad, eyeing the champagne thirstily. 'So, anyway, your mum and I decided we should make the best of it, and get married. And here we are, thirty years later.'

'Twenty-nine,' I say, looking at the two of them incredulously.

My mum puts a hand on my arm. 'It's not such a big deal, though, Ben, when you think about it.'

'Not such a big deal?' I look at them both, wanting to say that, in actual fact, it *is* – particularly now. I've spent the last however many years following my match-made-in-heaven – or so I thought – parents' example, and believing that like them, I'd eventually meet my one true partner, when in actual fact, their whole marriage is a sham. Or not a sham, exactly, but it hardly started under the most romantic of circumstances. 'I'm sorry,' I say, noticing the looks on their faces, suddenly feeling like I'm the guilty one. 'It's just a bit of a shock.'

'Not as much of a shock as it was for us back then,'

says my dad. 'I mean, there we were, not knowing whether we'd have a future together, and then suddenly we didn't have any choice in the matter.'

'Thanks very much,' I say, miserably.

'No, Ben,' says my mum, walking over and sitting down next to me. 'We should be thanking you.'

'What do you mean?'

'Because we might not have had these wonderful thirty years together if you hadn't come along.'

'Twenty-nine,' corrects my dad, a split second before I do.

'And if that's not worth celebrating,' she says, picking up the bottle and filling up the champagne glasses, 'then I don't know what is.'

My mum hands me a glass, but I stop short of taking it from her. 'But isn't it all a little, well, false?'

'Why?' She smiles. 'Who's to say we wouldn't have stayed together if we hadn't had you?'

'You just did!'

'Yes, well I didn't mean it quite like that. Don't be so sensitive.'

'I'm sorry, Mum. I just . . . I mean, I've been looking for what you and Dad have for all this time, and all of a sudden, it's not what I thought it was. And now, I can't help feeling that I might have been wasting my time. I mean, you just got on with it and made the best of things. Maybe that's what I should have been doing all along.'

My dad takes the champagne glass from my mum, and

presses it into my hand. 'Ben,' he says, surprising me with the use of my actual name. 'Even though your mum and I have been very happy together, we've been lucky. And I think if there's one thing that we'd both agree on, it's that it's always better to have a choice.'

'Yes, but . . .'

'So, here's to us,' he says.

'All of us,' says my mum.

I look at the two of them, force a smile, and reluctantly clink my glass against theirs, downing the contents in one before heading miserably off to the toilet. Of course it's always better to have a choice, I think to myself, as I stare miserably at my reflection in the mirror. But the problem is, at the moment, I just don't think I've got one.

When I eventually walk back into the lounge, my dad is fiddling with the stereo, playing one of his old Frank Sinatra albums. He's convinced that music sounds better on vinyl, scratches and all, as opposed to from one of these 'seedys' as he insists on calling them. On top of this, he refuses to get a modern stereo, mainly because they don't seem to have record players on them any more. Instead, his is a hulking great black unit that takes up most of the far wall, full of flashing lights, little levers and knobs, and even a double cassette deck – the kind of thing that wouldn't look out of place in NASA mission control. When I don't say a word, but just slump down on the sofa, he comes and perches on the armchair opposite.

'Everything all right?'

I half–smile back at him. 'Where's Mum?'

My dad nods towards the serving hatch. 'Making us all something to eat.'

'Oh. Right. I'm not really hungry.'

My dad suddenly looks concerned. 'You sure you're okay?'

I meet his gaze for a moment, and then exhale loudly. 'I suppose so. I just . . . Well, I didn't think this would all be so complicated, that's all.'

He grins, sheepishly. 'Accidents happen, son.'

'No, not that. I mean *me*. Life. Everything.'

My dad shrugs. 'It's a difficult thing to get right, son. But it's worth the work. And when you finally do settle down, and maybe even start a family, it'll be the best thing you ever do.'

'But if that's the case, why did you stop at me?'

'Pardon?'

'Why did you just have the one child, if having me was so great? Did you resent the fact that I'd come along and forced you into marrying someone you couldn't possibly have been in love with?'

As soon as I've said those words, I regret them. Because not only are they unfair, they sound particularly harsh. But my dad doesn't look angry. Quite the opposite, in fact.

'Well, seeing as tonight seems to be the time for big revelations . . .'

I look up at him. 'What now? Don't tell me I've had

an evil twin all this time, and you keep him locked up in the attic?'

My dad smiles. 'Not quite. But you remember what your mum used to say to you all the time when you were growing up?'

'Eat your greens? Or that rubbish about going blind if . . .'

'Not that. I mean whenever you did something bad.'

'Oh. You mean "You'll be the death of me". She still does, from time to time. What about it?'

'Well, you nearly were. Your mum had a terrible time when she was pregnant. There were times when I thought I was going to lose her – and you, of course – and so I swore that if she pulled through . . .' My dad swallows hard. 'Well, I knew I could never put her through that again. And by the time you came along, and your mum had recovered, well, I was so happy that she'd survived, and so grateful to her for giving me you, how could I not be in love with her?'

'I'm sorry,' I say, awkwardly. 'I had no idea.'

My dad reaches over and ruffles my hair. 'You've got nothing to be sorry about, son. It wasn't your fault. And in fact you coming along made me realize how lucky I was, to have met your mother. And I might have let her get away if not for that.'

'But you really didn't have any idea? Beforehand, I mean? That Mum was the one for you?'

He smiles. 'No. But she did, and when you think about it, that's the important thing. We're men, Ben.

We might have discovered fire, or invented the wheel, but that was probably only because some woman some-where moaned at us that she was cold, or fed up with walking back from the shops. And, similarly, we don't go out looking for love. Sometimes it finds us. The trick is to recognize when it does, and put all your energy into making sure it doesn't get away.'

'Yes, but how?'

'Simple. Just remember one thing.'

'What's that?'

He smiles at me, then lowers his voice, conscious that my mum's in the kitchen. 'Happy wife, happy life.'

'I heard that,' comes the voice from through the serving hatch.

'Yes, but . . .' I sit there for a second, wondering how to phrase this. 'It just sounds a bit, well, strange. I mean, you find someone, marry them, and then have to work extra hard in an attempt to keep them happy, just so you can be happy. Why not cut out the middle man and just not marry them in the first place?'

'Where's the fun in that?'

'How do you mean?'

My dad nods towards the stereo. 'You're listening to a great example.'

'Frank Sinatra? Someone who was married about a hundred times, and yet always sang about love as if he knew all about it?'

'I was talking about the hi-fi,' says my dad, standing up and walking over to turn the volume up.

'Huh?'

He reaches down, and points to the graphic equalizer, where a series of lights are blinking on and off. 'Look. Here you're able to make minute adjustments to each aspect of the sound. If there's too much bottom, or the vocals are too loud . . .'

'You'd better not be talking about me again,' shouts my mum from the kitchen.

'. . . and so what you can do is get the ideal sound for everything you listen to. If you're not quite sure, just give it a little tweak, and see what response you get.'

'And what's your point?' I say, hoping myself that he's not talking about Mum now.

My dad smiles. 'My point, Ben, is that the record's the same for everyone, but after a bit of fiddling, you can get it to sound right for *you*. And that's just like marriage. The trick is making it how you want it. That way, you'll enjoy listening to it for the rest of your life. And when you get it right?' He stops and listens to Frank hitting one of his high notes. 'It's worth all the effort.'

'But how do I know what the right sound is for me? And where to adjust the, er, knobs?'

My dad shrugs. 'That's something you're going to have to work out for yourself. But before you can do that, there's one important thing you've got to do.'

'And what's that?'

'Buy yourself a record.'

'It's not that simple, Dad . . .'

'Yes, it is,' he scoffs. 'You already know what kind of

music you like. So just make sure you get something from within that genre and you'll be okay. For example, if you like Frank Sinatra, obviously you might enjoy someone like Tony Bennett. But you can't expect to get a Julio Iglesias album and hope it's going to sound the same. Or that Morrison's chap that you like.'

'*Morrissey*, Dad.'

'That's what I said.'

'And it's really as simple as that?'

He shrugs. 'Yup. Sometimes, you might not like it on the first listen. Or even the second. But, eventually, it's going to grow on you. And you'll end up loving the sound of it.'

I think I'm finally beginning to follow his drift. 'And even if you don't, you can use one of those graphic equalizer things to change her? I mean, it.'

My dad shakes his head. 'Not exactly.'

'Well, how exactly?' I say, trying to keep the desperation out of my voice.

'Because playing with your knobs,' he says, then looks at me admonishingly as I can't hide a snigger. 'I mean, making these fine adjustments doesn't actually change what you're listening to. It's still Frank. Or Tony. Or . . .'

'Morrison's,' I say, not wanting to fight a losing battle.

'Exactly. But what it does do is change how you *hear* it.'

As I watch him tap his foot along to 'Love and Marriage', which apparently go together like a horse and carriage, I think about what he's said. Maybe I *have* been a little too fussy. Perhaps I've been too intent on finding the perfect woman from day one, without realizing that maybe I could have just adjusted *my* perception. And if that's the case, have I already let her get away?

Look at my mum and dad. They were forced together, and yet they've made more than a decent go of it. Which surely means that if I've at least made an informed choice to be with someone – someone who I know wants to be with me, as opposed to someone whose feelings I don't have a clue about, or has added 'complications' – then I'll have a better chance of success.

I stare at the hi-fi, thinking about my recent exes. And while with Hope I'd have had to spend the whole time with her 'mute' button pressed, there is one rather obvious candidate.

I'd always thought you could never go back. But at the moment, I don't seem to be making much progress forwards. And although it might not be my ideal choice, right now, it looks like my only option.

Chapter 28

I spend a sleepless night thinking about it, and then as soon as I get up the next morning, fire off a text to the still-familiar number, and by the time I've emerged from the shower, my phone's already bleeping with a reply. I take a deep breath, and click on 'read', and sure enough, there's a response from Amy. *Call me* it says, perfectly punctuated as ever, even though it's just a text. *It'd be lovely to see you.* And while to anyone else, me getting back in touch like this might seem a bit cheeky – rude, even – to Amy, it of course makes sense. Because she'll think that's what I've finally seen.

'Ben,' she says, picking the phone up almost immediately. 'This is a pleasant surprise.'

I take the word 'pleasant' as a positive, although the tone of her voice suggests it's anything but a surprise, and plough on. 'Hi, Amy. How are you?'

'Never better.' With Amy, that's probably true, as not a day goes by without her doing a fitness class at the gym, or a training course at work, or even just reading some self-improvement manual. 'What can I do for you?'

Ah. Straight down to business, then. 'Well, I've just been, you know, doing some thinking. About us. And what you said.'

'Oh yes?'

'So I wondered if we could, you know, meet up. For a chat. If you're not busy, that is.'

There's a pause, which could be as much due to Amy consulting her diary as considering whether she wants to. 'Of course. That'd be lovely. Shall we say this evening? Seven o'clock? At Marcello's?'

I shudder. Marcello's is this little Italian wine bar on the High Street run by, well, Marcello, not surprisingly, although Marcello's real name is actually Martin, as I found out when my dad met him one parents' evening. Which might explain his bad Italian accent, and even worse Italian food.

'Sure,' I say obediently, remembering Amy's controlling ways. She was always a little frustrated that I never seemed to slot into her timescales, so I'd better start as I mean to go on.

'Great,' says Amy, breezily. 'See you later.' And before I can say anything else, or even change my mind, she's gone.

I stare at the phone for a few seconds, then slip it into my pocket, before heading off to my studio, where I spend the day reworking the abstract I started on a while ago. Although I still can't get it quite right, I resign myself to the fact that it'll do, which is kind of the conclusion I've come to where Amy's concerned. I mean, we had a good thing going. While it wasn't great, sometimes 'good' is perhaps as good as it gets. And there's a limit to the number of times you can start again.

By six-fifty, I'm already in the bar, nodding hello to Marcello as I take a seat in the corner. I'm hoping I don't have to make small talk with him as I wait, although I needn't have worried, as he seems more interested in fussing over Barney, the bar's resident Great Dane, who I'm sure Marcello only keeps to save on the hoovering bills, seeing how good he is at locating any scraps of food that manage to fall from the tables.

Amy arrives on the dot of seven, her face lighting up as she sees me. She still looks the same – but then Amy's looked the same for as long as I've known her, as if she's found a look that works, and she's sticking with it. Her hair's styled in a perfect bob, and she's wearing a shirt-and-trouser combination that shows off her gym-toned figure, and while I'm relieved that I still find her attractive, that's possibly not the major consideration any more. Amy was always pretty matter-of-fact. Calculating, even, although not in a nasty way. She just seemed to have this way of evaluating everything, even our relationship. And yet again, she seems to have been right.

I pick up my car keys and hide them in one hand, just in case I lose my nerve and need to turn a trip to the toilet into a quick getaway, then stand up to kiss her hello.

'Ben,' she says, her eyes flicking momentarily from my face to my hair, then back again.

'Thanks for coming. You're looking well,' I say as we sit down at the table, then curse myself under my breath. 'Well' is hardly the most complimentary of descriptions, given what I'm planning to ask her. And first impressions, and all that.

'Thanks.' Amy pats her stomach. 'Although a little too well, maybe. I've put on a few pounds, I'm afraid. Too many business lunches, not enough time at the gym.'

As I stare at her non-existent spare tyre, I have to stop myself from smiling. Amy always seemed to know the precise number of calories in any particular food, and then exactly how long she'd need to spend on the treadmill in order to work it off.

'Rubbish. You look . . .' I struggle for the appropriate word, wondering whether it's too late to start with the compliments, but then think *what the hell*. 'Great.'

'Thanks.' She does a quick inspection of what I'm wearing, rather than automatically replying. 'So do you. And your hair's so long now.'

I'm not quite sure how to respond to that, so don't, and instead pour her a glass of white wine from the bottle I've already ordered, refilling my glass at the same time. 'How's work?'

'Good. Busy. I'm a partner now.' She picks her glass up, and takes the tiniest of sips. 'But you didn't want to talk about work, did you, Ben? Unless you're thinking of coming back.'

I'm pretty sure she means 'to work', but then again, she might have sussed me out already. 'Well, no. But

I did want to talk to you about being a partner. My partner.'

It's a bad attempt at a joke, admittedly, but it makes Amy smile. 'Ben, we've been through that. You weren't looking for a commitment, remember? And I was.'

'Ah.' Suddenly I spot the potential flaw in my plan. Just because I haven't moved on, that doesn't mean Amy hasn't. Maybe she's agreed to meet me to rub my face in it. Teach me a lesson. Show me what I've lost. 'So, are you seeing anyone else?'

Amy shrugs. 'There's this one guy. But I wouldn't call it "seeing", exactly.'

I resist the temptation to ask Amy what she would call it. 'And is it . . . serious?'

She takes another sip of her wine. 'I haven't decided yet,' she says, as if it's completely up to her. Although knowing Amy, it probably is.

'Great. Because I've been doing a lot of thinking. About you and me. And where we, I mean, I, went wrong.'

As I pick my glass up and take a huge gulp, Amy puts hers down on the table and smiles at me triumphantly. 'I *knew* that that was what this was about. Weeks of no contact, and then this.' She shakes her head. 'I hoped you'd see sense eventually. Even though we had to split up for it to happen.'

I look at her across the table, wanting to tell her it's not all about seeing sense. But the truth is, I've begun to wonder whether she's right. Love and marriage might be two incompatible things – despite what Frank Sinatra has to say on the matter. After all, according to my dad, what you sometimes think is love at first sight is really only lust, and when that passes, what do you have left? Friendship? Respect? And maybe that's enough – or even what grows into love. Besides, I've never been in love, so how am I expected to recognize it when it comes along?

And let's face it – I've been going along with all this 'arrangement' stuff for the last few weeks, looking for some kind of 'spark', when what I should actually have been doing is taking it a little more literally. Because surely that's what marriage is – an arrangement. A contract between two people, designed to produce a common benefit – a life together, with a family, and a home. And while love might not be the important thing at the start, well, maybe that develops. Perhaps all it is is a mutual respect through an honouring of that contract. An appreciation of the other person, based upon all that they've done for you in the course of the marriage, and vice versa. And it's occurred to me that in actual fact, that's possibly not a bad thing.

Say that Amy agrees to marry me, and we get together, and buy a house, and start a family – maybe even get a dog. I've always wanted a dog. And while we might not be 'in love' when we start, surely after a while we'll feel that we are, because we'll have all these things together – a lovely home, great kids, and a dog. And because I'll appreciate what we've built together, and be grateful to her, even, then maybe that's the best I can hope for.

'Ben!'

'Huh?'

'You seem to have drifted away.'

'Sorry, Amy. I was just wondering about something.'

'What?'

'Whether you'd ... I mean ... we got on well, didn't we?'

'I suppose,' she says, a little puzzled.

'And we didn't have any problems. You know, in the bedroom department,' I say, conscious that I sound like my dad.

Amy blushes slightly. 'Not that I can recall.'

'And, in fact, the only problem I remember was with my lack of commitment.'

'Yes.'

'So if we, I mean I, you know, *fixed* that, do you think we might have a chance?'

Amy sits back in her chair. 'At what?'

'Well, at us. You know, er ...' I take a deep breath. 'Giving things another try.'

Amy regards me suspiciously for a moment. 'Don't play with me, Ben.'

'What do you mean?'

'You know what I mean. When we split up, I told you why it was. And are you now telling me that you've changed?'

I nod, a little frantically, it has to be said. 'Yes! I've

been doing some thinking. A lot of thinking, in fact. And I realized that I was just too immature at the time to make a proper commitment.'

'And you've matured in these last few weeks, have you?'

'Well, yes. So I wanted us to try again. You know. See if we couldn't make a go of it. More . . . permanently.'

For a moment, Amy looks like she can't quite believe what she's hearing. 'I'm sorry. You're asking me if I want to get back with you. For good?'

'Well, for better and for worse, actually. But there wouldn't be any "for worse". We've been through that. And now I realize what I want in a partner. A w . . .' I can't quite get the word 'wife' out of my mouth. '. . . oman. And it's someone like you.'

'Someone like me? Or actually me?'

'Actually you.'

Amy looks as if she almost seems to have been expecting this – a suspicion that's confirmed when she suddenly breaks into a smile. 'Oh, Ben, I knew you'd come round eventually.'

'Pardon?'

'When I dumped you, I was just being cruel to be kind. Trying to force you into action. Make you see what you – what *we* – had. And it's worked.' She beams across the table at me. 'But tell me one thing.'

'Sure.'

'What do I get out of it?'

'Huh?'

'What's my incentive. If we do get back together.'

'Well . . .' Ah. This strikes me as a little unfair. I mean, a couple of months ago, Amy wanted a commitment out of me, and now I'm giving her one, she's suddenly put the shoe on the other foot. Plus, I haven't really prepared anything. 'I'd love, honour, and obey, obviously.'

Amy raises her eyebrows at me, evidently thinking that the 'obey' part goes without saying. 'I could buy a pet that would give me that. I mean, for example, will you keep me in the style to which I've become accustomed?'

I give Amy a quick look up and down. As far as I can work out, that handbag's one of those expensive leather ones, and those shoes look more designer than Dolcis. 'Well, I'm quite happy for you to have a career, if that's what you want. I mean, if that's what you'd *prefer*.'

Amy gives me a flat-lipped smile. 'That's generous of you, Ben. But what if I decided to stop working?'

I start to laugh, because the idea of Amy giving up her career is about as preposterous as, well, me going back to accountancy, then stop abruptly when I see her expression. 'Well, you could, of course. If you wanted to.'

'And you'd support us both with your painting, would you?'

Ah. I should maybe have seen this coming. 'Well, if we lived frugally. Tightened our belts a little.'

'A lot, you mean?'

'I'm sure we'd get by.'

Amy shakes her head. 'I don't want to "get by", Ben.

So I want to know there's a possibility of you going back to work. Doing what you were trained for. What you're good at. A proper job. *If* it was required,' she adds sweetly.

I think about this for a second. And while I'm pretty sure there's no way Amy would ever want to give up her job, I can tell that she wants me to make some concession. Give her some reassurance that, yes, I'd support her if that was the case.

'Yes, Amy,' I say, crossing my fingers childishly under the table. 'There's a possibility.' About a one per cent possibility, I reckon, but don't dare say that out loud.

'And what happens if it all goes wrong?'

'Why would it go wrong?' I say, unable to imagine anything Amy ever doing not working out.

Amy shrugs. 'They do, don't they. Statistically, I mean. So, if we're going to go into this as some arrangement, then we need to make contingency plans, don't we?'

'That's not very romantic, is it?'

Amy puts her hand on mine, a gesture that seems rather inappropriate, given the subject matter. 'I'm just being practical, Ben.'

'Ah. Right.' I don't quite know what to say. Normally people only plan the details of their wedding. Not what's going to happen if they split up. But maybe she's right. Maybe this is the way to go about it, rather than risk becoming one of that ever-growing statistic. This way, there won't be any surprises. Although why does that last sentence fill me with a sense of dread? Perhaps because I like surprises. 'Fine. Well, we can sign one of those agreements, if you like.'

'And when are we going to do it?'

I look at my watch. 'Well, I hadn't worked any of that out, actually. I mean, a wedding takes planning, doesn't it? Organization.'

'Leave that to me,' says Amy, as if she's mentally ticking items off a list. 'It is supposed to be my big day, after all. And what about children?'

'Well, sometimes they can spoil it, can't they? I mean, crying in the church, and then messing around at the reception, or being sick from eating too much cake . . .' I stop talking, because Amy is shaking her head slowly.

'No, Ben. Not at the ceremony. *Our* children. I mean, that's one of the reasons for getting married, isn't it? To start a family.'

'Of course. But I thought we might want to have some . . .' I stop myself adding the words 'fun' and 'first'. 'I mean, thought we'd have some. Obviously.'

Amy smiles, showing me her perfect teeth this time, which tells me I've said the right thing. 'Because neither of us is getting any younger. And it's something we need to think about sooner rather than later.' She stops talking herself and looks at me strangely, possibly because when I catch sight of my reflection in the mirror on the wall behind her, I've gone a deathly shade of white. 'You do *want* kids, Ben, I take it.'

'Of course,' I say, realizing that to say anything else

would be to risk Amy getting up and walking away from the table – and, in fact, the whole arrangement. 'I was just wondering how . . .'

Amy rolls her eyes. 'Well, the traditional way. We have sex, and nine months later . . .'

'No. How *many*.'

'Well, I think two is a good number,' says Amy, who unlike me, has quite clearly thought about it. A lot. 'A boy and a girl. You can't really just have one, and with three, you risk the two-against-one scenario. No,' she says, as if her decision is final, 'three isn't really fair.'

On the parents, I want to say. *Because then they're outnumbered.* 'Right.'

'Which means we ought to start looking,' she continues. 'Soon.'

'Looking? For . . . a baby? Can't you, I mean, are you . . .?'

'For a house, silly. And one with at least four bedrooms. Because we don't want to have to move. Not with young children.'

'Right,' I say, thinking I don't want to have to move ever, with or without young children.

For a moment, this strikes me as ridiculous. Here we are, talking about how many children we're going to have, when we don't even know if we can have them, whereas Amy has already assumed – and wants to plan for – what's going to happen when we do. And this strikes me as so funny, that I can't help but laugh. Which clearly is the wrong thing to do.

Amy pulls her hand away, folds her arms and stares angrily across the table at me. 'What's so funny?'

'No, sorry, I was thinking of something else.'

'What else?'

'Er . . .'

'Come on. Something was obviously funny. So share it with the rest of us.'

It's like being told off at school, and I cringe in my chair, wondering if this is how all women think, and how far they plan in advance. 'I'm sorry, Amy. It's great that you're being so, er, professional about all of this. Really it is. It's just, well, don't you think we should be a bit more spontaneous? Try to have at least a little bit of, you know, fun?'

As soon as that particular 'f' word has left my lips, I worry I'm in trouble. But Amy seems to see the funny side of it.

'Oh, there'll be a lot of fun, Ben,' she says, although she makes the word sound a little scary. 'I'll make sure of that. I mean, you still fancy me, don't you?'

'Of course.' That's easy to answer. Amy's pretty, with a nice figure, and breasts that are slightly too large for the rest of her – what's not to fancy? Plus her attractiveness is amplified by the fact that apart from Dawn, where I nearly died in the act, I haven't had sex for a while. But judging from her reaction, 'of course' isn't the correct response.

'What's that supposed to mean?'

'What's what supposed to mean?'

'"Of course".'

'Pardon?'

'I said do you still fancy me, and you said, "of course". As if you were bound to. Not "oh yes", or anything positive like that, but "of course", as if I ticked a few of your standard boxes. Like it was an automatic response, or something.'

What do I say now? Because while I know Amy is making me work a little, and looking for a compliment or two, to be honest, with most men, it *is* an automatic response. But I have a sneaking suspicion that's not going to be a good enough explanation.

'Well, er, what I meant was that, you know, physically, there are obvious elements of your body shape, that do, you know, turn me on.'

I've meant it as a compliment. But judging by Amy's reaction, she hasn't taken it as one. 'But that sounds like you're just objectifying me. Like you have no control over whether you get a hard-on when you stare at my chest.'

'I don't. Mean that,' I add, quickly. 'I mean, for us blokes, a lot of it is to do with the physical response. Don't blame me, blame a hundred thousand years of evolution. I mean, what do you want me to say, that I'm turned on by your intellect?'

'Some men find smart women sexy.'

Ah. And while she's partly right, in that some men say they find smart women sexy, that's actually because they like their tits, and want to charm them into bed by saying they're turned on by their intellect, whereas, actually, they're playing on the fact that they're stupid enough to be taken in by that sort of lame line. But I can't explain this to Amy. Not without giving away secrets that are passed down from generation to generation. And at least *I'm* smart enough to recognize that I have to tread carefully here.

'Amy. You are. Very sexy, I mean. And smart. And while even if you were brain dead, or admitted to liking *Emmerdale*, or something, which amounts to the same thing, I'd still fancy you. And that's not a bad thing, but a compliment. Physically I find you very attractive. And certainly more than attractive enough to sleep with.'

I look at her carefully, hoping I've got away with it, even though as a man, that description would probably apply to more than seventy-five per cent of the female population. Maybe more, depending on how long it's been.

'I'm sorry, Ben,' she says, visibly relaxing a little. 'It's just that, well, it's not the same for a woman. We're not quite so, you know, fickle.'

Yeah, right, I'm thinking. If Brad Pitt suddenly walked in and sat down at the next-door table, I'm sure I'd have your full attention.

'I know,' I say. 'So you shouldn't be so attractive, should you?'

Amy smiles at me, then reaches over and takes my hand again, and because I've seen that smile from her before, I know I'm home and dry. It's been easier than

I thought – a little too easy, perhaps – and maybe a little scary at the same time. But there's nothing for it.

'So, you will?'

She raises one eyebrow. 'Will what?'

'Go back out with me. With a view to, you know, a more permanent arrangement.'

She squeezes my hand even tighter, squashing my car keys – which I'd forgotten I was still holding – painfully into my palm. 'Of course I will, you idiot. I don't know what took you so long.'

'Great. Well, we ought to celebrate,' I say, for some reason feeling the opposite. 'Champagne?'

Amy looks at her glass of wine, and I notice that she's hardly touched it. 'Not for me. I've got a Yogalates class first thing in the morning. You go ahead, though.'

'Oh. Right.' I'm suddenly reminded of one of the reasons I got Amy to dump me, to use Ash's words. We didn't do anything spontaneous. And while the fact that she won't even celebrate our getting back together is more than a little depressing, it also occurs to me that maybe she's right. Why should we do what everyone else does, and drink a glass or two of expensive fizzy wine just to toast the fact that we're going to get married? Far better that we just celebrate by drinking in each other, so to speak. 'Well, should we at least kiss? You know, to mark the occasion?'

Amy looks horrified. 'Not here, Ben. Some of my clients might be watching.'

I look around the deserted bar, and apart from a

bored-looking Marcello, there's no one else around. 'Well, shall we go back to mine?'

'No, thank you,' says Amy.

'Well, what about yours?' I say, hoping her reaction is to do with my flat.

She lets go of my hand. 'Weren't you listening, Ben? I've got an early class. Besides, we've only just met.'

Yet again, Amy's matter-of-factness slaps me in the face, or, rather, pours a bucket of cold water over my groin. 'What do you mean, only just met? We went out for the best part of a year.'

'Yes, well, I don't want you thinking that I'm easy, do I? I mean, you could just be spinning me a line.'

'I wouldn't.'

'You're a *man*, Ben. Of course you would.'

'But . . .'

'In fact, I've just had an idea. So it's "yes" on one condition. You're going to have to prove yourself to me.'

'Prove myself? How?'

'If you're really as committed as you say you are, then you'll just have to wait until we're officially engaged.'

'Wait for what?'

'Sex.' Amy sits back in her chair and folds her arms, obviously pleased with the brilliance of her plan. 'Yes. If you can wait until you've actually put a ring on my finger, then that'll prove to me that you're serious.'

'Are *you* serious?'

Amy looks at me across the table. 'Deathly.'

As I meet her gaze, I tell myself that I can do this. Even if it means not doing it, if you see what I mean. And besides, the jeweller's will be open first thing Monday morning.

Chapter 29

First I have to tell my mum and dad, of course, and after the fun they've had over the past few weeks, I'm hoping they'll be pleased, not to mention relieved. But when I let myself in through the kitchen door, the first thing I hear is a strange noise coming from the front room, followed by my dad's voice.

'You're not holding it in the right way.'

'I'm holding it just like it says in the book,' says my mum. 'And, anyway, I'm the one on top. So you keep your comments to yourself. And watch your aim.'

My dad laughs. 'I'm pointing it at the hole,' he says. 'But I can't seem to get it in. And why is it making that funny noise?'

'It vibrates when you do it wrong.'

'I'm not doing it wrong.'

'Well, maybe you're doing it too hard,' says my mum. 'No wonder your balls are flying everywhere.'

Oh *no*. It sounds like they're, well, I don't want to think about what it sounds like they're doing, particularly given the strange porno-film music I can hear in the background. Telling them about Amy and me can wait, I decide, and what's more, I'm going to have to make my escape as quietly as possible. But as I tiptoe back towards the kitchen door, I accidentally bump against a chair, which makes a loud scraping noise on the floor. *Bollocks*.

'Is that you, Ben?' calls my mum. 'Because we've already had our dinner.'

For a moment, I think I might be better off not answering, but then they might think they're being burgled, and I don't want to frighten them. 'Er, yes.'

My dad pops his head through the serving hatch. 'Come and join us,' he says, looking a little red in the face. 'You can have a go with your mum. Give me a rest. Although be warned, she's rather good.'

'How about it, Ben,' calls my mum. 'Want to play around?'

Oh. My. God. I'm either having a nightmare, or I've stumbled into the kind of thing that apparently happens round at Dawn's parents' house. 'Er, no. That's okay.'

'Well, come and watch me and your mum at it,' says my dad, disappearing back through the hatch.

'No. Thanks,' I say, thinking about making a run for the door, when my dad walks into the kitchen. Fortunately, he's fully dressed.

'Come on,' he says. 'It'll be fun.'

Unable to see a way out of this, I follow him nervously back into the lounge, only to find my mum standing in front of the television. 'What are you doing?'

'Your dad and I are weeing,' says my mum, proudly. 'It's great fun.'

'What?'

'It's one of these new Nintendo game things,' says my dad, pointing to the small white box plugged into the TV. 'Your mum and I won one. In the bowls club raffle.'

'And I've just beaten your dad at golf,' announces my mum.

'Beginner's luck,' says my dad, winking at me.

'And tennis. And ten-pin bowling,' says my mum proudly.

'Yes, well,' huffs my dad, picking his remote control up. 'Did you want a game, son? Or were you just after something to eat?'

'No. Thanks. I've, er, got something to tell you.'

My mum smiles, then turns back to the screen. 'Oh yes?' she says, practising a couple of golf swings, narrowly missing the light fitting with the white plastic golf club she's holding.

'Yes. Well, Amy and me. I've, I mean, we've decided to give things another go. In fact, more than another go. We're, er, getting married.'

For a moment, my mum and dad don't say a word, but just stare at each other, and then my dad puts the remote control down on the coffee table and walks over to where I'm standing. 'Congratulations, son,' he says, shaking me firmly by the hand.

'Yes, Ben,' says my mum, following him over and enveloping me in a huge hug. 'Congratulations.'

'You don't seem that pleased,' I say, a little surprised at their muted reactions.

'Neither do you, Ben,' says my mum.

'I am. I'm just trying to get used to it. That's all. But you're okay with it?'

'Of course,' says my dad. 'We love Amy.'

'Just as long as you do too,' says my mum enigmatically.

'I will,' I say. 'I'm sure.'

'You will?' says my dad. 'But you don't now?'

'Well, we've only just got back together, haven't we? I mean, it's all a bit, well, sudden.'

'You haven't got her pregnant have you, son?' asks my dad.

'No, of course not. Or at least, not yet.'

He folds his arms. 'So, you're doing this for the right reasons?'

I look at them both. 'Yes,' I say, perhaps still trying to convince myself. 'Yes, I am. Because the one thing this whole process has taught me is that marriage is just an arrangement whereby we men give up our freedom in return for companionship. And that's the best we can ever ask for. So marriage, kids, the whole nine yards, here I come.'

My dad sits down on the sofa, and indicates for me to sit down next to him. 'An impartial observer might say you were a little bit cynical.'

'Or realistic,' I say. 'In fact, I'm just repeating how
Amy feels about it. She's a businesswoman, after all, and
that's what this is to her. Just another deal. An arrangement. And we've done our due diligence, or whatever it
is when two companies decide to perform a merger, and
it looks like being a goer.'

'A what?' says my mum.

'A goer,' I say, even though Amy quite obviously
isn't. Although, as I say this, I start to get a little worried.
Because what if this is the way Amy feels about everything. What if I really am just a hopeless romantic who
happens to believe in a little more than this? But then
again, look where that's got me. In fifteen years of
dating, I've not met anyone who's made me feel that
way. So maybe it's me who's wrong. And Amy's got it
right.

My mum sighs. 'Why you've remained unmarried for
so long amazes me. And how many children does Amy
want?'

'One of each.'

'Three, then?' jokes my dad.

'Really?' My mum widens her eyes. 'She's that
specific?'

'Yup,' I say, sure that she's probably even picked out
names for them.

'And when is she planning to start this family,
exactly?' asks my mum. 'Assuming you're not – what is
it you young people say – firing blanks, that is.'

My dad puts a protective arm around my shoulder,

which makes a pleasant change from the usual hair-ruffling. 'No son of mine would fire blanks.'

'Er, well, she's just been made a partner at work, so I imagine she'll want to consolidate her position there for a while, and then maybe fit them in around the end of the financial year.'

My mum rolls her eyes. 'That's very organized of her.'

'That's Amy.'

'And what if you fail to provide her with the precise mix of offspring she's after?'

I shrug. 'I don't know. I mean, it's hardly up to me what kind of kids she'll, I mean, we'll have. That's down to the man upstairs.'

My mum looks surprised. 'Mister Williams?'

'No, Mum. Not upstairs from my flat. God.'

'I'm sorry, Ben,' says my dad. 'I just don't think you can map things out like this.'

'You have *met* Amy, haven't you?'

My dad laughs. 'No, I mean that life has a way of throwing things at you that you weren't expecting.'

'Like me, for example?'

My dad suddenly looks a little hurt, and I feel instantly guilty. 'Well, yes. But we coped with it. And were so pleased with the way it turned out. Whereas if you're expecting things to happen to order ...' He and my mum exchange glances. 'Life's just not like that.'

I want to tell them that Amy's is, and if I'm along for the ride with her, then surely mine will be too. But at the same time, I know exactly what he's getting at, and that these surprises are what makes life so much fun. This unpredictability is what enriches things – unless you're Amy, of course – but for some of us, if you always know what's going to be around the corner, why bother going there?

My dad puts his arm around my shoulder again. 'Listen, son. If this is what you want then of course we'll give you our blessing. But you've just got to be sure. After all, once you have children, there's really no backing out of this.'

I smile back at him, remembering this evening's discussions with Amy, and the promises I've made, and realize that actually it's probably already too late. 'Thanks, Dad.'

'Well, in that case . . .' My mother walks out of the front room and into the kitchen, but instead of starting to make some tea, she starts rummaging around in one of the sideboard drawers. 'Here,' she says, walking back into the lounge and placing a small black felt-covered box down on the coffee table in front of me.

'What's this?'

My mum nods towards the box. 'Open it.'

I do as I'm told, to reveal a gold ring with a small cluster of diamonds on the top – the kind of thing that makes the crowd on the *Antiques Roadshow* gasp. I'm no jewellery expert, but from what I can tell, it's quite old. And quite beautiful. 'Mum, I can't . . .'

'It was my mother's,' explains my mum. 'And she'd have wanted you to have it.'

'But . . .'

'Well, not you, exactly,' she explains. 'But the girl you're going to marry. And if Amy's going to be that girl then . . .'

As my mum stifles a sniff, I snap the box shut and give her a hug. It's a wonderful gesture, and a fabulous ring, and given its history, it's not surprising that my mum's quite emotional about this.

Although as I put the box carefully back down onto the table, I can't help but wonder if Amy's going to feel the same way.

Chapter 30

Amy's busy on Sunday, so we've arranged to meet in Marcello's on Monday at seven to 'seal the deal' – her words, not mine. I'm running late, as I've forgotten the ring, and have to rush round to my parents' house on the way, but no one's home, so I just let myself in and grab the small black box from where my mum's left it on the sideboard, before racing round to the restaurant. Unusually, Marcello's is quite busy for a Monday evening, but as usual Amy's there on time.

'I thought you'd got cold feet,' she says, as I come hurrying across to the table, nearly tripping over Barney on the way.

'No.' I pat my pocket to check the box is still in there. 'Not at all. You still . . .' I struggle to find better words than 'up for it?', and fail, and, besides, don't want to appear desperate, so decide to change the subject. 'Shall we order?'

'Why not?' says Amy, picking up the menu.

In fact, so successful is my changing the subject, and so much appears to have happened in Amy's life since

I saw her last, that it's not until we've finished our pizzas that I decide to broach the subject.

'So,' I say. 'About the other night.'

Amy leans across and dabs at a spot of tomato sauce on the side of my mouth with the corner of her napkin, a regular habit of hers which I always found annoying. 'What about it?'

'I mean, do we, you know, have a deal?' I say, realizing I should be grateful that she doesn't lick the napkin first.

Amy smiles at me. 'I suppose so.'

'Okay then.' I fish around in my pocket to retrieve the ring box, then push my chair back and get down on one knee beside the table.

'What are you doing?' says Amy. 'Have you dropped something?'

'No. I just thought I'd do it properly.'

'People are *watching*.'

'Let them,' I say, suddenly aware that all eyes in the busy restaurant are on me, although I'm sure it's not going to be as embarrassing as I always imagined it might be given that Amy's already told me that she's going to say 'yes'. However, what I haven't reckoned on is Barney, who seems to think that my coming down to his level means that we're on for a game. Before I can stand up, he rushes over and jumps on me, tail wagging frantic- ally, his huge paws on my shoulders, and knocks me over onto my back. 'Barney. No!' I say, although a little too late, as he proceeds to lick my face enthusiastically, doing a better job of cleaning it than Amy's napkin had earlier.

'Ben, just get up, will you?' hisses Amy.

'I'm trying,' I say. 'But it's tough when you've got half a ton of Great Dane on you.'

'Barney! Sit.' Amy stands up and clicks her fingers, and the huge dog looks up, a little scared by her tone, as, to be honest, am I, then sits down obediently.

'Sorry about that,' says Marcello, rushing over and grabbing Barney by the collar.

'That's fine,' I say, getting back on one knee as he leads him away. 'No harm done.'

'Now will you get up?' says Amy.

'No. Now, where was I?' I ask, determined to soldier on – after all, I'm only going to be doing this once in my life, hopefully, and I want to do it right. 'Amy. Amy Watson. Miss Amy Watson ...' I try all three versions, trying to work out which one sounds right. 'Will you marry me?' To a smattering of applause from the other diners, I flip open the lid of the ring box with a flourish and hold it out to her, then watch in horror as her face falls.

'Ben, I ...'

'You're not going to say "no", are you?'

'I can't say yes.'

'Why not?'

'Because you aren't offering me anything.'

I'm rather taken aback by this. 'Yes, I am. I mean, I might not have the best job in the world, but I'll be a good husband, and ...' I stop trying to justify myself, because it seems a little unfair to ask me to do that now. 'I thought we already discussed this?'

'No. In the box. There's nothing there.'

'What?' I flip it round to face me and peer disbelievingly at the black felt slit where the ring should be, then put the box to my ear and give it a shake, just to check the ring hasn't somehow fallen through.

Amy glares down at me. 'Is this some kind of joke?'

'No!' I get down on my hands and knees, careful to check that Barney is nowhere nearby, and search around on the floor underneath the table, but can't find anything apart from a shrivelled piece of pepperoni that he's somehow missed, then stand up and run my hands frantically through my pockets. 'It was my grandmother's engagement ring. My mum's going to kill me.'

Amy's face falls. 'Your . . . grandmother's?'

'Yes. It was gold, with a cluster of diamonds . . .' I stop describing it, partly because I don't want to ruin the surprise, but also because I can sense that Amy isn't best pleased.

'You were going to give me a *second-hand* ring?'

'No. Well, yes. I mean, it was antique, rather than second-hand . . .' I say, then stop talking, imagining my mum's face when I tell her I've lost the ring. 'I'll explain in a moment. Wait there.'

I leave a stunned Amy at the table, then race outside and find my car, hoping it might somehow be in there. I drive to the nearest petrol station, where I can hunt through the car under the glare of their lights, but that doesn't turn the ring up either, and after a few more minutes of frantic searching, realize there's nothing for it. I'm going to have to come clean, and so jump into the car and head back to my parents' house. When I walk into the kitchen, my mum looks up from where she seems to be going through the kitchen drawers.

'Hello, Ben,' she says. 'Everything all right?'

I realize that I'm sweating, and breathing heavily. 'Yes. Fine, thanks. You?' I say, chickening out from telling her straight away.

'Yes.' My mum frowns. 'Except . . .'

'Except?'

'I can't seem to find the ring box.' She stares quizzically at the sideboard. 'It was here earlier, and now it's gone. You wouldn't know anything about that, would you?'

'Er . . .' I can't quite bring myself to admit that I might have lost the most precious thing my mother owns. Not until I've at least had a bit longer to look for it myself. 'No.'

My mum shrugs. 'Oh well. I can always get another one, I suppose.'

'Huh?'

'I'll just head into town tomorrow and pick one up. If you're sure you need it?'

'Yes. Yes, I do.' I'm a little confused, particularly considering the big deal she made of giving it to me in the first place. 'But, another one would do, I suppose,' I add, remembering my prospective fiancée's initial reaction to the offer of a 'second-hand' – her words – ring. 'Although perhaps I should get it?'

'Don't worry,' says my mum. 'It's no bother.'

'You're being very good about this. I mean, what about the sentimental value?'

She smiles. 'Oh, it's not the original one. I lost that a long time ago. This was just a cheap one I got from the pound shop. Though I don't know if I can show my face in there again, given what happened between you and that Dawn.'

'The *pound shop*?' Just as well I didn't present it to Amy. 'Well, you might as well have this back, then,' I say, pulling the ring box out of my pocket and putting it down on the kitchen table.

'There it is,' says my mum, shaking her head at me, before fishing around in her handbag and removing a small plastic bag with my grandmother's engagement ring in it. 'I wondered what had happened to the box. What on earth were you doing with it?'

'Well, I . . . What were you doing with the ring?'

'It needed a clean, didn't it? So I've been soaking it in some of that stuff your father uses to oil the lawnmower. Seems to have done the trick, too,' she says, holding it up to the light and admiring the shine.

I take it from her, careful not to cover it with finger-prints, and slip it back into the slot in the box. 'Great. Thanks.'

'I do hope Amy likes it,' says my mum, smiling proudly at me. 'Such a nice girl.'

Amy. *Bollocks!* I've left her sitting in the restaurant. On her own. For the best part of half an hour. I lean over and kiss my mum on the cheek.

'Gotta go,' I say, stuffing the box back into my pocket, then sprinting outside to where I've parked the car. Fortunately, when I run breathlessly back in through the restaurant door, Amy's still sitting at the table.

As she smiles up at me, for a moment I think that maybe I have got away with it. After all, I've only been gone for thirty-two minutes, and I could just have been in the toilet, I suppose. I take a couple of deep breaths in an attempt to regain my composure, then stroll nonchalantly back towards the table.

'Sorry about that,' I say loudly, placing a hand on my stomach, and puffing out my cheeks. 'That pepperoni must have been playing tricks on me.'

'You had the quattro formaggi, Ben,' says Amy, acidly. 'So unless you ate that piece you found on the floor . . .'

I sit back down at the table. 'Ah. No. Of course not. Must have been the cheese. In fact, that's a disease, isn't it? Mixing my cheeses?'

Amy smiles, but there's no humour in her expression. 'Myxomatosis, Ben. And that's something that rabbits get.'

'Ah.'

Amy folds her arms and glares at me across the table. 'So, you want me to believe that you've been in the toilet all this time?'

'No,' I whisper back, glancing around the room, where the assembled diners still seem to be looking at us. 'I want them to believe that.'

'What, as opposed to the fact that you got down on one knee to propose to me – without a ring – and when I said no, you legged it out of the door, leaving me sitting here on my own?'

'Er, yes. As opposed to that. But I had to go and find it.'

I reach into my pocket again, then have a momentary heart attack when I can't locate the ring, but realize that that's only because I'm looking for it in the wrong pocket. But when I put the box down on the table, Amy waves me away. 'Not here, Ben. Or, at least, not again this evening.'

'I'm sorry, Amy. My mum . . .'

I start to explain, but Amy turns away, though that's primarily to put her PIN into the credit card terminal that an awkward-looking Marcello has just brought to the table. And later, as I drop her home, I know better than to ask to come in – after all, I've already had enough rejection for one night. Besides, given Amy's 'condition', what would be the point? I've still got the ring, which means I'm still not fully engaged.

I just hope that's not true in both senses.

Chapter 31

When I meet Ash at the pub the following evening, he's looking rather pleased with himself, probably due to the fact that Priti's coming down next weekend for their engagement party. I, on the other hand, must be giving the opposite impression, as his face falls when he spots me walking in.

'What are you looking so depressed about?' he says, sliding the pint he's bought me across to my side of the table.

'Amy and me are back together,' I say, downing half of my beer in one go. 'And I'm not depressed.'

Ash does a double-take. 'Amy? Your ex-girlfriend Amy?'

'Yup.'

'The one about whom you said, and I quote, "If I ever go near her again, shoot me, because if you don't, I might shoot her"?'

'I don't think I was quite that harsh, was I?'

He nods. 'That's the polite version. And I thought the

only way she'd take you back was if you agreed to marry
her?'

'So, congratulate me.'

Ash stares at me for a second or two, although judging by his expression, breaking out the champagne
is the last thing on his mind. 'What happened to her
being too manipulative. Too controlling. Not enough
fun?'

I shrug resignedly. 'Ash, all that kind of stuff matters
when you're going out with someone, admittedly. But
this is different. I'm getting married. And those things
aren't important any more.'

'They are to me. And they used to be to you. Besides,
you sound like you're trying to convince yourself.'

'But it's different with you and Priti, isn't it? I mean,
you've got all that to look forward to, before it starts
getting a bit, well, routine, and by the time it does, it'll
be too late for you to do anything about it.'

Ash grins. 'Thanks very much. Now *I'm* depressed.'

'And, anyway, with Amy I know I've got my whole
life mapped out. To a timetable. And it means I can plan,
you know?'

'Plan what – your funeral? Because you're going to
die of boredom. And sooner rather than later.'

'This means you don't want to be my best man, I
take it?'

Ash looks at me strangely, as if he can't believe that
I'm actually serious. 'So you're actually engaged?'

'Yes. Well, not officially,' I say. 'But we will be. And

sooner rather than later, hopefully,' I add, explaining Amy's condition to him.

'And have you discussed when it's going to be? The big day, I mean?'

I shake my head. 'Again, sooner rather than later, I think. After all, no point in hanging around. Besides, that's Amy's department.'

'But you're happy to leave everything up to her? Let her run the show?'

I nod. 'Why not? Might as well get used to it. I mean, think about it. With Amy on the case, I can get on with my career. Stop wasting time on this stupid wife hunt, and concentrate on my art. There's something comforting about knowing that I pretty much just have to turn up and do my thing at allotted times. Everything – the house, even starting a family, will be run by her. And so I can just get on with my life, safe in the knowledge that she's in control.'

And the more I think about it, the more I see how it can work. Because it'll be like having a secretary. A place for everything, and everything in its place. I won't have to worry about any of the major decisions in life, because quite frankly Amy's already made them. *And* I'll get to sleep with her, assuming she's got a slot available, so to speak. In fact, it's a brilliant plan. Although Ash doesn't seem to agree.

'A control freak, you mean?'

'No. She's not. She just knows what she wants. And maybe that's a good thing for someone like me. To have all those practical decisions taken out of my hands, so I can just focus on the creative side of my work.'

'Jesus, Ben. It sounds like what you need is a house-keeper more than a wife.'

'Yes, well, I couldn't have sex with a housekeeper, could I?'

He grins. 'You can't have sex with Amy either, can you?'

'That's not the point. Besides, she's not being un-reasonable, if you think about it. All she's doing is asking me to prove myself to her. My commitment. And it's a small price to pay.'

'So why aren't you rushing round to Amy's tonight to give her the ring, instead of sitting here having a beer with me?'

'Because there's plenty of time for that kind of thing,' I say, trying to convince Ash as much as myself.

Ash looks unconvinced. 'Okay. Say the two of you do get married. How long before she tries to make you give up your art and go back to accountancy?'

I shudder at the thought, and decide not to tell Ash about the promise I made her the other day. 'She'd never do that. I mean, she knows that it's what makes me, well, me.'

He raises one eyebrow. 'What happened to all that stuff you were saying about how she wants to turn you into a slightly different you? A you who has respon-sibilities. Commitments. And that might mean you getting a proper job. After all, what happens when you start a family? Who's going to be the breadwinner then?'

'I don't think Amy will ever give up work.'

'Hello?' Ash leans over, and knocks twice on the table. 'What about the actual birth. She'll have to take a least a few months off.'

'I'm not so sure. Knowing Amy, she'll probably arrange to have the child in her lunch hour so she can be back at her desk for the afternoon.'

'But . . .' Ash stares at me for a second or two, as if he's deciding whether to tell me something or not. And then obviously makes his decision. 'You don't think you're rushing into it?'

For some reason, that hits a nerve, and I can't help but have a go back at Ash. 'Look who's talking.'

'Pardon?'

'I mean, tell me, Ash. Why are you getting married, exactly?'

Ash looks at me strangely over the top of his pint glass. 'Well, like you said the other day, it's what you do, isn't it?'

'Okay. And why is Priti doing it. Same reason?'

Ash shrugs. 'I guess so. Plus, she really wants kids, so . . .'

'And what about you?' I ask, thinking how familiar this sounds.

'What about me what?'

'Do you want kids?'

Ash takes a mouthful of beer, and nods. 'I guess so. I haven't really thought about it.'

'Why not?'

He shrugs again. 'I dunno. You just don't, do you? Anyway, why the twenty questions?'

'That was only four. And I've got a lot more than twenty.'

Ash puts his pint down. 'Okay,' he says patiently. 'Fire away.'

'It's just . . .' I pause for a minute, wondering where to start. 'I mean, the kids thing, for instance. How many blokes do you know who actually, genuinely want them, rather than just go along with it?'

Ash thinks for a moment. 'Er . . .'

'I mean, do you absolutely, genuinely, definitely want to have children?'

He shifts uncomfortably in his seat. 'Well, I suppose so.'

'Suppose? That doesn't sound very definite.'

'Yeah, but . . .' Ash picks up his pint again. 'I mean, I'd never really thought about it, to be honest. And then, when Priti brought it up, I realized that yes, I might fancy it after all. Plus, it's part of the deal, isn't it? You know. The whole marriage thing.'

I shake my head. 'But that's where you're wrong. It's not that good a deal, is it? Because a good deal suggests you both get some kind of return from it. And what do you get out of it?'

'What's your point, Ben?'

'All I'm saying is, if you're a businessman, and if you look at it in a business sense, well, it doesn't make any.'

'Why not?'

'Okay. Businesses are all about assets, right? So what you're doing is investing your hard-earned funds in one asset . . .'

'Priti, right?'

'Exactly. And over the years, she's going to get older. Lose her looks. Maybe put on weight. Start . . . depreciating.'

Ash actually looks depressed now, and I feel a little guilty for ruining his earlier good mood. 'Thanks very much.'

'I don't mean it personally. I just mean that, from an investment point of view, it doesn't make any sense. It's like buying a car. The older it gets, the more mileage it has, the more value it loses.'

'And women are the same?'

'Yes. And men, come to think of it. Unless they add value in another way. Bring something extra to the table.'

'Well, in this case, we both do. I get a gorgeous wife, who's going to be a fantastic mother, and Priti gets, well, me. And that's a win–win situation any way you look at it,' he says, clinking his glass against mine.

'So, it really is an arrangement? In both senses of the word.'

Ash nods. 'Isn't that what all marriage should be? As you say, it's just like a business deal, after all.'

'But isn't that a bit, well, practical?'

He looks at me, an amused expression on his face. 'So come on, let's hear it.'

'Hear what?'

'Your theory.'

'What theory?'

He smiles, then sits back in his chair. 'Every time you do this, it's because you've worked out some great theory about life. And the problem is that they're exactly that. Theoretical. Not in the real world.'

He's caught me. 'I'm sorry, Ash. And I don't mean to have a go at you, or what you and Priti are doing. Because it's great. It really is. I just . . .' I shake my head. 'I mean, I do want to get married. And to Amy. I'd just be a lot more comfortable if I could see some logic in it. And at the moment, the only reason I can see that people get married, and do the whole family thing is because they're afraid of being alone. And I wish there was a little bit more to it than that.'

'Afraid of being alone?'

'Yup. We're social animals.'

'Some of us more animal than others,' says Ash, trying to lighten the mood a little. 'Dawn, apparently, for example.'

'I'm serious. We need other people. And what's the only way to guarantee we'll have them as we grow older? Tie ourselves to one – even though it doesn't make a lot of sense – by doing this thing called marriage.'

'Huh?'

'Think about it. In the past, people had big families because the survival rate for children wasn't all that great, so you had to hedge your bets. Nowadays, you don't need that. And, in fact, the greenest thing you can do is not have kids, otherwise the earth is going to be over-populated and run out of resources. And yet people are still having two, three, or even more. And do you want to know why that is?'

Ash grins. 'If I said no, you'd only tell me anyway.'

'It's because divorce is more common. And so by having the children, there are more people around who aren't going to leave you.'

Ash shakes his head. 'But what about all these people who actually *want* to get married? Are you telling me that they're just deluding themselves?'

'Yes!'

'What about those who are, you know, "in love"?'

'Well ...' I open my mouth to start talking, and then shut it again.

'Don't tell me,' says Ash. 'You've got a theory about that, too.'

'Well, not a theory so much as an ... observation.'

Ash takes a deep breath. 'Go on, then.'

'Well, answer one question first. Do you love Priti? Honestly.'

'It's early days,' says Ash.

'But you're still going ahead and marrying her?'

'Yes.'

'Without being in love with her? Why?'

Ash considers this for a moment. 'Because I can see that I might.'

This stops me in my tracks. How on earth can you

marry someone purely on the basis that you might, conceivably, one day, love them? 'Surely if they tick a few basic boxes, then you can say the same about most women?'

Ash laughs. 'Perhaps.'

'Well, in that case, that's my point. And I think too many men confuse love with gratitude. They're grateful that a woman will go out with them. Marry them. Have sex with them, even. And agree not to do any of this with anyone else at the same time. And how can you still love someone who cheats on you? Who gambles away the money you'd use to feed your kids? Because that's an abuse of trust. And yet when you see this happen, what's the one thing the wronged party always says? "But I still love them." Pathetic.'

'You've been watching too many episodes of *EastEnders*.'

'Maybe so. But it's still a valid point.'

'So I shouldn't get married?' says Ash.

'Not at all. You and I are doing the same thing. Because when you think about it, it is an arrangement. Tit for tat. And that's why love shouldn't come into it. Because that only muddies the waters.'

'So what you're saying is that marriage isn't anything personal. It's just business?'

'Precisely.'

Ash shakes his head. 'But this is for life, Ben. Not just for Christmas. Especially if you have kids, because then you've got to at least stick around until they're off your hands, so that makes, what, twenty-five years, give or take? And are you prepared to spend the next twenty-five years with this woman? And it's not just twenty-five, is it? Because usually, by that time, life, the kids, and the marriage have tired you out so much that you don't have the energy to leave.' He takes another mouthful of beer. 'It's like they say. You could murder someone, and still be out in half the time. In fact . . .'

'In fact what?'

'That's a great business idea. You could murder her. And then at least you'd get away without having to pay the divorce settlement.'

'What?'

'I'm serious. Marry Amy, then murder her, rent your house out while you're in prison – twelve years later, you'll be free – and mortgage free as well. Brilliant.'

'Don't be ridiculous. And who are "they", exactly?'

Ash looks at me. 'What are you talking about?'

'You said "It's like they say". Who are they? These people who know everything about everything.'

Ash shrugs. 'Well, it's just a figure of speech, isn't it?'

'Well, it's a stupid figure of speech. Marriage isn't something you enter into thinking "Oh well, if it goes wrong, there's always divorce". That's not what it's about. There's no money-back guarantee.'

'Quite the opposite, in fact,' says Ash.

'I'm serious. That's why the divorce rate is so high. Because people treat it like this disposable concept, that they can just go into on a whim, and bugger the consequences. So when you've finished laughing at me, and you're living in your bedsit behind Lidl while your ex-wife and ex-kids are living it up in the family house that you worked so hard to pay for and then gave to them because that's what the judge decided, who'll have the last laugh then?'

I look up, to find Ash staring at me strangely. 'Okay, Ben. Calm down. I was only joking.'

'Yes, well, it's not a laughing matter, is it?'

'Maybe not. But it sounds to me like you need to work out if you're actually doubting marriage, or doubting marriage to Amy.'

I stare at him for a second. 'Says the man marrying someone he's not sure how he feels about. And besides, I'm not doubting marriage. I'm merely putting it in context. Rationalizing it. Going into it with my eyes wide open and my feet on the ground.'

Ash smiles patiently at me. 'Ben, it's great that you're such a romantic,' he says sarcastically. 'But love is one of those things that grows. Out of appreciation, maybe. If Priti loves me, then I'll love her back. If she presents me with a couple of kids, then I'll love her for that too. And if I give her a good home and a nice standard of living, then maybe she'll feel the same way about me. But getting married just for love … Well, there's a recipe for disaster, as far as I'm concerned.'

'But that's my point. It shouldn't be.'

Ash sighs. 'How many people do you know get married for love?' Ash shakes his head. 'Not my parents, for one. But over the years, they've become very fond of each other. They respect each other. And if that's not as good as love, then I don't know what is.'

'But it's a different kind of love, isn't it? Different from the "when you set eyes on them your heart leaps" – more of a comfortable, appreciative love. It's like "I love my BMW", versus "I love this old pair of 501s". And while I'm not sure I'm looking for comfort just yet, I know that one day, I probably will be. And that's why Amy will do me just fine.'

Ash shakes his head at me. 'Sounds like you want it all, Ben. Which might explain why you've never met the perfect woman.'

I smile back at him. 'Maybe. Or maybe it's Amy?'

'Well, if you think that, then you don't have to convince me. Although it sounds like you're still trying to convince yourself.'

'Ash, out of all my failed relationships, this one has failed the least. And, besides, how can you *ever* be sure when it comes to getting married?'

'*I* am,' he says, looking at me strangely, before taking a deep breath and exhaling loudly. 'Anyway. A toast,' he says, picking his glass up and holding it out towards me. 'To you and Amy.'

'To me and Amy,' I say, picking up my beer, and clinking it against his. But as I do it, I can't help noticing something.

My glass is half empty.

Chapter 32

'Morning, handsome.'

It's Thursday lunchtime, and I'm heading into Julia's Scissors, the salon at the top of the High Street where, at Amy's request, seeing as she 'doesn't want to accompany a hippy to Ash's engagement party on Saturday' – her words – I'm getting my hair cut. My dad had offered to do it for me, but I'd politely refused, remembering all too clearly the time when he'd arrived home with some 'automatic barber' device he'd purchased from Woolworth's, and the subsequent trip to A&E.

As I walk in, Jo, my hairdresser, makes the 'haven't seen you for ages' face, and just as I'm thinking that it can't have been that long since I was last in here, I catch sight of my reflection in the mirror on the far wall, and realize that it probably is. I haven't had my hair cut since I quit my job, and while that's partly symbolic – a rebellion against the conventional environment I was leaving behind – it's also partly because haircuts were an expense I could do without.

I smile back to where she's attending to some old lady

who appears to be having her hair dyed a shade of pastel blue. Jo is very pretty – although unfortunately very married – and I used to feel particularly flattered by her 'handsome' comment. Until I heard her saying it to my dad as well.

I shut the door behind me, then make my way over to the sofas at the back of the salon, trying to avoid treading in the huge clumps of hair on the floor. Normally it's the trainee's job to sweep these up, but they've begun to collect, possibly because she seems to be being instructed by one of the other hairdressers in the mysterious art of how to use a broom. Given the rapt attention she seems to be paying, it's as if she's completely unfamiliar with the concept of 'brushing', but then again, by the looks of her own gel-spiked hairstyle, she quite possibly is.

I brush a few offcuts from the sofa and sit down, causing some hair to go up my nostrils, which makes me sneeze loudly, then look around for a magazine to read, but as usual there's just a few dog-eared copies of *Hello*, along with a couple of hairdressing titles. I pick one of them up and flick through, wondering whether I'll find a new style to cheer me up instead of the old short-back-and-sides-but-slightly-messy-on-top that Amy's expecting me to get, but then picture her face and chicken out.

As Jo looks over and mouths 'five minutes' to me, I settle back to watch a bit of MTV on the screen on the wall, remembering how much I used to love getting my hair cut. Although thinking about it, what I really liked was Jo washing my hair beforehand, which always felt more like a massage than a simple shampoo. I used to kid myself that she'd give me extra special attention because she fancied me, but in reality I'm sure all the caressing, stroking, and 'accidental' brushing of her breasts against my ear was just to alleviate the boredom she must have felt from a day that consisted primarily of asking her clients where they were going on holiday.

But not today, apparently, as instead Jo asks the trainee to take a break from her advanced sweeping class to wash me, so reluctantly I walk over to the sink, where the girl drapes one of those strange poncho-like things over my shoulders, then Velcros it slightly too tightly around my neck. Despite the fact that I'm worried her hairstyle might take my eye out, she's not unattractive, and as I settle down into the chair, and she leans over me to wedge a towel down the back of my neck, I'm afforded a view down her rather low-cut top. But then, and to my surprise, instead of walking round behind me, the girl straddles my legs, evidently preparing to wash my hair from the front rather than the more traditional from-behind-the-sink approach. I'm just about to protest, and ask whether she's actually done her shampooing training yet, but before I get a chance she grabs the shower head and directs a stream of lukewarm water over the back of my head.

'Is that too hot for you?' she asks, her breasts inches away from my face.

'No, it's fine,' I say, assuming she's referring to the

water, and not the proximity of her considerable cleavage. In truth, it's a little cold, but I don't want to risk her having to lean in even closer to adjust the tap on the back of the sink, so just shut my eyes and hope she doesn't decide to chat, although to be honest it'd be hard to hear anything she said given the amount of water running into my ear canal. Instead, I tell myself to relax, trying not to concentrate on the slow, sensual movements of her fingers through my hair which, combined with the kind of occasional touching that I imagine you only get in a lap-dancing bar, mean she's not the only one in danger of working up a lather.

I can't cross my legs, given the way she's standing over me, and so I try and think of something – anything – to take my mind off my growing excitement, eventually settling on an image of Ash in his underwear, and as she rinses the shampoo out of my hair, I foolishly think I've just about got away with it. The mistake I make, however, is to nod 'yes' when she asks me if I want conditioner, thus accidentally sticking my wet ears – albeit briefly – in between her pillow-like breasts. As I open my eyes and mumble an apology, she takes a pace backwards, and the first thing I see are a couple of wet patches where her nipples are.

When, finally, she rinses me off, I stand up, thankful for the billowing folds of the gown I'm wearing, then make my way awkwardly back to the sofa and sit down, shaking the water out of my ears as I do so.

'Hello, Benjamin.'

I look round to see Sarah from my art class sitting next to me. 'Sarah. Hi. What are you doing here?'

'Same as you, I imagine. Getting my hair cut.'

'Of course,' I say, realizing not for the first time that I'd do pretty well in the 'dumb questions' Olympics. 'Sorry. How's things?'

'Oh,' says Sarah. 'Not bad. You?'

'Good. I . . .' I stop for a second, wondering whether I should be sharing my news with her given how deeply affected she still seems to be by her husband dying, but then she's going to find out some time. And probably through Terry shouting 'don't do it' to me at the top of his voice at class tomorrow night. 'I'm getting married.'

'Well, congratulations,' says Sarah. 'Is this someone you've met through your parents?'

'No, actually,' I say, realizing I'm quite relieved by that admission, before explaining that Amy and I are back together. But when I've finished, Sarah folds her arms.

'So, this is for good, is it?'

I shrug. 'I hope so. She's agreed to give me a second chance, anyway.'

Sarah shakes her head slowly. 'And that's going to be your story?'

I'm a little confused. 'My "story"?'

'The best marriages always have a story. About how the bride and groom first met. And the more romantic the story, the longer it's going to last.'

'Ah,' I laugh. 'Amy and me are doomed, then.'

Sarah smiles. 'Do you know how my husband and I first met?'

'I do, actually,' I want to say, as she's told me their story before, and it almost made me cry, but I shut up, realizing she's going to tell me again no matter what I say or do. So I sit and listen patiently as she tells me how, fifty or so years ago, her dad was ill, and so she went off to the chemists to pick up some prescription of leeches or something, and the soon-to-be Mr Sarah just happened to be working behind the counter, but on the way home the leeches escaped, and she had to go back and ask the dashing young man if he wouldn't mind giving her some more. Anyway, apparently he thought it was just a ruse to come back in and see him, but he did it anyway, and the next day she came back in to say thank you, and he asked her out for a date. That was nearly fifty years ago. And they were happy right up until he died last year.

'So you see,' says Sarah, as I struggle to swallow the lump that's been building up in my throat. 'These things, they happen by chance. Not by design. Because they're such random events that you can't possibly try and predict when and where they're going to be. Or indeed make them happen.'

'And . . . He was a pharmacist?' I say, making a sudden connection.

'Oh yes,' says Sarah. 'They make the best lovers.'

'Pardon?'

'Have you never heard the phrase "Pharmacists do it over the counter"?'

'I, er ...' I shake my head, trying to get rid of the image of Seema that's just popped into it.

Sarah chuckles to herself. 'That was his favourite joke. But seriously, Benjamin, fifty years is a long time. So you need to be sure about what you're doing.'

'But Amy and I are determined to give it a go.'

'Give it a go?' Sarah smiles. 'You young people, you meet in one of your discos, go back to your place for a bit of how's your father, and you're lucky if you can remember the other person's name the next morning. Back in my day, you had to be courting for weeks before you even got to hold the other person's hand.'

'Yes, but back in your day, you had rationing, and thought blancmange was the height of sophisticated dining. Times change. People change. And therefore they work in different ways nowadays too.'

Sarah listens to my outburst patiently. 'Fair enough. But how many people my age do you know who are divorced?'

I shrug. 'I don't actually know many people your age apart from you. Oh, and mad old Mrs Hodges from next door.'

'What I'm trying to say, Benjamin, is that there's a reason we're in it for the long term, or lasted the course, if you like. Because we started from a position of romance. Not this wham-bam-thank-you-ma'am approach you lot have, or just drifting into it. My daughter's the same.'

'You've got a . . .' I stop myself from saying 'daughter?' – just. Because I'm with Amy now, and shouldn't be interested in other women. 'Point.'

'Dating for you is like shopping,' she continues. 'Buy it, then just throw it away if you don't like it. We didn't have a lot of money in those days, so we had to be certain that the thing we wanted *was* the thing we wanted. And then we stuck with it.'

'Tell me something,' I say, 'when exactly did you think he was the one? Your husband, I mean.'

Sarah rests a hand on my arm and gives me a squeeze. 'I didn't,' she says. 'Right up until he proposed. But he was so nervous about asking me to marry him, and when I suddenly saw how much he didn't want my answer to be no, that showed me just how much he didn't want to lose me.'

As Sarah picks up my discarded magazine, and starts to leaf through the pages, I sit there, stunned, because I've suddenly realized something myself. When I proposed to Amy, I was nervous too. But nervous that she'd say yes.

'Come on, Ben. I'll do you now.'

'Pardon?' I look up to see Jo standing next to me. 'I mean, great,' I say, following her over to the chair and sitting down.

'So, how have you been?' she asks, smiling at me in the mirror.

'Good,' I say, although to be honest, after my chat with Sarah I'm feeling anything but.

'And to what do I owe this honour?' she says, starting

to comb her fingers through my hair. 'I thought you were growing it.'

'I was. But I'm, er, getting married.'

'What?' Jo makes a mock horror face. 'Well, congratulations,' she says, leaning over and kissing me on the cheek. 'So what am I doing – a special look-good-in-the-wedding-photo haircut?'

'No, we haven't actually set a date yet. My, er ...' I can't quite bring myself to use the word 'fiancée' – mind you, I have only just given Amy the ring this morning, dropping it off at her office rather than doing the whole down-on-one-knee thing again, as I've had to have it re-sized to fit her unusually fat fingers, which she insists are just slightly above average thickness, and even then, that's just from using a calculator so much. 'I mean my *girlfriend*, Amy, just wants me to get it cut. She says she prefers it shorter.'

Jo looks at me strangely. 'And what do you want, Ben?'

'Er ...' What *do* I want? 'Well, I quite like it long.'

'So tell me,' says Jo, standing behind me with her scissors poised. 'What am I doing?'

And as I stare at my reflection, I realize I should really be asking myself the same question.

Chapter 33

I can't concentrate on work for the rest of the day, such is my nervousness about seeing Amy this evening for what she's expecting to be a celebratory dinner. Thinking back over my relationship history, I've never actually dumped anyone, so don't have the faintest idea how to get, well, disengaged.

Whenever I'd wanted to finish with a girlfriend in the past, there was always something stopping me – something more than just cowardice, that is. Bad timing – perhaps their birthday was coming up, or we'd booked a holiday, or Valentine's Day was around the corner. It always seemed to me that just at the moment I decided I had to end it, there'd be something that would make me appear even more heartless if I did it just then. So, inevitably, I hung around, until it was them who finished with me.

Something that always made it all the more difficult was the fact that you're not just splitting up with the person, are you? It's all their friends, who have come to know you as a couple. And their parents, who you might like, and, assuming they can get over the fact that you're sleeping with their daughter, maybe quite like you too. Then there's my parents – I've lost count of the times that my mother has cried more than I have over me splitting up with a particular girlfriend. And as they've told me on countless occasions, they love Amy. I just wish that I did.

And the thing that makes the prospect of this evening worse, is while I know that Amy sees this marriage as much as a business decision as anything emotional, I've seen how angry she gets when she loses out on a deal at work. And that's not something I want to be on the receiving end of. Or put her through, to be honest.

I spend most of the afternoon pacing around my studio, wondering what the best approach is. I could send her an email, I suppose. I mean, that's how people communicate formally nowadays, isn't it? Or a text. Maybe even a fax. But the trouble is, whatever medium I use, I'm just not that good at giving bad news to people, because I always feel like I'm letting them down. And while the last thing I want to do is let anyone down, I know now that if I do go through with this marriage, the person I'll be letting down most is myself. And Amy too, of course, because after all, she has agreed to spend the rest of her life with me – after I asked her to. And now, just a few days later, I'm withdrawing the offer.

Plus, she's going to want a reason. A bona fide excuse. Something that she can hold on to, or rationalize, as to why I don't want to marry her. I could try the 'love' angle, I suppose, but she'd probably think I was silly for wanting it in the first place.

Trouble is, she's good at arguing too, so I'm likely to lose if we get into any sort of debate, and unless I'm firm from the outset, there's a danger I'll end up staying with her simply because she'll refuse to accept my reasons for wanting out. So I'm just going to have to be strong – for my own good, not just hers. Cruel to be kind, I suppose. And if she's upset, I'll just have to deal with it. Because that's the nature of 'dumping' – you leave someone down in the dumps.

In a way, of course, Amy's response will tell me if I've made the right decision. If she's all emotional about it, then obviously she does really care about me, and while that'll be tough to take, at least it means I'm worth caring about. I've had women in the past dump me simply because they wanted to see my reaction; if I was all cut up about it, and pleaded with them to take me back, then they'd at least have the satisfaction of knowing I was interested in them. But, as was more often the case, if I was more relieved than upset, well, again they'd know they'd made the right decision too. So all I have to do is tell Amy straight out that I don't want to get married to her, and watch her reaction, and if it's what I suspect it'll be, then that'll be fine. If it isn't, however, I'm in trouble.

As I walk up the High Street and into Marcello's, I try and look on the bright side. At least I've come to this conclusion now, and not a few years down the line, when I'm unhappy, and she's unhappy, and maybe our kids would be unhappy too. And, in effect, that means what I'm intending to do is a good thing, because I'm sparing both of us even more hurt in the future. But somehow, now matter how many times I tell myself this, it doesn't make me feel any better.

I'm a little early, which gives me just enough time to gulp down a glass of wine before Amy arrives – as usual – at seven o'clock precisely.

'Ben,' she says, sitting down at the table without even kissing me hello. She's wearing my grandmother's ring, but doesn't seem to want to show it off to me, the 'second-hand' element obviously still a little bit raw.

'How do you manage it?'

'Manage what?'

'To always be exactly on time. For everything.'

Amy glances at the clock on the wall, and then her watch. 'I didn't know I was.'

I wait to see if she's joking, before remembering that Amy rarely jokes. About anything. 'Listen, Amy, I . . .'

'I thought you were supposed to be going to get a haircut?'

'I did. Go, that is.'

Amy peers closely at me. 'Ben, when I asked you to get a haircut, I didn't mean *a* hair cut,' she says reproachfully.

'No. I mean, I went to the salon, and everything, but . . .' I stop talking, conscious that I shouldn't have to be explaining to Amy – or anyone – about my hairstyle.

'Ben, we can hardly have you looking like that for the party. Or the wedding, come to think of it.'

'Who's we?' I say, my nervousness turning to irritation at the assumptions that Amy's making.

Amy frowns across the table at me. 'Pardon?'

'Who can't have me looking like this for the wedding? Who have you discussed the suitability of my hair with? Ash? My mum and dad? The vicar? Or are you deciding on my behalf?'

'No, I just thought . . .'

'*You* thought. And what else did you think? Do I need to lose a bit of weight? Or get a bit taller, perhaps?'

'Don't be ridiculous, Ben. I just don't want you to let yourself down, that's all.'

'Let you down, you mean.'

Amy rolls her eyes. 'Well, someone's got to tell you.'

'Tell me what?'

Amy sighs, and leans in towards me, as if she's explaining something to a child. 'That you need to make a few . . . changes.'

Here we go. I sit back in my chair and stare at her for a second, conscious that this is my big chance. 'And that's exactly why this marriage is going to be in trouble before it's even happened.'

'What?' Amy suddenly sits bolt upright. 'Why?'

'Because marriage should be about finding someone who'll let you be yourself. Not someone who wants to change you. I mean, I'm not asking you to make any changes, am I?'

Amy looks at me blankly, as if to ask why she'd need to. 'I'm not trying to change you, Ben,' she says huffily. 'I just want you to see that you need to change yourself.'

'What's the difference?'

Amy stares at me, then at the menu, as if she'll find the answer in there. 'Well . . .'

'We're all individuals, Amy. And the secret of a happy marriage is letting someone be who they really are. Not trying to make them into your idea of who your perfect partner is. Because then there's resentment. And pretence. And those things aren't the basis for love.'

'Love?' Amy looks at me in disbelief. 'This is a marriage we're talking about, Ben. What's love got to do with it?'

'And there, ladies and gentlemen, is the name of the song they'd play for our first dance as husband and wife,' I say, as if to the whole restaurant. 'Tell me something, Amy. When you walked in here this evening, what was the first thought that went through your head when you saw me?'

Amy frowns. 'The first thought?'

'Yes.'

'Apart from your hair?' She shrugs. 'Well, I was a little surprised you were early, I suppose. Oh, and that you hadn't ironed your shirt very well.'

I sigh, then lean across and put my hand on top of hers. 'And that's why this just isn't going to work, I'm afraid.'

'Because you can't iron a shirt?'

'No. Because that's what you noticed about me. You should have been happy to see me. Excited about our life together. Not . . . Critical.'

Amy looks at me levelly for a moment or two, then slowly removes her hand from underneath mine and pulls my grandmother's engagement ring off her finger. There's an awkward moment when it jams momentarily at her knuckle, but with one last tug, it's off. 'Your loss,' she says, handing it back to me.

'I know. And I'm sorry.' I slip the ring carefully back into my pocket, relieved to have it back in my possession. 'Really I am. I just need to find someone who loves me for, well, me. And so do you.'

Amy shrugs. 'That's okay. Plenty more fish in the sea.'

'You mean for me, right?'

Amy stands up abruptly, then leans over and kisses me on the cheek. 'I hope so, Ben.'

'I hope so too,' I say.

I watch her leave, feeling slightly guilty, but knowing it's for the best – and not just for me. Amy needs someone a bit more, well, mouldable. Someone who doesn't mind that she'll run things. Boss them about, even. And there are people out there like that. I know – I've read about them on the Internet.

And even though I'm on my own again, I feel more than a little relieved, because I'm starting to understand that there's only one thing worse than being on your own, and that's being in a relationship with the wrong person.

Because you're even more lonely then.

Chapter 34

'Here,' I say, handing over the creased Boots carrier bag.

'Thanks.' Seema removes the box of condoms and frowns at it. 'But I didn't get you anything.'

'No, I . . .' I can't stop myself from blushing. 'It's for, well, a refund. Like you said.'

She puts the box down on the counter. 'Have you got the receipt?'

I peer inside the bag, then check my wallet. 'Er, no. But you sold them to me. Remember?'

Seema smirks at me from behind the till, then shakes her head slowly. 'I'm teasing you, Ben.'

'Oh. Right. Very good.'

'Can you write down your details for me?' she says, reaching under the counter and handing me a pad and pen. 'I need your address, and telephone number.'

'Er . . . Okay.' I'm a bit stunned by her matter-of-factness, but flattered too. 'But I spend most of my time at my studio, so shall I give you that address instead? I mean, if you wanted to come and see me, then that's probably the best place.'

'I need them to process the refund, Ben. For head office.'

'Ah. Of course. Sorry.' I fill in my details on the pad, slide it back across the counter, then wait nervously as she rings the condoms through the till.

'Have you got two pee?'

'No, thank you. You just make me a little nervous, that's . . . That wasn't what you meant, was it?'

'Two *pence*, Ben. So I can give you a tenner back.'

As Seema watches me patiently, I check in both my pockets, but apart from an old tube of paint and a rather impressive bit of fluff, don't find anything. 'No. Sorry.'

'No problem,' she says, counting out a fistful of change from the till drawer and handing it over to me. I resist the urge to check it, and just stuff it into my pocket, realizing that now's my big chance, but when I can't think of anything else to say, Seema smiles. 'Well, say hello to Ash for me.'

I'm just about to say 'Of course', when something occurs to me. 'Why don't you say hello to him?'

Seema regards me for a moment. 'Well, I haven't seen him for a while.'

'You could see him tomorrow. It's his big engagement party.'

'I know, but . . .' She shakes her head. 'I might not go. Especially with all my family there. I don't know if he said, but I'm regarded as kind of . . .'

'The black sheep?'

'Are you trying to be funny?' says Seema, making me suddenly very aware of the colour of her skin.

'No. Sorry. I didn't mean . . .'

Seema rolls her eyes. 'Relax, Ben. You're so easy to get. It's just . . . Well, my family and me don't really see eye to eye. In fact, I'm surprised he even mentioned me.'

'Of course he did. I mean, does. He cares about you. And so do your parents.'

'My parents?' Seema's expression changes. 'What were you doing talking to them about me?'

Oh *no*. And just when it was going so well. Well, relatively. 'We weren't really. They just came round for dinner a couple of weeks ago. To my mum and dad's. And you happened to come up in conversation.'

'I bet I did. And I bet they also told you all about how I'm the bad daughter because I don't want to follow their traditional ways, especially now because Ash is.'

I'm starting to wish that another customer would come along and rescue me from this conversation, but unfortunately the shop's almost deserted. 'Not at all.'

'Well, what, then?'

'Er . . .' I'm faced with a dilemma. Spill the beans about what I've been up to and risk Seema thinking I'm an idiot, or lie, and pretend it was something to do with Ash's forthcoming wedding. But I've never been very good at lying to women. And besides, I'm pretty sure Seema already thinks I'm an idiot.

'Seriously, Ben. I'm interested. In what context was my name mentioned?'

Seema's tone leaves me in no doubt that she won't be happy until I've given her an answer. And given the lack of people behind me, I can't see any way out of it. Unless . . .

'I can't go into it now. But meet me for a coffee later, and I'll tell you?'

As soon as I've said this, I realize it's a brilliant plan. Because apart from the fact that she might agree to have a coffee with me, it'll also give me a good few hours to think of something less embarrassing than the truth. But when Seema looks at her watch, and waves one of her colleagues over, I'm stuffed.

'Okay. I'm due a break in five minutes. See you in the Costa on the corner,' she says, in a tone that leaves me no room for negotiation.

Five minutes later, I'm sitting in Costa Coffee as instructed, at a table by the window, sipping my cappuccino nervously. I'm worried I've been rude by ordering before Seema gets here, but there was no other way to keep the table given the withering looks I was getting from the barista.

As I stare out of the window, I can feel myself starting to perspire nervously. Still, I console myself, as the scent of Africa wafts from my armpits, at least this time I've got some protection.

When Seema finally arrives, she's not dressed in her white coat any more, but instead is wearing a low-slung pair of jeans and a short white T-shirt under an even shorter leather jacket, revealing what looks like a tattoo of a butterfly on her left hip.

'What can I get you?' I say as I stand up to meet her, hoping she hasn't caught me staring at it.

'Don't worry,' she says, walking straight past me towards the serving counter. 'I'll get my own.'

'Are you sure? I . . .'

'Quite sure, thanks.'

By the time she's sitting down opposite me, a steaming espresso and a chocolate brownie in front of her, I've finished most of my coffee, but I worry that it might be rude if I go and get myself another one. Plus, I don't want her to bite my head off again.

'So,' she says, tucking ravenously into the chocolate brownie. 'Spill.'

I look down at my cup instinctively, although I'm pretty sure she's not asking me to pour the rest of my cappuccino on the table. 'Well . . .'

'Yes?'

'Er . . .' I'm a little stuck, having not been able to come up with a single plausible alternative, so decide that the truth's my only option. 'Well, we were kind of discussing Ash's wedding. To Priti?' I add, unnecessarily. 'And how it was, you know arranged. And how both of them seemed so, you know, happy about it.' I look up to give Seema a chance to butt in, but her tactic of not saying anything means I feel pressurized to keep speaking. 'And we were talking about' – I clear my throat nervously – 'me, and how I hadn't met anyone to settle down with yet, and wondering whether, you know, it might be something that I, I mean, my mum and dad, might want to look into. For me. To meet someone, I mean. And my dad jokingly asked whether Ash had a sister, and your dad went pale – well, not pale, exactly, and not because of you, I hasten to add, but because the thought of me, um, marrying you wasn't to his, er, liking, evidently. And they ended up nearly having an argument because, well, my mother was a bit put out about the fact that they didn't think I was, you know, worthy of, well, you.'

I can't think of anything more to say, and besides I think Seema's probably got the gist of it, so I stop talking, but all she does is sit there and sip her coffee while regarding me over the top of her cup. And even though it's only an espresso, it seems to be taking her ages to finish it.

'So you see,' I say, unable to stand the awkwardness any longer, 'they obviously do think highly of you.'

'In what way?' says Seema, breaking her silence for the first time in what seems like hours.

'Well, in that they don't think, I mean, think that I'm not, you know, the required standard. To marry you,' I say, blushing furiously.

Seema considers this for a moment, before half-smiling at me. 'Don't sweat it, Ben. And I wouldn't worry about not being' – she makes the 'speech marks' sign with her fingers – *worthy*. It's probably just because they don't want me seeing someone who's not Indian. I mean, imagine the shame if I brought someone like you home.'

'It could be worse,' I say. 'At least I'm not an account-ant any more.'

Seema laughs. 'But they'd have thought you being one was a *good* thing. Honestly,' she says, shaking her head slowly. 'My parents. Think yourself lucky, Ben, that your folks are normal.'

'Well, you haven't met them. I mean, "normal" is a relative term, isn't it?'

'Not when you're talking about my relatives, it isn't.'

'I'm sure they've only got your best interests at heart.'

Seema narrows her eyes sceptically at me. 'Yeah, right. In fact,' she says, sitting up suddenly, 'that's exactly what we should do.'

I do a double-take at the word 'we'. 'What?'

'Get married.'

'Get *married*?'

Seema shrugs. 'Why not? I mean, you're apparently desperate to tie the knot, and I'm keen to teach my folks a lesson, and that would really stick it to them. No offence, obviously.'

I stare at her for a second, wondering whether she's serious. 'None taken. And, well, while that sounds really, er, romantic, I don't think it's the best basis for a long and happy . . .'

Seema shakes her head, then allows herself a slight smile. 'I'm messing with you again, Ben.'

'I knew that,' I say, giving the impression of the exact opposite.

'Of course I don't mean that we should get married. But we could pretend that we were going out, or even engaged. That'd really put the wind up them. Yes,' she says, evidently growing more and more pleased with the idea. 'Then, when I eventually tell them that, of course, we're not, anything else I want to do in the future is going to be a piece of cake. And by the sound of it, it'll get your parents off your back for a while too.'

'Ah.' I don't quite know how to admit that this is one area where I asked for my parents' help.

'So, how about it? Shall we announce our engagement?'

'Shouldn't we, you know, at least go on a date first?'

'What do you call this?' laughs Seema, nodding towards the coffee cups. 'And at least we met more than once beforehand. Unlike a certain brother of mine and his fiancée.'

'You don't like Priti much, I take it?'

Seema shrugs, and picks at the crumbs from her brownie. 'I've never met the girl. I just wish she could have been a bit more . . .'

'Independent?'

'Exactly. Like I said before, you're not as stupid as you look, Ben.'

I smile back at her. 'You'll have to stop with these compliments. I'm getting big-headed.'

'Sorry.'

'And you shouldn't be so down on your family, you know. They only want what's best for you. Or rather, what they think is best for you.'

Seema shakes her head. 'But that's their problem. Because surely you're the only one who truly knows what's best for you?'

'Maybe so,' I say, particularly in the light of the past few weeks. 'But you can't blame them for trying.'

'They set me up to marry a gay man, Ben.'

'Yes, but that wasn't their fault. I mean, I'm sure they didn't know.'

'Maybe not. But they could have checked.'

'How? By getting Ash to make a pass at him first? Some things you can't tell beforehand, no matter how much research you do,' I say, mindful of my recent bad date experiences. 'Trust me.'

'No, Ben, you're right. I can't blame them. But I can resent them. Especially after what happened. Why do you think I moved out in the first place?'

'Er, because you're independent and free-spirited?'

'You think so?'

It's a wild stab in the dark, but it seems to have provoked a favourable reaction. 'I do. And so do they, come to think of it.'

'Yeah,' says Seema, reluctantly. 'But not in a good way, I fear.'

'Any parent has got to be proud that their child can stand on their own two feet. Make their own way in life. Their own decisions.'

'You think so?'

'I know so.'

'I tell you something, though. If I ever do get married again, it'll be on my own terms. To someone I choose. And my parents will just have to live with that,' she says defiantly. 'At least they'll be grateful that they don't have to pay for another wedding for me. Do you know how much those things cost?'

'Maybe you could just ask them for the money instead?'

Seema laughs. 'That's very funny, Ben.'

'So this whole experience hasn't made you, you know . . .' I swallow hard. 'Anti-marriage?'

'Not at all. In fact, I think the concept of two people wanting to be together for ever makes perfect sense. As long as they're straight with each other from the beginning.'

'Or even just straight. In the groom's case, I mean.'

'Not so funny, Ben,' says Seema, trying to hide a smile. 'Honestly. My parents.'

'Even so, you might want to cut them a little more slack. And I'm sure they'd love to see more of you. Ash too.'

She stares at me across the table. 'Ben, with all due respect, I've known you for five minutes, and you're trying to give me advice on how to deal with my family?'

I look at my watch. 'It's probably closer to fifteen minutes, actually. And I wouldn't dare give you advice, Seema. But it's obvious they care about you.'

'Yeah? How?'

'Well, from the fact that they didn't want you associating with the likes of me, for one thing.'

She laughs. 'Well, they can't know you that well, if that's the case.'

As we sit there in silence, me a little uncomfortable at receiving an actual compliment, and Seema perhaps feeling awkward at having given it, for the first time I spot a little vulnerability. A chink in the emotional armour that Seema seems to be wearing whenever I see her. And it's at this exact moment that I know – if I wasn't before – that I'm well and truly hooked.

And I also realize that this is what I've been looking for all this time – and what was missing between Amy and me: this feeling of complete helplessness – not in Seema, but in me. While it's exhilarating, it's scary too, but I realize that feeling scared *should* be a part of it. Because that's what stops you from becoming complacent. Taking the other person for granted. If you're scared that you might lose them, then surely you'll work harder to keep them, and besides, as Sarah pointed out, there's nothing more flattering than knowing someone's scared to lose you. Especially if you're afraid of the same thing.

I know now that I have to ask Seema out, even though I'm going to be devastated if she says no. But I can hardly ask her to Ash's party, can I? I mean, if she really doesn't get on with her family, she's hardly likely to want to come to a party where they're all going to be, so if she does turn me down, she might be saying no simply because she doesn't want to see them, rather than me. And what if I ask her out and she says no, but then *does* go to the party? That'll leave me feeling even worse.

Of course, she might say yes – if only to rub her mum and dad's faces in it. And so what if she does want to go out with me purely to spite her parents? Well, at the end of the day, I still get a date with her out of it, and once I'm 'in', so to speak, well, surely that's my chance to prove that I'm worth a second date for more than simply revenge purposes. And people get together for reasons a lot weirder than that.

Just as I'm working up the courage to say something, my mobile rings, and my dad's number comes flashing up on the screen, but when I don't answer it immediately, Seema frowns.

'Shouldn't you get that?'

'It's just my dad.'

'Quick. Maybe he's found you a bride?'

'Ha ha,' I say, wondering why on earth he's calling. I've already told him and Mum about Amy and me splitting up, and they seemed surprisingly okay about it – a little relieved, even. But as the ringing continues, I can't ignore it. Particularly after my mum's recent arrest. 'Sorry, I ought to . . .'

'Be my guest,' says Seema, glancing at her watch, then standing up abruptly. 'I've got to get back to work anyway.'

'Wait, I . . .'

Before I can say anything further, Seema leans across the table and kisses me lightly on the cheek. 'See you, Ben,' she says, before making for the door.

I watch her leave, then stab the 'accept' button on my phone angrily. 'What?'

'We were just worried about you,' says my dad. 'I mean, it's nearly lunch time, and there's no sign of you.'

'Very funny. I was just having coffee, actually. With a friend.'

I can almost hear the cogs whirring in my dad's brain. 'A *girl* friend?'

'That's what I was trying to establish when you rang.'

'Ah. Sorry. Who is she?'

'She's Seema Mistry.'

My dad laughs. 'All girls seem a mystery to you, son.'

'No, Dad. Her name's Seema Mistry.'

'Well, why don't you ask her what they are?'

I sigh loudly into the handset. 'Do you do this on purpose?'

'Is she pretty?'

'No, Dad,' I say, deciding to give him a taste of his own medicine. 'That's Ash's fiancée. This is Ash's sister. Although she is. Pretty, I mean.'

'Oh. Right,' he says. 'Well, don't let me interrupt you.'

'Too late, Dad. She's gone.'

'Well, what are you waiting for?' he says, exasperatedly. 'Go after her.'

'Dad, didn't you hear me? It's Ash's sister. It's not that simple.'

'Yes it is, Ben,' says my dad. 'At the end of the day, whatever the complications, it's still just *boy meets girl*. And what could be simpler than that?'

Chapter 35

'How'd you get on with that woman?'

'What woman?'

'You know,' says Ash, shouting into his mobile to make himself heard above the music playing in the background. 'The one who you pictured spending the rest of your life with.'

'Amy? She's not in the frame any more.'

'Ah.' There's a pause, and then: 'So you're not doing it?'

'What do you think?'

'Pleased to hear it,' says Ash. 'Where are you anyway?'

'Just on my way.'

I grip tightly on to the door handle as Terry throws the taxi round another corner, then screeches to a stop outside the Indian Queen. I wouldn't have risked calling him, but I'm running late, and besides I've been under strict instructions from Ash not to drive this evening, as apparently there'll be a *lot* of alcohol. Plus, Terry's been only too pleased to chauffeur me here for free now that he knows my wedding's off. 'Think of it as a lucky escape,' he'd told me, which is ironic, because given the way he's been driving this evening, I'm thinking exactly the same about getting out of the cab in one piece.

'Good,' says Ash. 'Because I've got a surprise for you.'

'Not another one of your duff leads . . .' I start to say, but it's too late, because he's already ended the call.

I wave goodbye to Terry, speech impossible due to the volume of the music thumping from inside the restaurant, then push through the front door, with its 'Closed for a private party' sign, and when I get inside, I'm pleasantly surprised to notice a painting of mine on the wall in the reception area with a 'Sold' sticker on the bottom of the frame. With a spring in my step, I walk on into the main restaurant area, before stopping to take in the atmosphere. It's like a scene from a Bollywood movie: the men in either sharp suits or sporting traditional dress, and the women dressed in vividly coloured saris, whirling around to the kind of music I normally hear coming from Ash's car stereo, although – and I didn't think it was possible – somewhat louder. My mum and dad are already here, talking to Ash's mum and dad in the corner, no doubt comparing notes as to whether there's still any hope for me, and by the way Ash's dad has what appears to be a consoling arm round my dad's shoulder, I'm guessing that the answer is 'No'.

'Ben!' Ash catches sight of me from where he and Priti are sitting, sipping brightly coloured drinks, and waves me over. 'Glad you could come, mate!' he shouts, a bit shell-shocked by the occasion, as I sit down next to him.

'Your engagement party? I wouldn't have missed it for the world,' I say, leaning over and kissing Priti on the cheek. 'And thanks for my surprise.'

'What are you talking about?'

I nod towards the reception area. 'Another sale.'

'Oh that,' says Ash. 'That's not your surprise.'

'Well, what is?'

Ash grins. 'Wait and see.'

As I try to work out what Ash is talking about, Priti holds her glass up and smiles at me. 'Would you like a lassi?'

'Well, that's very kind of you to offer to fix me up with one of your Scottish friends,' I say, 'but I think I'll probably have a drink first.'

'No, Ben, I meant . . .'

'I know what you meant. I was joking. Although, if there *are* any single women here . . .'

Ash smiles enigmatically. 'There's going to be one less very soon,' he says, standing up and leading Priti towards the dance floor to a round of applause from the assembled guests.

As I watch them squeeze in between the other dancers, it strikes me that this is what an engagement party should be: a raucous celebration of the coming together of two people. And yet, as I look around the room, it's quite clear to me that this is more than that. It's the coming together of two families. To produce a whole new, bigger, better family.

And it's a big celebration. Huge, even. Which is quite

right, because I've come to realize that marriage is a huge thing, so it's only appropriate that the party you have to announce it should be on the same scale. And while fundamentally it's all about the two of them, it seems like here, everyone's involved. As if each guest is a crucial part of the celebration. Even single, miserable me, if only to make Ash look better.

Which is why I know I've done the right thing, where Amy's concerned. Because if this had been our – or rather, Amy's – engagement party, it'd have been nothing like this, and even if no one else had turned up apart from me and her, I'd have still felt like just another guest, watching the proceedings from a distance. Whereas here, even though I've just arrived, I feel part of it. Involved. And happy to be here. And I'm pretty sure that I wouldn't have been happy to be there.

I catch Ash's eye as he spins past my table, holding tightly on to Priti, and he looks like he's having the time of his life. And I'm happy for him. Really I am. Because if anything, his experience makes me see that there is someone out there for everyone. While finding them can be the tricky part, the looking's actually not so bad. And although it might end up costing me a fortune in toiletries I don't need, or condoms I'll never use, I'm pretty sure I've got a good idea where to look.

As Ash and Priti fly past me again, Ash sweating profusely, and Priti looking like she fears for her life, I pick up one of the selection of whisky bottles on the table and pour myself a large glass, wondering whether this was what Ash meant when he said Indian weddings were usually quite spiritual. I pull out a chair, and sit down, sipping my drink while I watch my mum and dad trying their best to match the skilful dancers either side of them, my dad wincing whenever he tries to put his weight on his bad knee, which he's aggravated in a vain attempt to beat my mum at computer tennis. After a few minutes, he catches sight of me and – leaving my mum to dance with Ash's dad – limps over, evidently grateful for the break.

'How's it going, son?' he puffs.

'Not bad,' I say, although 'not good' is perhaps a better answer.

'No joy, then?' he asks, looking over my shoulder.

'Her name's not Joy, Dad. It's ... Oh, that wasn't what you meant, was it?'

My dad pulls out a chair and sits down next to me. 'You haven't even asked her?'

'Not yet, Dad,' I say, a little ashamed of myself, because the truth is, since our coffee together, I haven't worked up the courage to even walk down the High Street, let alone go into Boots and actually speak to Seema.

'Why ever not?'

'Because I don't even know if she's interested in me. And I don't want to die on my feet in front of her.'

'Just remember,' he says. 'Faint heart never won fair lady. Or dark lady, come to think of it.'

'Yes, well, I'm just trying to work out my approach. You know. How to tell her that I'm interested.'

He nudges me. 'There's something we teach in English, about getting the message across. And it's one of the simplest, most effective maxims there is. Show, don't tell.'

'What's that supposed to mean?'

He puts a hand on my arm. 'It's very simple, Ben. If you like this girl, don't tell her. *Show* her. Actions speak louder than words, and all that. Which reminds me.' He peers furtively around the room, then reaches into his jacket pocket and removes a piece of paper. 'Here.'

'That better be your will, given how red in the face you are,' I say, looking suspiciously at the folded sheet of A4.

'Don't be cheeky,' says my dad. 'In fact, it's something better.'

I take the piece of paper and unfold it. It's another of his CVs. 'Dad, I . . .'

'Just read it.'

I shake my head slowly and glance disinterestedly through the details, smiling when I see the word 'tattoos' in the 'hobbies' section, and I'm just about to hand it back to him when I notice that this time, there's a name at the top. Seema's name.

'What's this?'

My dad smiles. 'We promised to find you a bride. Looks like you beat us to it.'

'If Ash's mum and dad put you up to this, then I'm afraid Seema's not going to . . .'

'It wasn't them,' he says.

'Well, in that case, it's very nice of Ash, but . . .'

He grins. 'Wrong again.'

'Well, who?'

My dad sighs, then levers himself painfully to his feet. 'I know you're an artist now, Ben, but surely I don't have to draw you a picture?' he says, before making his way back to where my mum is.

I'm just about to follow him, when there's a tap on my shoulder, and when I turn round, for a split second I don't recognize her. Gone are the low-slung jeans and the leather jacket, to be replaced by a beautiful gold-edged sari, and while there's no sign of the tattoo, the intricate henna designs on both her hands are quite beautiful. She's breathing heavily, which I guess is from a turn around the dance floor rather than her excitement at seeing me. But one thing I'm sure of – she looks stunning.

Seema points at the whisky bottle on the table behind me. 'Drowning your sorrows?'

I pick it up and pretend to study the label. 'Thinking about it.'

'Well, pour me one as well, will you?' she says, grabbing herself a glass from the centre of the table, then collapsing into the chair my dad's just vacated. 'I'm parched.'

'What are you doing here?' I say, pouring us both a healthy measure.

Seema clinks her glass against mine. 'I couldn't let my little brother get married without at least checking out his wife-to-be, could I?'

'I suppose not,' I say, smiling at the idea of Ash being anyone's 'little' brother.

'Besides . . .'

'Besides?'

Seema winks at me. 'I thought we had an arrangement?'

'Oh.' I get a sudden sinking feeling, assuming she's referring to our discussion yesterday. 'You're talking about your parents.'

'No,' says Seema, pointing to the piece of paper I've forgotten I'm still holding. 'But I have been talking to yours.'

I stare at her for a second, not quite believing what she's just said, then look over at the other side of the room, where both my mum and dad *and* Ash's parents are doing a very bad job of trying to appear as if they're not watching us. 'You know, I've never really liked these things,' I say. 'They always seem so . . . Dull. A last send-off for the condemned couple. But this?'

'What?'

'It seems to be all about having fun. Which is what it should be, surely?'

Seema smiles. 'Maybe you'll have your own one day.'

'You've obviously never been to an English engagement party.'

'No,' says Seema, nodding towards the dance floor. 'I meant maybe you'll have one like *this*.'

I laugh. 'I doubt it. I mean, I'd have to marry someone, you know, *Indian*.'

Seema shrugs, then downs her whisky in one, and stands up. 'Well, you could start by asking me to dance,' she says, holding her hand out to me.

Which is exactly what I do.

Acknowledgements

Thanks, as usual, to Patrick Walsh and the team at Conville & Walsh. To Kate Lyall Grant, Libby Vernon, Emma Harrow, and everyone at Simon & Schuster. To my mum, dad, and Tina, for your continuing love and support. To Loz, Tony, Chris, Linda, and Seem – with friends like you, these books almost write themselves. To Hugo, for helping me move into my new premises. To John Lennard, for his expertise with both a paint-brush and a tennis racquet. And to the Board – the best bunch of people I could ever hope to share a (virtual) office with.